HARD EVIDENCE

"Come on, Trace," the countess said. "Let's trick."

Trace kissed her hard. She slid into his arms as easily as a family car rolling into the house garage.

"You serious?" she said.

"I never joke about important things," Trace said.

"Then let's make this a very important thing."

While Felicia slipped out of her clothes with her back toward him, Trace reached under his shirt and yanked the tape recorder and surgical tape from his waist and stuck the activated machine in his jacket pocket. Then he hung it over a doorknob so that the microphone was aimed at Felicia's bed.

Then she turned toward him, and he looked at her waiting, beautiful and naked, her lips half parted, her eyes half glazed, and it was time to get down to business. . . .

TRACE
AND 47 MILES OF ROPE

Exciting Reading from SIGNET

TRACE

AND 47 MILES OF ROPE

WARREN MURPHY

Ⓞ

A SIGNET BOOK

NEW AMERICAN LIBRARY

To M.C. Always and only. 242.

PUBLISHER'S NOTE

This novel is a work of fiction. Names, characters, places, and incidents either are the product of the author's imagination or are used fictitiously, and any resemblance to actual persons, living or dead, events, or locales is entirely coincidental.

NAL BOOKS ARE AVAILABLE AT QUANTITY DISCOUNTS WHEN USED TO PROMOTE PRODUCTS OR SERVICES. FOR INFORMATION PLEASE WRITE TO PREMIUM MARKETING DIVISION, NEW AMERICAN LIBRARY, 1633 BROADWAY, NEW YORK, NEW YORK 10019.

 SIGNET TRADEMARK REG. U.S. PAT. OFF. AND FOREIGN COUNTRIES
REGISTERED TRADEMARK—MARCA REGISTRADA
HECHO EN CHICAGO, U.S.A.

SIGNET, SIGNET CLASSIC, MENTOR, PLUME, MERIDIAN and NAL BOOKS are published by New American Library, 1633 Broadway, New York, New York 10019

First Printing, April, 1984

1 2 3 4 5 6 7 8 9

PRINTED IN THE UNITED STATES OF AMERICA

LATE NEWS BULLETIN

The body of Early Jarvis, about fifty, was found dead early this morning in the desert home of Countess Felicia Fallaci, where he worked as a servant.

A safe in the countess's home was found open and empty, and police believe Jarvis may have surprised a burglar and been injured in a scuffle. Officers at the scene said that Jarvis apparently bled to death after being struck on the head.

What, if anything, was missing from the safe could not be determined since Countess Fallaci was on vacation in Great Britain and could not be reached immediately.

1

The stereo was playing soft rock at hard volume. Some persons danced in the center of the large living room. Others stood in twos and threes and talked loud to be heard over the general din.

"Hey, I heard some kind of nutty long-range forecast coming over here. It might snow this winter."

"Come on, what are you smoking? It never snows in Las Vegas."

"Don't argue with me. Argue with the weather people. Maybe the almanac people. They said it, not me."

"Hear this? It's supposed to snow this winter. How much is it supposed to snow? They tell you that?"

"The way it always snows in Las Vegas. One line at a time."

"I got called to the school by the nun."

"What about?"

"About Margaret. The nun said that they were having music class and all the kids in the class had to stand up and sing their favorite song. And when Margaret's turn came, she got up and sang 'Push, Push, in the Bush.' "

"What'd you say?"

"What could I say? I said, What's the matter, she get the lyrics wrong?"

"So what do you do with some eighteen-year-old kid who comes to visit you in Las Vegas? A snotty little creep. So I take him to a saloon, what else can I do? Just like his old lady, he sits there swilling it down and I think maybe I ought to say something to him, 'cause he's my kid, or at least the old lady says he is. So we're watching a hockey game and Wayne Gretzky is playing."

"Yeah?"

"So this kid's looking at the screen and I says, That's Wayne Gretzky; when he was eighteen years old, he was the greatest hockey player that ever lived. And this snot says, So what? So I says, And you're eighteen years old, you cheap bastard, and you won't even buy a drink. Go back to Minnesota."

On the other side of a counter pass-through, in the kitchen, two men were standing within earshot of these conversations. One was Devlin Tracy. He was six-foot-three and blond, and there were laugh wrinkles in the corners of his eyes, even when he wasn't laughing. He gave the impression of being a man who knew the world was crazy and had decided to become part of the problem, rather than the solution.

He towered over the other man, who reached five feet only with a full stretch. His name was Walter Marks; his lips were stretched continuously into a look of disgust, and his narrow eyes shifted around quickly as if the world were filled with hired gunmen, all of whom had his photograph.

"I've never understood why you hate me," Devlin Tracy was saying. "I treat you with the utmost kindness. Despite everything."

"What despite everything?" Walter Marks said. "What? What?"

"I'd rather not talk about it if you wouldn't mind. I just don't think it's fair to repay my kindness with vicious hatred the way you do," Devlin Tracy said.

"I don't think it's hating you because I won't invest money in your stupid schemes. The last thing were those stupid automobile signs that you could read in mirrors. And before that, what was it before that? Oh, yeah. The CB Bible of the Air. 'Fisherman, fisherman, this here is Palm Leaf, Old Buddy. Beware the Ides of March.'"

"It wasn't the Ides of March. That was *Julius Caesar*. It was Passover."

"Whatever it was, who the hell would buy that?" Marks said.

Tracy shrugged. "I don't know. People buy Lola Falana records, I'm told. You never know what might make it."

He waved over the pass-through toward the living room, where a voluptuous brunette in a miniskirt and white patent-leather boots stopped dancing with her partner momentarily and tossed a very large bump and grind in Tracy's direction.

Her dancing partner was a distinguished, white-haired man in a three-piece pinstripe suit. He looked like what he was: the president of an insurance company. He grabbed the girl's hand and yelled out to the kitchen, "Hey, Trace. Tell her to save some of that for me."

"Plenty to go around," Trace yelled back, and the brunette moved into the white-haired man's arms again and ground herself against his body.

"Looks like Bob's having a good time," Trace said.

"Disgusting," Walter Marks said. "Who is that creature?"

"She dances in the show at the Araby Casino," Trace said. "Her name's Flamma. She does the Dance of the Seven Veils. Hold the veils."

Marks said, "Mr. Swenson's had a little too much to drink. Is he . . . you know, is he going to get into trouble with her?"

"I hope so," Trace said. "That's the way I set it up."

"He's got a family back in New York."

"I don't think he's going to take Flamma back with him," Trace said.

"I'm not worried about him taking her back. I just don't want him to take anything else back that she might give him. I knew this party was a mistake. When they decided to hold the insurance convention in Las Vegas this year, I said, Uhoh, it means that we'll be around Trace and that means we'll all be getting into trouble. I knew it. The convention doesn't even start until tomorrow and already Mr. Swenson's acting like this. I'm going to have to watch him every minute."

"Hey, Groucho. Bob's free, white, twenty-one, and owns his own insurance company. Let him be."

A petite Oriental woman, wearing a long blue evening gown cut low off one shoulder, stepped into the small kitchen, elbowed Trace aside, and began washing glasses. Her long black hair splashed about her shoulders as she stood at the sink, hair as black as a mine at midnight, as shiny as hard coal. Trace stepped behind her, pushed her hair aside, and kissed the back of her neck.

"Good party, Trace," she said without turning.

"Enjoy it now, Chico. My mother and father are coming pretty soon."

"Where are they, anyway?"

"My mother wanted to see the trapeze act at Circus Circus first."

"For that, she passes up your almost-birthday party?" Chico asked.

"Some things in life are important, more important than other things."

The young woman turned from the sink. Her face was smooth and delicately featured with large dark eyes set intelligently wide apart in her face. She smiled a dazzler at Walter Marks.

"Can I make you a drink, Mr. Marks?" she asked.

"No, thank you," he said stiffly.

"He's not drinking for two," Trace said. "He's worried about Bob."

"Mr. Swenson? He's all right," the young woman said.

"How can you tell?" Marks asked.

"He just offered me two dollars to go into the bedroom with him."

Marks looked pained. "Ohhhh," he said.

"Did you take it?" Trace asked.

"I told him to make it five and I'd go home with him."

"Don't give it up for less than ten," Trace said. "He's rich."

"I know. He told me. He told me anytime I wanted to get rid of you, he'd set me up right," Chico said.

"Don't believe his promises. He's an insurance

11

man. He'll tell you anything," Trace said as the girl breezed out of the room with a tray of clean glasses, destined for the bar in the far corner.

"How can you talk to her like that?" Marks asked Trace.

"We live here together. Shacked up. Roommates. What am I supposed to do, give her heavy-breathing phone calls and anonymous notes under her cereal bowl?"

"But . . . Well, never mind," Marks said. "I want you to—"

"I know. You want to talk business. I told you that you hate me, Groucho. Here I am, having a party for a few friends—"

"It looks like, what do you call it, Walpurgis-nacht," Marks said.

"I admit, all you insurance types here do lend a kind of decadent air to the festivities, but it's only four days to my birthday and you want to ruin this celebration with business."

"Yes."

"That's the trouble with you, Groucho. You've never learned to enjoy yourself. You're surrounded by Las Vegas royalty and you want to talk about some stupid insurance policy."

"Royalty has fallen on evil times," Marks said.

"Las Vegas royalty. Those two blond twins out there talking about the kid. They're the most famous hookers in Las Vegas. Maybe the most expensive in the world. Twenty-five hundred dollars the pair. One night's rental. And a waiting list ever since OPEC and the sheikhs decided they like Nevada sand better than Arabian sand. And they took the night off, two thousand five hundred dollars' worth, to come here expressly to meet you. That's right. I told them you were coming, and you can't take even ten minutes off from business. They'll be crushed. And let's see. That fat thing over there, you see him, complaining about his son?"

"The disgusting dirty one?" Marks asked.

"Ahah, you think he's dirty and disgusting, but that's just a disguise."

"Spaghetti stains on a dirty white shirt is a disguise?" Marks said.

"That's right. You know, everybody's got this idea that casino bosses are the shrewdest people in the world, but most of them are as worthless as a wet handkerchief. Like if you're not wearing a rented shirt with frills and genuine imitation-gold two-pound cuff links, they think you're some dumb tourist who came to make a donation to the Casino Good and Welfare Fund. The casino bosses around town laugh at this guy. He comes into their joints, a different one each night, and he buys in for five hundred or so at the blackjack table and he's sneezing and coughing and eating and spilling drinks, and none of the bosses wants to get too close to him 'cause maybe they'll catch something, and he plays for a while, and then all his chips are gone and he stands up and says, You guys cleaned me out again. So he leaves, and the bosses snicker to the dealer, What a jerk. And this guy's got a special pocket built inside his jacket and he's made maybe eight hundred, nine hundred dollars, and he has somebody else cash the chips in the next day and the bosses never know he takes five grand a week out of their casinos."

"Don't the dealers know?" Marks asked.

"Sure, the dealers know," Trace said. "But they don't talk."

"Why not?"

"First of all, they hate the bosses, so they don't

tell them anything. Second of all, this guy's a good tipper. If he gets tossed out of their casino, the dealers lose those tokes. Why should they tell?"

"Because they work for the casino. They should be loyal to their employer," Marks said.

"Very good, Groucho," Trace said. "*Segue* into company loyalty and into work assignments and into whatever you've got in your pocket for me to read and make my life miserable. All right, what is it?"

Marks reached into the inside pocket of his tightly cut charcoal-gray suit with cuffs on the sleeves and pearlescent buttons whose glimmer matched the light figure in his soft silk tie, and handed Trace a newspaper clipping.

Trace glanced at it and handed it back. "I know all about this," he said. "I knew Early Jarvis. So what?"

"The clipping's a little vague," Marks said, "but there was a million in jewelry taken from this woman's house. This countess."

Trace shrugged. "Garrison Fidelity does life insurance. I investigate life-insurance claims. What's missing jewelry got to do with me?"

"Just this. Jarvis was carrying life insurance with us. Seventy-five thousand. He left the money to the countess. I think you ought to look into it."

Trace didn't like the tone in his voice. There was something smug and self-satisfied about it. "What's going on here?" Trace asked. "This is like a freebie you're doing for somebody else, isn't it? I check out Jarvis' death and that means I'm going to have to check out the jewel robbery too, so I'm going to wind up working free for some other insurance company that's going to go for its lungs on a stolen-jewelry claim. Why are you doing this to me?"

"Don't worry, Trace," said Marks. "If you were lucky enough to find out who stole the jewelry, which I very much doubt, I'm sure the other company would pay you a nice fat fee."

"And you wouldn't mind? You wouldn't bitch and try to cut my fee? I know you. I can hear you now, Groucho. 'Trace, you already got paid from so-and-so, why are you trying to get paid from us too?' I can hear it."

"I wouldn't do that," Marks said. It looked as if he were making an effort to sound wrongfully accused, but it just didn't work.

"Yes, you would," Trace said, "but I've got your word you won't, right?"

"You've got it."

"Who's doing what with the jewels?" Trace asked.

"There's a local guy, some detective, he's working on it."

"What's his name?" Trace asked.

"Roberts. R. J. Roberts," Marks said.

"Aaaah, I don't want to work with him."

"Why not?"

"He's stupid," Trace said. "He couldn't find a bull moose in a bread box."

"Work with him," Marks said.

"You know, the only thing that matters to us is if the countess killed Jarvis," Trace said. "Anything else, we pay, right?"

Marks' face squinched up like a cat sniffing a cigarette. "Countesses," he said. "I never met one who wouldn't do anything for money. She probably did kill him. Seventy-five thou ain't hay."

Trace leaned over the kitchen counter and crooked a finger into the living room in the direction of a woman wearing a long white beaded gown. Even by the elevated standards of the women in Trace's living room, the woman was a great beauty. She was tall and shapely with red hair, the color of the last three minutes of sunset. Her eyes were spectacularly green, appearing even more jadelike in the delicate healthy tan of her face. She seemed to be wearing no makeup, but her eyelashes were astonishingly thick and full and her lips were a natural dusty-rose color.

She saw Trace gesturing to her and came out into the kitchen with her glass in her hand.

"Felicia, I'd like you to meet someone. This is Walter Marks. He thinks you're a murderer. Can I freshen your drink?"

Countess Felicia Fallaci turned on a truly breathtaking smile and handed Trace her glass.

"Darling, if you would," she said. "Just enough to pour over his head."

Walter Marks started to turn blue.

Not nearly so drunk as he acted, Robert Swenson, president of the Garrison Fidelity Insurance Company, still puffing heavily from his dance-floor workout with Flamma, leaned against the wall on the far side of the living room and recovered his full glass of Scotch from behind some books, where he had hidden it.

He looked out across the noisy room toward the kitchen, where Trace and Marks were still talking.

Chico walked over to join him.

"Anything I can get you, Bob?"

"Michiko, my darling, the only thing I want in the world is you." He sipped his drink. "And a new heart, new lungs, and a liver transplant."

Chico allowed her gaze to follow his out into the kitchen.

"Do you detect a smile, however subtle, on the face of Walter Marks?" Swenson asked.

"A smile or a gas attack," Chico said.

"I've seen his gas attacks," Swenson said. "His brows lower. No, that's a smile. I'll have his ears for that. He's not supposed to smile on company time."

"Maybe he's finally figured out a way to dethrone you as president," Chico said. "Today, vice-president for claims; tomorrow, the world."

"Too short," Swenson said. "No one looks up to little executives. No. He's up to something sneaky and duplicitous."

"I can't believe it," Chico said. "At an insurance-company convention, something sneaky and duplicitous? It's hard to believe."

"It's something," Swenson said stubbornly, still looking into the kitchen.

"Why don't you just ask him?" Chico asked.

Swenson shook his head. "Bad management practice. The way to deal with people like Walter is to ignore them. That constantly fills them with a sense of their own worthlessness. Act as if you know they're alive, and sooner or later they'll start to believe it, and *that's* when they try to dethrone you. Trust me, girl."

Affectionately, he put a fatherly arm around her shoulder, then asked her suddenly, "How many days to Trace's birthday?"

"Four."

"And then he's forty?"

"Right."

"And you're twenty-six?"

"Yup."

"He's over the hill, girl. Too old for you," Swenson

17

said. "But it's not all over for you yet. You could have me. Rich, powerful, handsome, intelligent . . ."

"And booked for tonight," Chico said.

"Ah, you noticed. Well, yes, Flamma and I do have an appointment. She promised to show me how she belly-dances with Sterno in her navel. Scientific research, you understand, in case we ever write a policy on her. But any night after tonight. Every night. I'll be chaste and loyal and pure. People will say of us, The perfect couple. They'll write songs about our romance."

"What about your wife?" Chico asked.

"Actually I was hoping that she'd never find out," Swenson said.

Chico shook her head. "Thanks, but no thanks," she said, and nodded toward Trace, who was just walking out of the kitchen. "He's a poor thing but he's semi-mine."

"Forty. He's done for."

"You know it and I know it. I don't think his body knows it yet," she said.

"Wait till I put saltpeter in his vodka. Don't come sniffing around to me then, girl, pleading and begging. Then it'll be too late."

"You wish," Chico said, and giggled. "I snap my fingers, you'd slither across the desert on your belly for me."

"God, it's true. Remind me to give Trace a raise. So he can treat you right."

"I will," Chico said. "By the way, you're doing just right."

"What do you mean?"

"You're acting just drunk enough so that none of these people bother you with insurance nonsense," she said. "Keep it up."

18

"I retract my offer. I can't stand women who can see right through me," Swenson said.

Chico saw Walter Marks talking earnestly to someone who had been introduced to her as the head of Garrison Fidelity's West Coast operations, so she excused herself from Swenson and began drifting around the room, talking to people, working her way closer to Marks, approaching him from behind his back.

He was talking softly when she got there, but she could hear a few words.

". . . to hang himself. I've got the bastard now."

The other man was about to answer when Trace came up alongside Chico and said, "I've got to talk to you."

Marks heard Trace's voice and Chico saw him nod to the other man to be quiet.

Chico took Trace's arm and walked away.

"Your timing is, as ever, impeccable," she said.

"Speaking of timing," Trace said. "Right now, I'm thirty-nine and you're twenty-six."

"Right. You remembered."

"But in four days I'll be forty and you'll still be twenty-six."

"And lovely. Don't forget lovely," Chico said.

"Right, lovely. Did you ever think this might be the start of a trend? Another dozen years and I'd be fifty-two and, God, you'd still be twenty-six, half my age."

"I don't think it works that way."

"No? Then how come you haven't had a birthday in three years?" Trace asked.

"Oh, you're vicious," she said. "And a liar to boot. Why is Walter Marks looking like a Cheshire cat?"

"Groucho? I don't know. Is he?"

"He is," Chico said.

"He ruined our party by giving me a job to do. I'll never forgive him."

Chico had no chance to comment because the door to the apartment swung open and a bull-elephant roar filled the room.

"All right, you degenerates, you're all under arrest."

Standing in the doorway was a tall, burly, gray-haired man with big powerful hands. His face was weathered and handsome. Behind him was a woman who seemed all bosom. She wore a hat that gave her the general configuration of a Coast Guard ice-cutter.

The thirty people in the room looked toward the door and Trace called out, "Okay. The party can start now. My father's here."

"And your mother," said the warship standing behind the man in the doorway.

"And my mother," Trace admitted reluctantly.

2

Chico slapped Trace hard on his bare stomach.

"Ouch. What's that for?"

"That's for getting me into this," she said. "You saw those insurance looneytoons tonight. I'm going to have to put up with them for a week. A week of fighting off Bob Swenson."

"You love it. Don't lie to me," Trace said. "Imagine. You. Official convention hostess to five hundred of the noblest of God's creations: insurance men. I don't know if you're really deserving of the honor."

"I'm underpaid," she said.

"You're getting two thousand dollars for four days' work."

"Exactly. I make five hundred dollars a week dealing at the Araby, and no heavy lifting. I should get five thousand for having to look at Walter Marks' pissy little face."

"Don't look at him. *Then* you'll be overpaid," Trace said.

"And it's wonderful that your folks are in town," she said sarcastically.

"I thought you liked Sarge."

"I love him. You know that, even if he is as bad as Swenson. It's that mother of yours."

"A peach," Trace said. "A veritable peach."

"You're like all smart people who learned to read young," she said. "You know the words but you mispronounce them. What your mother is is not pronounced 'peach.' Not unless you grew up in Puerto Rico."

"I'm shocked," Trace said. "My mother?"

"She wasn't here ten minutes, you saw her, she was rearranging the dishes in the closet. Then she started to rewash all my clean glasses. It's a good thing the party broke up, she'd be cleaning my oven. Why does that woman hate me?"

"She can't forgive you for being Italian," Trace said.

"I'm only half-Italian. I know, that's why she only half-hates me. Anyway, I'd watch myself if I were you."

"What are you talking about?"

"With Felicia's jewel robbery and all," Chico said. "Marks is up to something."

"What makes you think that?"

"I saw that look on his face when he was giving you that job. It was a nasty look."

"He always looks nasty," Trace said. "He hates me like my mother hates you."

"This was a special kind of nasty look. Then I was listening to him talk to that cretin who runs your West Coast office."

"What'd he say?"

"I was just finding out when you came stumbling along, yapping a mile a minute, and he clammed up. But he said something about somebody hanging himself and he said, 'I've got the bastard now.' "

"He couldn't have been talking about me. I can't recognize myself in that reference at all," Trace said.

"He was talking about you. He's got something going on. Even Swenson noticed it."

"What'd he say?" Trace asked.

"He didn't know what Marks was up to either."

Trace said, "Then it can't be important. Groucho wouldn't do anything important without clearing it with Swenson."

"I don't know. Just watch yourself."

"I will. You know, the worst part is having to talk to R. J. Roberts."

"Who's he?"

"He's a grundgy private eye who works in town. The insurance company's got him working on the jewel theft."

"What's wrong with him?"

"He's not a nice person," Trace said. "I don't like dealing with those elements. I've got my standards."

"Trace, you're an alcoholic, degenerate gambler. You'd hump a hamster if it smiled at you. How bad can this R. J. Roberts be?"

"He wears plaid shirts, for Christ's sake. Listen, we going to make love or are you going to talk all night?"

"I was thinking of talking all night."

"I know how to stop that," Trace said.

"Trace, it's the phone. Bob Swenson."

"I didn't hear the phone ring," Trace said. He put a pillow over his head.

Chico removed the pillow and put the telephone next to his ear.

"You don't pay me enough to take this abuse," Trace growled into the phone.

"Rise and shine," Swenson said. "Today's the first day of the rest of your life."

"Test it out for me and call me back in twenty-four hours," Trace said.

He snaked out a hand to replace the phone, but Chico took it from him and put it again on the pillow next to his head.

"You're all against me," Trace mumbled.

"That's what I wanted to talk to you about," Swenson said brightly. Even the tone of his voice annoyed Trace. Swenson could drink for a weekend and after two hours' sleep sound as fresh as if he had just come from spending a month in meditation at a monastery.

"What?" Trace asked.

"Marks is up to something, but I don't know what it is yet."

"You and Chico. Maybe you should both start a mind-reading act," Trace said.

"Maybe," Swenson said. "But he's got something on his mind."

"Well, you're the boss," Trace said. "It's your company. Ask him what he's got on his mind. Tell him to get it off his mind."

"I can't do that," Swenson said. "I get involved in things like that, and before you know it people will start coming into my office, asking me questions about rate structures and advertising and what kind of paper we ought to print policies on. And before you know it, I won't have time to do anything except think about insurance. Being president isn't easy, Trace. Let your guard down for a moment, and right away they start thinking you give a rat's ass."

"All right, skip it," Trace said. "How'd you make out with Flamma last night?"

"Does a gentleman tell? Did you know she can really dance with Sterno in her navel?"

"Doesn't it run out?" Trace asked.

"Well, it would if she stood up, I guess," Swenson said. "Basically, she just stays horizontal most of the time. Keep an eye out for Walter."

"I will," Trace said.

"And tell Chico I'll see her at the luncheon."

He clicked off and Trace replaced the phone and started running down his check list of functioning body parts, preparatory to getting out of bed.

When he finally made it to the kitchen, Chico was there, standing at the stove cooking eggs, incongruously wearing a blood-red long gown. There was a cup of coffee on the small breakfast table and Trace sipped at it. The first sip of coffee made him feel better, and so did watching Chico. He wondered how many people had this mistaken impression of Japanese women as white-faced, sickly, sort of tubercular Kabukis. How wrong they were. Chico's complexion was tawny, vibrant with life, vitamins, and good genes. He felt healthier just looking at her and told her so.

"Don't worry, it'll pass," she said. She slipped eggs from the skillet onto a plate, plopped it in front of Trace, and poured him a glass of orange juice from a container in the refrigerator.

"Eat it all," she said. "Your mother will probably ask questions later. Oh, and thanks."

"For what?"

"For staying sober last night."

"I'm going to stay sober forever from now on," he said. "That's part of the new me."

"There was nothing wrong with the old you," she said, "but keep sober anyway."

"You off now?" he asked.

"Yes. I'm off to my new career as zoo keeper. Official convention hostess for the ninth annual convention of Garrison Fidelity Insurance Company being held this year, to my great joy, in my home city of Las Vegas, Nevada. I am off to get my ass pinched in as many ways as he can think of by Robert Swenson and to go look at Walter Marks' curled lip. I'll talk to you later, if I'm still talking to you for getting me into this, and you be careful today."

She stood in front of Trace, her neat little dancer's body separated from his face by only a few inches and a few thin scraps of fabric, and he grabbed her around the hips and said, "Want to fool around?"

"Your fortieth birthday's in three days," she said.

"I promise we'll be done by then," he said.

"You ought to think about tapering off," she said, but she made no move to pull away. "You're entering the fifth decade of life."

"No, I'm not. I'm going to be forty."

"Exactly," she said. "There was the zero decade, age oh-one and oh-two and like that. Then the teens and the twenties and the thirties. Thursday starts your fifth decade."

"Only a Japanese-Sicilian with a warped mind could think of a grisly way of looking at it like that."

"And I'm still twenty-six," she said, and leaned over and licked his neck.

After she left, Trace pushed his eggs around his plate for a while before eating two forkfuls and dumping the rest in the sink disposal unit. He sipped orange juice and decided he would tell Chico to buy grapefruit juice from now on, grapefruit juice being more corrosive and better able to blast away the residue on the inside of his mouth.

He drank all his coffee, was very proud of himself, and thought of leaving Chico a note telling her that he had finished all his coffee, but he couldn't find anything in the kitchen to write with.

Trace spent a long time in the shower, thinking about his upcoming birthday. It was one thing to joke about it, but was he going to go crazy like a lot of people he had known, buying gold chains for his neck, a little Italian convertible, and hanging around schoolyards handing out chocolate bars? He thought that maybe Chico would keep him sane, and the thought instantly depressed him. Swell. All that stood between him and middle-age lunacy was a twenty-six-year-old Eurasian black-jack dealer who occasionally turned tricks to supplement her income. And who was just too smart by half.

Before dressing, he went to a plastic bag hidden on the top shelf of a bedroom closet. From it he removed a small portable tape recorder and a roll of surgical tape. He tore off two long strips of the tape and fastened the recording unit to the back of his bare waist, just over his right kidney.

He inserted a wire into the machine, then dressed and drew the wire through the front buttons of his shirt. After he put on a tie, he pressed the wire through the back of the tie into a slit in a tie clip fashioned in the shape of a golden frog. The frog's open mouth was covered with a thin golden mesh and under the mesh was a tiny, sensitive microphone.

Trace tested the device.

"Devlin Tracy donning the tools of ignorance one more time. Am I live or am I Memorex?"

He pressed another button through his shirt and the recorder repeated his message into the empty bedroom.

Satisfied that he was still live, he rewound the tape and turned the recorder off, then put on his jacket and drove downtown.

3

It was only midmorning, but the electric sign outside the bank reported the temperature at 91 degrees. It would get close to 110 before the sun set on this August day, Trace knew.

The downtown streets were already cluttered with tourists, most of them underestimating the sun and wearing walking shorts as they went in and out of the small stores selling the hand-carved silver jewelry that was Las Vegas' third major attraction, after gambling and sex.

R. J. Roberts was twenty pounds too heavy and two days too dirty. His hair looked unwashed, but that might have been because it made a matching pair with his moustache, a sparse little cluster of brownish weeds that sat on his upper lip like a hair transplant that hadn't taken yet. He was sitting behind his desk wearing a loud red plaid shirt. A brown suit jacket was tossed over the back of a chair in the grubby second-floor office. Trace took one look at him and disliked him again. If he had been a movie producer, R. J. Roberts was the sort who'd have a casting rug because he didn't want to spend the money to buy a couch.

"Yeah, of course I remember you," Roberts said. "It was . . . let's see . . ."

"It was two years ago. One of your hookers rolled one of my insurance people and I took the money back from her. I'm sure she mentioned my name to you."

"That's not the way I remember it," Roberts said. His teeth were yellow and Trace didn't want to get too close to him because he could imagine what the man's breath was like. "I kind of remember a client of mine saying she was assaulted by you, but I advised her not to pursue the case. That's how I remember it." Yellow smile. "Anyway, what can I do for you, Tracy?"

"Early Jarvis," Trace said.

"What about him?"

"The company I work for carried his life insurance. The countess is the beneficiary. I'm checking that out. You're checking out the jewel theft. My company thinks it would be good if the two of us pooled knowledge. Sort of on the theory that two heads are better than one. Especially if one of them is yours."

Roberts hunched forward in his chair behind the desk. "I didn't hear anything like that from my company," he said.

"Listen," Trace said. "Ground rules. I don't give a damn about the jewelry and I don't give a damn about whatever deal you've got with the insurance company. And I don't give a damn what kind of scam you run on them."

"What do you mean, scam?" Roberts snapped.

"Is this going to be one of those conversations where everything is a question?" Trace said. "All right, Roberts, I'll tell you exactly what I mean. You're a private investigator but I don't know how you got your license. You make most of your living by running a handful of hookers. Your hookers steal. If one of them makes a big score, you get the insurance company that's handling it to hire you. Then you get the stolen stuff back from your girl, whoever she is, and you send most of it to the insurance company and get a fee. The rest of it you keep and sell, and split with the hooker. Sound familiar, so far?"

"You've got—"

"No, not a helluva nerve. I live in this town and I know most of the time what's going on. So let's just save ourselves all the trouble. You do whatever you want with the insurance company. All I want to do is clean up that it wasn't Felicia who killed Jarvis, and then I'm done. You do what you want."

Roberts shook his head. "I don't want to work with you. We won't get along."

Trace shrugged his total unconcern. "Suit yourself. I can get what I need from you or I can get it from the cops. No difference to me. But if you don't cooperate with me, the first person I go to is my company's vice-president for claims—he's my closest friend—and I tell him what kind of insurance dodge you run and then you know what'll happen. He'll tell some other vice-president for claims, all those insurance bastards stick together, and he'll tell another vice-president for claims and pretty soon the story will get to the right vice-president for claims and you'll be out of a job and a fee, past, present, and future. Work with me, you do what you want. Work around me and I guarantee you, you'll get zip code. If you don't believe me, I'll call Walter Marks right now. He's my boss and he has absolute faith in my word. You'll be gone so fast, your head will swim."

Yellow smile. "You don't have to take that attitude, Tracy. As long as you lighten up, we could work together on this. What about fees? How do we split?"

"We don't. You get paid for what you do; I get paid for what I do. I'm not interested in robberies. The only reason I'm here is because I've got to find out something about the jewels before I can find out anything about who killed Early Jarvis. You tell me and we'll share information. Sort of one hand washes the other." The image was instantly repellent to Trace. The thought of engaging his hand with Roberts' mitt in any kind of cooperative endeavor was vomitous.

"All right," Roberts said. "That sounds fair enough." He turned to a file cabinet, opened a drawer, and was pulling out a thin folder when the door to his office flew open and a woman's voice yelled, "All right, what's this shit?"

The woman standing in the doorway was tall and blond and too-tan because her face had started to wrinkle and was showing every one of her forty-plus years. She was wearing a costume of some kind of zebra pattern knit with a short-sleeve top that showed a lot of cleavage and skin-tight long pants that Trace thought would cut off the circulation to a normal person's feet. If that hadn't already been taken care of by her shoes, transparent glass-looking numbers with heels a full five inches high.

She wore night-time makeup—a lot of blues and greens around the eyes—and it did nothing to soften the angry scowl on her face.

Roberts spun around, tossed the folder on the

desk, and snapped, "Goddammit, bitch, I've got business here."

The woman looked at Roberts and at Trace a long while before her face relented a little.

"I've seen you around," she said to Trace.

He nodded. "How are you, Lip Service?"

"Not as good as I could be. Come to talk some business."

"Outside," Roberts said. "Outside. I'll talk to you outside." He got up and thumped toward the open office door. "I'll be right back," he told Trace, and grabbed the woman's arm and took her into the hallway. He closed the door after him, but Trace could still hear parts of their conversation. Through the frosted glass of the window, the two together merged into the outline of one foggy lump of humanity, and Trace remembered Shakespeare's "beast with two backs" and thought this was more like a beast with no brains.

"What is it . . . why she running . . . ?"

". . . does it better than you."

". . . doing it seven years . . . just toss me off like that?"

". . . no tossing off. Easier to get along with . . . like her better."

". . . cut their goddamn throats, they like me fine."

". . . done . . . all there is to it . . . no more complaints."

". . . ain't telling that bitch nothing."

". . . working? Stop complaining."

". . . tossed aside like an old rag."

". . . talk later . . . business now . . . yeah, right . . . tonight."

Through the frosted glass, Trace could see the lump of humanity disengage slowly into two lumps

33

and then half of it moved away down the hallway. Roberts stayed fixed in one spot for a moment, then opened the door and came back inside.

Yellow smile. "Sorry about the interruption," he said. "She's having some problems she asked me to look into and she's getting a little impatient. You know. Women."

And because that polite fiction served Trace's main purpose, which was to get out of Roberts' office as rapidly as he could without contracting a social disease, he nodded and said, "Clients are pains in the ass sometimes. So fill me in on Jarvis."

Roberts oozed himself back into his chair, moved aside a red spiral-bound notebook, and opened the file folder. It contained only two yellow sheets of paper and the detective shuffled them a long time before starting to recite.

"Okay. It happened on the twenty-seventh. That'd be two weeks ago. The countess and Jarvis were in England, she was on vacation and he always traveled with her. He wasn't feeling good, the countess said, so she told him to take a couple of days off, but instead he said he wanted to come home and see his doctor. She told me it was all right with her. I got all this from her when she got back. And also from the cops, but they don't have much. So, anyway, Jarvis flies back. Next thing is that Spiro . . . You know where the countess lives?"

"Yeah. Big place outside town," Trace said. "I've been there."

"Okay. Well, this Spiro is like the gardener and the watchman and whatever, so he was staying there while they were away. Anyway, it's late and he gets a call from Jarvis, who says to pick him up at the airport. So Spiro drives out there, but no

Jarvis. He musta got tired of waiting or something. Spiro hangs around for a couple of hours, but when Jarvis don't show up, he drives back to the countess's. When he gets inside, he goes back to the kitchen and makes himself a drink because he wants to sit by the phone for a while 'cause he's afraid that Jarvis'll call and chew his ass out and tell him to get to the airport again. But for some reason—maybe he hears a noise or something—he walks around the other side of the house, you know how it's kind of split into two sections, and there's the living room and it's a mess. You know that big fireplace the countess has got at the end of the room?"

"Right."

"Well, her safe was under a stone panel in that fireplace, see? And the panel is open, and the room looks like there was a fight. One of the big plants, some kind of tree or something, is tipped over near the fireplace. So Spiro looks around and then he sees Jarvis' body. The sliding doors out to the pool are open and Jarvis is laying there and he's got his head near the goldfish pool—they've got freaking goldfish in their yard, would you believe that shit? —and his head is all bloody and he looks dead, so Spiro calls the police and they come."

"What'd they find out?" Trace asked.

"The safe had been opened, but there weren't any fingerprints on it. Spiro didn't know what was in it and it was only when the countess came back that the cops find out that she's missing a million dollars or so in jewels. But there's no prints. They said that Jarvis got his head bashed in, but Spiro could see that. And that's what they got and that's all. Oh, yeah. Jarvis rented a car at the airport. Cops found it parked out on the road near the house. They don't know why he parked there and neither do I."

"You find out anything else? What about Jarvis?" Trace asked.

Roberts lit a cigar before answering. Like everything else about him, it was foul-smelling. "Nothing yet. I looked around town for anything on him, but there wasn't anything. He didn't gamble and he didn't bop around with women. He spent all his time out at the plotzo. That's what the countess calls her place, she kept calling it a plotzo. You know what a plotzo is?"

"I think she means a palazzo. It's Italian for palace," Trace said.

"Yeah, maybe that's what she meant," Roberts said. "But this ain't no palace, though. It's just a nice big house with a high wall and a gate, but it ain't no plotzo."

"Nobody you heard of wanted to kill Jarvis? No gambling debts or loan sharks or anything like that?" Trace asked.

"Nothing I can find out yet. Like I said, he was always out at the plotzo."

"All right," Trace said. "You hear anything on the street about the jewels?"

"No," Roberts said. "I should have, too. I let everybody know that I was working on this. Now, if it's a townie who hit the plotzo, he read the papers. He knows it's a million dollars the insurance company's going to have to cough up and he knows if he tries to go on the street, this is a murder rap maybe and nobody's going to want to mess with him. So he should get hold of me and I'll get him a few dimes on the dollar and he doesn't have to fence and the insurance company saves a lot and the countess gets her jewels back and everybody's happy except the cops but fuck them, who cares? But I ain't heard nothing from nobody. I can't understand it."

"Maybe whoever took them was from out of town," Trace said.

"Maybe, but there's a lot of word out on these now, these jewels. They were pretty special pieces, I guess. There was a diamond terror with a lot of stones."

Terror? "A tiara?" Trace said.

"Right. A diamond terror and like two big diamond necklaces like queens wear. Wait. Here's a newspaper picture of the terror and one of the necklaces." He shoved a clipping toward Trace, who saw Felicia Fallaci bedecked in jewels and smiling beautifully. The caption said the photo was taken at a charity ball for homeless children at which she had made a surprise appearance.

"They took that picture just before she went to Europe," Roberts said. "If those pieces show up, they'd be spotted right away."

"The thief'd just remove the stones and sell them piecemeal," Trace said.

"Yeah, probably."

"Anything else I ought to know?" Trace asked.

"That's all I got so far. I talked to the countess, but she don't know nothing and she said there wasn't anything going on at the plotzo, like people trying to stake out the joint or a lot of salesmen or surveyors showing up when they didn't used to show up. So she wasn't a lot of help."

"Basically," Trace said, "if you don't get a call from the thief, you don't have anything."

"That's about it," Roberts said. "If you find out something, then you could probably be a big help to me. Listen, Tracy, I got no problems with cutting you in for a piece of my fee. You help me, I help you."

Trace nodded. "Okay. Thanks, Roberts. I'll keep you posted."

"You got any ideas right now?" Roberts asked.

"Not yet. I think first I'll go to the plotzo."

4

"Hey, goombah. What brings you to these hallowed halls?"

Lt. Daniel Rosado shook Trace's hand in a tight grip, then nodded him to a chair in the dimly lit detective's office in the basement of police headquarters.

Without waiting for an answer, Rosado said, "I learned your trick. I've got vodka in the freezer. You want a pop?"

"Before lunch?" Trace said, and tried to look shocked.

"Trace, I know you. You drink before getting out of bed in the morning."

"Not anymore. I'm tapering off."

"You?" Rosado laughed, much too long for Trace's taste. "How come?"

"I'm getting old. I'm turning over a new leaf."

"You know what I found out in life?" Rosado said. "You turn over a lot of new leaves, and underneath them you still find the same old bugs."

"Don't undermine my courage now," Trace said. "The first day is the hardest."

"Horseshit. The first seven years are the hardest. Every day's harder than the one before it. You know how miserable you feel now? You're going to feel worse tomorrow and even worse the day after that. You'll cut your wrists by the weekend."

"I didn't say I was quitting, just tapering off," Trace said.

"Good. Then taper off later. Have a drink." Rosado went to the small refrigerator in the office, took a pint bottle of vodka from alongside the ice-cube tray, and poured some into a plastic throw-away glass and handed it to Trace. Trace sipped at it, then set it down.

"The things I do for a client," he said. "Now that I've got you all agreeable, I know you're going to help me. Felicia Fallaci."

"The countess?"

"Right. And Early Jarvis."

"I thought the Inspector Clouseau of crime-fighting was working on this. Roberts, that douche bag."

"He is. On the jewelry theft."

"Forget ever seeing that jewelry again," Rosado said with disgust.

Trace nodded. "Jarvis had an insurance policy with Felicia as beneficiary. I'm just checking it out before my company pays."

"What do you need?"

"Everything," Trace said. "I talked to Roberts. He's almost as dumb as he is dirty."

"I'd hate to have to live on the change," Rosado said. "Okay. You stay here. Help yourself to the vodka if you want more. I'll be right back."

Rosado walked out of the office. He was a handsome man with salt-and-pepper hair, almost as tall as Trace but leaner through the chest and shoulders. He was gentle and good-hearted, often reminding Trace of the owner of an underpriced Italian restaurant who gave most of his profits to the local Opera League. They had first met while Trace was looking into a string of systematic thefts from the Araby Casino, where Chico worked, and they had spent long hours together arguing about the merits of tenors—Rosado liked Jussi Bjoerling while Trace held out for Caruso.

He was honest and funny and happily married, hadn't had a drink in seven years, and his only professional flaw was that he was just not much of a detective. But, then, who was? Trace thought generously. Most police-department detectives were minimally talented and they didn't have Rosado's saving grace of being charming.

When the lieutenant came back into the office, he was holding an inch-thick sheaf of blue and pink papers, held together by a wide rubber band. He plopped it onto his desk, sat down, and sipped at his coffee.

"You want to read this stuff or you want to talk to me?" he asked.

"Let's talk first," Trace said. "Roberts gave me the bare bones. Time, body, blah-blah, safe unlocked, jewery gone, what Spiro said. Tell me things I ought to know that'll enrich my life."

"The countess must be good in bed," Rosado said.

"I wouldn't know. I don't score royalty," Trace said.

"You mutt, you'd mount a mongoose."

"Why do you say that about Felicia?" Trace asked.

" 'Cause she had like a million dollars' worth of jewels. It came to her as gifts along the way, she said."

41

"Some people give women things. When they look like Felicia, bigger things."

"I guess so. Anyway, the murder night. Here's some reports from cops on the scene. Let's see. Luggage. Here's the autopsy. Here's—"

"Wait a minute," Trace said. "Go back to luggage."

"When this Spiro ran into the living room, he tripped over a bag. Jarvis'. He must have come to the house, set the bag down in the living room, and I guess surprised whoever was breaking into the safe and got clubbed."

"What was in the suitcase?" Trace asked.

"Your police department never sleeps," Rosado said. He flipped through the sheets and pulled out a blue one. "Not a suitcase—a little leather bag, like a gym bag," he said. "A shaving kit, a bottle of aspirins, American Airlines magazine, that's all."

"Okay. What about the autopsy?"

"Here's a picture," Rosado said. He handed Trace an eight-by-ten color print.

It was shot from a slight elevation and it showed Early Jarvis lying facedown on the stone patio between the house and the swimming pool. His arms were extended up over his head, his gloved hands almost reaching the small goldfish pond built into the patio. His head was turned to one side and Trace could see it had been bashed in pretty thoroughly. He was lying in a large puddle of blood and there were blood smears on a ceramic fish statue next to the goldfish pool.

Rosado had found the autopsy report. "Doc Johnson did the autopsy," he said. "She said it looked like Jarvis was slugged inside the house, because there was blood there, and then there was a trail leading outside to the patio. Somehow he must have got-

42

ten out there and, she says, he fell again, cracked his skull on that stupid ceramic fish, and then just lay there and bled to death. There were traces of skull matter on the ceramic thing. No indication of what else he might have been hit with. Maybe a big flashlight."

Trace shrugged. "Why crawl outside? When you come to, wouldn't you just call the cops?"

"I asked Doc Johnson that, too," Rosado said. "She said you never can tell with head injuries because you don't know exactly what got injured in the brain. She said she had a case once where a guy was standing at the bathroom sink and got shot in the head by his wife. Well, he picked himself up, and then lathered his face and shaved. And when he was done shaving, then he called the police. And when they got there, he was dead. You can't tell with head injuries, she said. People do nutty things. Anyway, here's some more photos."

He slid a stack of eight-by-tens across the desk. They showed the inside of the countess's living room with the stone panel on the fireplace hinged outward, exposing the safe door. A cocktail table was overturned. A large Fiberglas pot on the left side of the fireplace had been knocked over and a six-foot-tall treelet was lying on the floor, dirt from its roots strewn about the floor. There were photos of the open sliding doors that led to the patio.

"No prints, I guess," Trace said.

"None."

"What was on Jarvis' body?" Trace asked.

Rosado looked through more papers. "I'm not allowed to let you look at official reports, you know."

"I know that. But if you read them to me, it

43

saves me the trouble of sneaking back here at night and stealing them."

"Yeah, here we are. He had his wallet, twelve dollars in cash, a driver's license, a photo of him and the countess, and an American Express card. That's all."

"Anything in his pockets?"

"Just his house keys and the keys to the car he rented. About eighty cents in change."

"Good," Trace said.

"Why good?"

"Where's his passport?"

"His passport, his passport." Rosado shuffled through more papers. "No passport."

"How'd he get back into the country?"

"Damned if I know. Can't get in without a passport, can you?"

"No. You in charge of this case, Danny?"

"Well, we've pretty well deep-sixed it. You know how it is. If you don't solve it in two days, you don't solve it at all. But technically I guess I'm still in charge. And I've got some guys out on the street, watching for the jewelry, but nothing yet."

"Okay, I'm going to nose around some, maybe see the countess today. Anything I get, I'll let you know."

"Okay," Rosado said agreeably. "And if anything comes up on this end, I'll tell you. Together, maybe we can beat that pimp out of his fee."

"A worthwhile ambition," Trace said.

"And Bjoerling was still a better tenor than Caruso," Rosado said.

"He wasn't even a better tenor than Mario Lanza," Trace said. "And, hell, everybody was a better tenor than Mario Lanza. Liberace's a better tenor than Mario Lanza."

"Prettier too," Rosado said. "Dinner soon?"

"After this week. Chico's doing some convention work for my insurance company. When we finally get all those lunatics out of town."

"Okay."

"But I'll be talking to you before then," Trace said.

5

"Son, if I see one more nickel slot machine, I'm going to cut my wrists. And trapeze acts at Circus Circus. If I knew your mother had a trapeze fixation, I never would have married her. I've got a mind to saw through some of those ropes."

"I told you to keep her away from that place," Trace said. "Where is she anyway?"

"Ladies' room. I think they give away free packs of Kleenex. This is the third time for her in an hour."

"Maybe all the excitement under the big top has unsettled her kidneys," Trace said.

The two men were seated at an otherwise-empty large table in the back of the main banquet room in the Araby Hotel. The tables on either side of them were empty also, but there was a high drone of voices in the room from five hundred other lunchers who sat in tables of ten, in front of a long head table, elevated three feet above the main floor. Robert Swenson sat in the middle of the head table, flanked on one side by Walter Marks and on the other by Chico.

She saw Trace and waved. He made a circle of

thumb and index finger and gave her the okay sign.

Trace's mother returned to the table. Without greeting her son, she said to her husband, "That woman didn't give us much of a table, did she?"

"Hilda," her husband said, "that woman's name is Chico. By the way, this is your son, if you want to say hello."

"Hello, Devlin," she said without looking at him. Instead, she picked up a coffee spoon and began to examine it for flaws.

"Actually, Mother, Chico gave you the best table in the house," Trace said.

"Way in the back here where you can't see anything?" she asked.

"Yes. Way in the back here where no one can see you, either, when you walk out in the middle of the speeches. She was being kind to you. Who wants to listen to insurance speeches? Eat and leave."

"God bless Chico," Trace's father said.

"Amen, Sarge," Trace said.

"You would say that, Patrick. You like her, for some unknown reason. Did you see our son's apartment?"

"It's her apartment too, Mother," Trace said.

"You can tell, with all those terrible striped fabrics and leather all around. A woman's touch would do wonders for your place, Devlin."

"It has exactly the woman's touch I want, Mother," Trace said.

"Hmmmph," his mother said conclusively. Alongside a plate two places away, she finally found a spoon that passed inspection, and used it to put sugar into her coffee.

"Are you enjoying your vacation, Mother?" Trace asked. He winked at his father.

"I wanted to go to Miami. Everybody I know is in Miami. But your father wouldn't go."

"Exactly," Sarge said. "Because everybody you know is in Miami. If everybody you knew was in Las Vegas, *then*, by God, I'd go to Miami."

"Everybody I know should go to a tavern somewhere. You'd go *there*," she said.

"Even the purest of us sometimes has to compromise on moral principles," he said. "You're right."

"Will you two just drink your coffee?" Trace said. "You're enough to send me back to the bottle."

"Hear, hear," Sarge said. "What are you up to these days, son? Working on anything interesting?"

"Nothing much. Just kind of scuffing around," Trace said.

"I figured you were working on something because you're wearing your microphone tie clip," the gray-haired man said.

"A couple of interviews this morning. An insurance dead end," Trace said.

"If you need any kind of help, you should call me," his father said. "You know I'm going to be here all week and I used to be pretty good."

"You wouldn't take the lieutenant's examination," his wife said. "You could have been a lieutenant, but you wouldn't take the examination."

Trace's father leaned over and whispered in his ear. "And it'll get me away from this harpie for a while. A day without nickel slots."

"What'd you say?" his wife demanded. "What'd you say?"

"I told Devlin that you've already dropped ten dollars on the nickel slots," Sarge said.

"If those slot machines would pay off once in a while, I'd be ahead. They never pay off here. Slot machines in Atlantic City pay off, but not here. In Atlantic City, you can win a million dollars."

"That's a lot of nickels," Sarge said.

"Play the machines by the front door," Trace said.

"What?"

"Play the slots near the entrance doors to the casinos. They rig those to pay off the most because it helps drag more players into the casino."

"Is that true?" his mother asked.

"Would I lie to you?"

"Why did you wait until now to tell me? I'm already ten dollars behind. I could have been a winner already. When I played in Paradise Island, I won enough to buy a piece of crystal. A beautiful piece of crystal."

"It looked like a glass carrot," Sarge whispered to Trace.

"I never win anything in this town," Trace's mother was saying. "I don't know how you can stand to live here."

"You forget, Mother, I made my living gambling here for three years. The place has its charms."

"Sand and sun," she said. "What charm?"

"No ex-wife. No What's-his-name and the girl."

"Must you refer to your children that way? They are your children, you know."

"That's arguable," Trace said. "Not that they're mine, but that they're children at all. I've always regarded them as particularly repugnant midgets. Now, drink your coffee or I'll pour salad dressing on your hat."

Mrs. Hilda Tracy looked horrified for a moment, then bent over her coffeecup with total concentration. Sarge leaned toward his son and whispered approvingly in his ear, "Firm, firm, very firm."

There was a clinking of glasses and Trace looked up as Bob Swenson began his speech of welcome to the assembled national sales force of Garrison Fidelity Insurance Company.

"It's a pleasure to welcome you all here," he said, his actor's voice resounding through the room over the speaker system. "And I think you'll all agree with me that we owe a special vote of thanks for the arrangements to our lovely convention hostess, Miss Michiko Mangini." He leaned over to his right and kissed Chico on the top of her head.

She looked embarrassed. Walter Marks, watching, looked pained.

Later, when Marks was reading off the names of everyone in the company who had sold more than a million dollars' worth of life insurance in the past twelve months, Chico met Trace at the doorway to the banquet hall.

"Ah, it's the famous Miss Michiko Mangini," Trace said. "Introduction, kiss on the head from the boss. What's next?"

"He had his hand on my knee all during lunch. I prefer the kiss on the head. I wish he hadn't mentioned my name, though. Now all these insurance lunatics will be after me to find their lost children, complaining about crooked dealers, what can their wives use for sunburn?"

"Two grand," Trace said.

"I still don't know if it's worth it," Chico said. "How's it going with you?"

"Just splashing around," he said. "Listen, if you

feel really depressed, look at Sarge over there. He's stuck with my mother. At least Swenson likes you."

"Trace, sometimes you have an absolute genius for making the sun shine."

"No extra charge. It's the kind of wisdom we elderly develop naturally as the years go on."

6

Countess Felicia Fallaci's home was fifteen minutes outside of Las Vegas, set back from a secondary road that sliced its way through the untidy, weed-cluttered desert. It was surrounded by ten-foot-high stone walls, topped with barbed wire, as was the large iron gate cut into the walls. Today the gate was wide open and Trace drove his white Mazda up the long straight drive and parked it next to Felicia's burgundy Rolls Royce, a Jeep convertible, and a small and totally impractical English sports car, the kind with the foot pedals so close together that one normal-size shoe could cover clutch, brake, and accelerator all at once. Which always left the question of what to do with the other foot, since there was no room for it on the narrow little sliver of auto floor.

The front door of the house was open too and Trace stepped into a hallway that passed through into the swimming pool and patio area, located between the two main wings of the house. Without bothering to ring or knock, he walked through the hall and out toward the pool, where a half-dozen people were lounging around on chaises.

Trace stopped in the open sliding doors and

looked at Felicia. She was at the far end of the pool, lying on her back on a padded lounge chair, wearing only a very skimpy white bikini bottom that looked garish against the warm copper tan of her body. Her bare breasts were tanned the same color as the rest of her body, and they were very good breasts indeed, Trace thought. Four other people were on lounges near her and there were two more on the far side of the pool, sitting at a table, but Trace couldn't see them because a sun umbrella was in the way.

"Felicia," Trace called.

She sat up, saw him, waved, and came toward him.

"Hi, Trace. You bring a bathing suit?"

"No."

"No matter. Take off your clothes anyway. You can climb on me and I'll walk you around the pool. Or not walk you around the pool, whichever you prefer."

"Will you explain it to Chico? When she sends her family of Samurai warriors around to remove our heads?"

Felicia sighed, a sigh that raised her bosom and lowered it again. Trace thought it was one of the two or three best sighs he had ever seen sighed.

"Rejected again," she said.

"Not that I love you less but that I love life more," he said.

She threw her arms around his neck and tried to insert her breasts into his chest cavity.

"Well, feel me up a little bit anyway," she said, and kissed him on the mouth hard.

"How come your door's open?" he asked. "Your gate too?"

She shrugged, one of the half-dozen really great shrugs. "Nothing left to steal," she said. "You here on work?"

"Yeah. You know, Felicia, I'm sorry about this, but once in a while my company gets a bug up its butt and I've got to check things out."

"Not your company," Felicia said. "That horrible little Munchkin, what's his name?"

"Groucho."

"Marks. Right. Walter Marks. I hope *he's* heavily insured."

"Who's your company?" Trace asked, nodding toward the other end of the pool.

"Usual crowd of hangers-on. Come on. If you're not going to jump my bones, I guess I ought to introduce you. But listen, if you change your mind and want to trick, we can go inside. You piss me off, Trace. I'm a fucking countess. I can get any man I want and you keep turning me down."

"That's why you keep coming back," Trace said.

"I'm different." He looked down at her. "God, what a set of knobs. I'm weakening."

"Eat your heart out, faggot," she said, took his hand, and walked him toward the back of the enclosed patio, sealed off in the rear by a wooden wall that matched the rough unhewn wood of the stucco house's exterior trim.

As he walked alongside her, Trace looked past her bosom and saw the sliding doors that led to the living room, and before them the small square goldfish pond with the large ceramic fish sculpture alongside it. The pond itself was filled with plants and floating lily pads, and the water seemed green and murky. He wondered if it held any fish. He had had an aquarium as a young boy, and whenever the water turned that color, the fish went belly-up. He heard a squawking sound near his head and looked up to see two parrots sitting in a tree.

"Hey, they chained?" Trace asked.

"No. They're quite gentle," Felicia said. "Eat right out of your hand."

"Yeah. Your palm. No, thank you."

They were at the feet of two people who lay side by side on a double-width chaise longue. The man was short and bald, but he made up for the scarcity of hair on his head by a surplus of it all over his body. Even his kneecaps were hairy. The woman next to him was short and dumpy. She wore a one-piece bathing suit with a skirt and her legs looked like the "before" advertisements from a cellulite clinic. If you are what you eat, Trace thought, this woman has been eating nothing but orange peels all her life.

"These two things are the Neddlemans," Felicia said. "They say they're in shipping, but basically they're just a pair of spongers who go anywhere there's a free meal."

Neddleman removed a pair of red eye-shields that had made him look like an extra from *The Village of the Damned*. With his right thumb and forefinger, he made a mock effort to pry open his right eye, bloodshot and rheumy. He fixed his eye on Trace, mumbled "Charmed, I'm sure" in a basso-profundo voice, closed his eye, and replaced his eye shields. His wife lowered her sunglasses and looked at Trace.

"Actually, we are in shipping," she said. "Felicia just has a strange sense of humor. Who are you?"

"Devlin Tracy."

"What are you in?"

Trace hated people who asked him what he was "in." "Ladies' underwear, when I'm lucky. Most of the time, insurance. Want to buy a sunburn policy?"

"How pedestrian," Mrs. Neddleman said. "Do people still buy insurance?"

"If they've got something to lose."

Mrs. Neddleman closed her eyes.

"Don't waste your time talking to them, Trace," Felicia said. "They're absolute scumbags as people. I keep them around because both of them are named Francis. Francis and Frances Neddleman. I think that's cute."

"No accounting for taste," Trace said.

"You say you're in insurance?" said a man who was lying on a large towel a half-dozen feet away. He was very tan and wore the smallest bathing suit Trace had ever seen on a male. He had wavy, long dark-blond hair, swimmer's muscles, and was good-looking. His accent was vaguely continental.

"You might say that," Trace said.

"At the airport, those lunatics scratched my luggage," the man said. The accent was Italian, Trace decided. "Can you help me collect?"

"No."

"What good are you?"

"I make a very good potato-chip dip. With chives," Trace said.

"Trace," Felicia said, "this is Paolo Ferrara. He says he's a count, but he's not. He's just a rich playboy."

"What's he into?" Trace asked her.

Ferrara answered. "Drugs, basically. Coke, grass, hash. Want something?" He reached for a little leather case that lay next to him on the pool deck's rough tiled surface.

56

"No, thanks. I'm into alcohol basically," Trace said.

There was another man lying on a towel on the deck. A copy of *Gentlemen's Quarterly* covered his face. He slid it down to his chin. Another foreign accent.

"Are you a detective?" he asked. He was a painfully lean man with a neatly trimmed moustache and beard and treebark-brown hair. He had laugh lines in the corners of his eyes.

"Kind of," Trace said.

"Investigating the murder, right?" The man's own words seemed to interest him, and he slapped the magazine aside, sat up, and shook Trace's hand.

"This one is real," Felicia said. "He's a baron. Edvel Hubbaker. He's after my body. This is Trace."

"Of course I'm after her body," Hubbaker said. "Did you ever see tits like that anywhere else?"

"Nice butt, too," Felicia said.

"Are you going to catch the killer?" Hubbaker asked.

"If you do," Ferrara said, "Please do it somewhere else. I'm not into sordid."

Trace ignored him and said to Hubbaker, "I don't know. I'm just looking around."

"You have a theory, though, right? All detectives have theories. What is it? Burglar surprised while cracking a safe. What does that mean, anyway? Cracking a safe? Why not busting a safe? Anyway, safecracker surprised, fights to escape, bops poor Jarvis on the noggin, and flees with ill-gotten gains. Like that?"

"It's as good as anything else," Trace said, and then he stopped talking to Hubbaker because the two people on the far side of the pool stood up and Trace could see them. Or, more specifically, one of them.

She was a platinum blonde, six feet tall, stark naked. Her body was an erotic fantasy, and looking at her bosom, Trace thought of words like "ballooning," "bazooming," "galoomphing." Standing still, she quivered with sexuality. She was either a natural blonde or had a very close relationship with her hairdresser.

"Gee whillikers," Trace said softly.

"You like that, huh?" Felicia said. "I'm disappointed in you, Trace. I thought you were into subtlety, hints of smoldering sensuality. A lowered eyelid, a pouty lip, that kind of thing."

"I am. But for her, I make an exception. Raw, sweating sex. Gee whillikers."

"Well, come on, I'll introduce you. But be warned, you're not her type."

"I can change."

"Did you ever read *The Golden Ass of Apuleus*?" Felicia asked.

"Yes."

"Then you know the struggle that awaits you," she said. She grabbed Trace's elbow and pulled him toward the woman.

"Sweetheart," she called out, "there's someone here I want you to meet."

The blond woman turned around to face them fully. She had a face of unreal innocent beauty. Her eyes were sky-blue, her cheekbones pronounced, but soft instead of angular. She was enough woman to fill the dreams of ten generations of farm boys, Trace thought.

"Trace, this is National Anthem."

"What?" he said.

"National Anthem."

"Give me five seconds and I'll be able to salute."

"Slob," Felicia said. "We call her Nash for short. Nash, this is my friend, Trace, who thinks you're absolutely spectacular."

He knew it. It was too good to be true. He could see it in the blonde's eyes. There was a hesitation, as if she were trying to figure out what the countess had said, whether it was good or bad, and what she should do about it.

She finally decided it was good and smiled radiantly, jiggled a little up and down, setting her breasts into alarming motion, and squealed.

"Eeeeeyou," the sound came out. It was accomplished somehow by inhaling on the "eeee" and quickly expelling the "you" sound at a higher pitch. "Pleased to meetcha, I'm sure."

So much for passion, Trace thought. It was no-man's-land between the girl's ears. Not a brain in her head. And a New York Forty-second Street accent.

She stuck out her hand for Trace to shake and he had the fleeting desire to pump her hand up and down hard to see how her breasts would react, but he restrained himself and shook hands gently. She squeezed him hard and fingered his palm with her index finger.

"Eeeeyou," she squealed again.

"Trace is into insurance," Felicia said. "Nash here is into films. And donkeys."

"I'm gonna be a star," Nash said. "That's what they tell me anyway. No more loops." She was still holding Trace's hand, still tickling his palm. Maybe she would keep doing it until he told her to stop, Trace thought.

Felicia explained to Trace patiently, with a hint of a smile in the corners of her lovely mouth, "Nash has just finished her first feature film. She takes on nine men and a donkey."

"Let me tell ya, the donkey was the nicest one of the bunch," National Anthem said with a giggle, happy and secure because she was obviously repeating a phrase she had used many times before to good response. And she squealed again, "Eeeeyou."

Felicia would show no mercy. "It's called *Asses Up*, starring National Anthem."

"It's going to be bigger than *Deep Throat*," National Anthem assured Trace. She was still tickling his palm. "It'll gross millions, won't it, William?"

And for the first time since meeting this astonishing creation, Trace noticed, really noticed, that there was a man standing behind her. Like Trace, he wore a jacket and tie, but unlike Trace, he was short and mousy-looking with thinning hair, average color skin, average features. He wore eyeglasses that seemed too large for such a small face.

"This is William Parmenter," Felicia told Trace. "Everybody calls him Willie."

"I keep forgetting," National Anthem said. "I keep calling him William."

Trace shook the man's hand. It was a surprisingly firm handshake from a mouse.

"William, ooops, Willie says my picture will gross millions, isn't that right, Willia . . . Willie?"

Parmenter seemed embarrassed to be discussing it. "I'm no expert," he said.

"Willie's an expert on everything else," Felicia said. "He works for Paolo over there."

"What do you do, Parmenter?" Trace asked.

"Whatever Mr. Ferrara wants me to do," the

man said. He was an American, Trace noticed, with the broad vowel sounds of the Midwest in his voice.

"Willie's like an accountant and a valet and an assistant and a gofer," Felicia said. "But he's nice." She put her arm around the short man's head and squeezed him, pulling him toward her bosom. His face reddened with embarrassment. National Anthem finally stopped tickling Trace's hand. She had found something else to do. She put an arm around Willie's head and squeezed him too.

There he was, with his tiny little head squeezed in between two wonderful chests. Mouseman's paradise, Trace thought.

"Willie," bellowed Ferrara's voice from the other side of the pool.

"Yes, sir?"

"If you can extricate yourself from all those tits, would you fix me a drink?"

"Yes, sir," Willie said. He nodded to Trace, slipped free of the two women, and walked quickly away.

"Eeeeyou, he's sweet," National Anthem said.

"Does he have something to do with your movie?" Trace asked.

"Huh?"

"Is he an actor? Or a producer? Something like that?"

"I don't know," National Anthem said. She looked at Felicia in confusion. "Is he?"

"No. He's just a little, put-upon, horny wimp of a man who'd say anything to get into Nash's pants. If she had pants."

"Eeeeyou. I didn't know that."

"You wouldn't," Felicia said.

"Too bad," Nash said. "I'm into donkeys." She smiled at Trace again.

"Come on," Felicia said to Trace. "I guess you want to look over the scene of the crime and like that." She pulled him away from National Anthem. "If you find evidence that makes me the killer, you'll give me time enough to run away first?"

"For you, Felicia, for enriching my life by introducing me to National Anthem, anything. Tell me. Is this what they mean by decadence?"

"Hell, no. This is just a quiet afternoon at home with friends. You want decadence, come after the sun goes down."

They walked past her two parrots again. One of them squawked, "Polly want a hit. Polly want a hit."

They were near the goldfish pool.

"Early's body was found here," Felicia said.

"I saw the police photos."

"I don't know. The cops think he maybe was dazed or trying to follow the guy that hit him. Then he hit his head on this goddamn statue and ripped it open and then bled to death."

"Could the thief escape from out here?" Trace said, looking around the yard.

"Well, he could go through that gate back there. That puts him out into the grounds. But he'd still have to get through the front gate, or over the wall."

Trace nodded and said, "Felicia, would you mind covering your chest? It's hard for me to concentrate when my mouth keeps watering."

He hadn't realized how hot it was until he walked after Felicia into the air-conditioned coolness of her living room.

There was a white shirt tossed over the back of

the sofa and she put it on. When she turned back to Trace, the shirt was open, unbuttoned, and even though her breasts were covered, she now seemed even sexier.

"The safe's in the fireplace," Trace said.

"Right. It's buried under the stone." She walked to the fireplace and reached under its front edge. "There's a clip in here," she said. As she spoke, an irregularly edged rectangle of stone pieces popped away from the rest of the fireplace facing. "It's spring-loaded," she said. The section swung back on hidden hinges, exposing the safe. It was a regular wall safe, a foot in diameter, with a combination dial in the center.

Trace looked at the face of the safe. On either side of the dial was a deep hole and he touched them with his fingers.

"That must've been where the burglar tried to force the safe," Felicia said.

Trace nodded. "The safe was unlocked when what's his name, Spiro, found it?"

"Actually, the cops found it open. And everything gone."

"Who has the combination?"

"Now, me. Early had it too."

"Not Spiro?" Trace asked.

"A mopper and flopper? No, thank you. He didn't have it."

"And it was a million in jewels?"

"More than that, actually. It was insured for a million, but it might have been worth a million two or three. Diamonds have been going up again."

"From what I hear, they haven't shown up yet," Trace said.

"What does that mean?"

"I don't know. Maybe somebody from out of

town stole it all. Or whoever stole it is waiting for the heat to die down before he dumps it somewhere," Trace said.

He had the sense that somebody was listening to him and he walked softly to the open patio doors.

"Hello, Baron," he said. "Why don't you come in, instead of straining your ears?"

7

Baron Edvel Hubbaker stepped into the room. He was as tall as Trace and very thin.

"I'm sorry," he said to Felicia.

She shrugged, and Trace said, "Mind telling us why you were eavesdropping?"

"Really, I'm sorry. I just wanted to see how a real detective worked. But I didn't want to intrude, so I just thought I'd listen in."

"Pitch right in," Trace said. "How do you think I'm doing so far?"

"I haven't learned anything new yet," Hubbaker said.

"Here's a new question for you," Trace said. "Where were you the night Jarvis was killed?"

"Oh, that's good. This is really getting good," Hubbaker said. He seemed totally unconcerned by the question.

"Sorry, Trace," Felicia said. "Edvel was in England with me. All these people were. We were staying at Lady Dishwater's."

"Lady Dishwater?" Trace said.

"We call her that. Lady Dicheter. We were all there. I invited them all to come with me when I had to come home, but they were all mutts and didn't want to get involved in any funeral. So I came by myself and they all just arrived."

"Sorry," Hubbaker told Trace. "She's my alibi."

"It was worth a try," Trace said. "I just generally mistrust people who try to listen in on my conversations. Why did Jarvis come home?"

"He got sick," the countess said. "I think it might have been food poisoning. First, Willie got sick as soon as we all arrived, and then Early came down with it. I told him to take a couple of days off and go out into the countryside, but he decided he wanted to come back and see his doctor."

Trace turned back to the fireplace, looked at the safe, then at the two plants on either side of the stone wall.

"This the plant that got knocked over?" he asked, touching the six-foot-high plant that sat loosely inside a Fiberglas pot.

"Yeah," Felicia said. "I don't know plants, but they're some kind of aspidistra trees or something. They're due for planting any day now and I just hope that one didn't get shocked. They cost a small fortune. And another thing. I forgot to tell this to the police. The thief stole one of my ashtrays." She walked to the end table by the sofa and picked up a heavy-looking milky-white marble ashtray. "There was another one just like this," she said, "and now it's gone."

"Why would a thief steal an ashtray?" Trace said. "Unless maybe he hit Jarvis with it."

"I don't know," Felicia said. "Maybe he was compulsively neat and didn't want to drop cigarette butts in the yard when he was leaving. My ashtray. My goddamn tree. I hate this."

Trace looked again at the two trees. All trees looked alike to him. He looked at the one that had gotten knocked over and then at the other one, sitting inside its green Fiberglas pot, its roots wrapped loosely in a burlap bag. It didn't look any healthier to him than the other tree. Maybe shock was good for baby trees; maybe it let them know it was a jungle out there.

Trace looked at the trees and at the ashtray and at the fireplace and at the safe again. He glanced through the sliding doors toward the pool and the fish pond. He felt Hubbaker's eyes watching him, and he felt required to do something detectivey.

"Umhum," he said with what he hoped was proper significance. "Yup. I see. Umhum."

"Oh, Trace, will you stop the bullshit?" Felicia said. "What are you doing?"

He looked at her. Her shirt had slipped open and her breasts were exposed again.

"Just thinking out loud," he said darkly. "Is Spiro working today?"

"Was the Jeep parked outside?"

"Yes."

"Then he's here." She went to a speaker box on a small table and called into it.

"Spiro, come into the living room."

Just then, Willie Parmenter came into the living room from the hallway at the front of the house. He was carrying a tall highball glass.

"Sorry, I didn't think to ask. Would anyone like a drink?"

"No, Willie," Felicia said. Hubbaker and Trace shook their heads.

The small man walked through the cool room and out onto the patio. Trace followed him and stood in the doorway, looking across the pool at National Anthem, who was doing jumping-jack exercises. The Neddlemans were still unmoving on their twin chaises. Maybe they weren't husband and wife, Trace thought. Maybe they were Siamese triplets. Francis, Frances, and the Chaise Lounge all joined at the back.

Ferrara took the glass from Willie Parmenter and sipped it. Trace heard him snap, "Jesus Christ, what'd you do, fill this with water?"

"Sorry, sir. Ice melts," Parmenter mumbled.

Trace felt Felicia brush alongside him.

"You know anything about Jarvis' passport?" he asked.

"No. What about it?"

"Police didn't find it on him," Trace said.

"I don't know. Maybe one of those dopey cops lost it."

"You called me, ma'am," said a voice behind them.

Trace remembered Spiro from the last time he had been at Felicia's home. He was a swarthy man in his early thirties, with a *Viva Zapata!* moustache and greasy black hair.

"Mr. Tracy here wants to talk to you. Trace, I'm going outside before the sun's all gone. Call me if you need anything. I've heard all this before."

"Mind if I stay?" Hubbaker asked Trace.

"If you want," Trace said. "Sit down, Spiro."

The man sat stiffly on the edge of a small wooden desk chair.

"Is Spiro your last name or your first name?" Trace asked.

"Both names."

"Spiro Spiro? How's that?"

"Well, if you really got to know, my name's Spirakos Spirakodopolous. My father was Greek."

"The hell you say."

"Yes, he was," Spiro said. Obviously no sense of

humor, Trace thought. "He was a fisherman in Maryland. My mother was a baker."

"Okay. How long have you been working for the countess?"

"About a year. Since right after she moved here. Jarvis hired me."

"You lived in town before that?" Trace asked.

"Yes."

"What were you doing for a living?"

Spiro hesitated slightly. "Mostly odd jobs," he said.

Trace changed the subject quickly. "The night that Jarvis called you from the airport, how did he sound?"

"What do you mean?"

"Did he sound nervous or in a hurry or anything?"

"He was always in a hurry. But, no, I guess he didn't sound nervous or anything. He was like he always was."

"What did he say? Wait. Before you answer. Where were you when the phone rang?"

"In the kitchen. I was just getting ready to watch a movie."

"What movie?" Trace asked.

"*Mildred Pierce*. It's my favorite movie. It just came on."

"I think Joan Crawford always overacted," Trace said. "You were alone?"

"You better believe it," Spiro said quickly. "This is a good job and I wouldn't have anybody here 'cause Jarvis and the countess say don't have anybody here. See, I only spend nights here when the countess and Jarvis was away; otherwise, I stay at my own place. I wouldn't go messing up my job by fooling around here."

"Okay. Spiro, I just want you to know I'm not accusing you of anything or anything like that. I just want to try to get this whole thing straight in my mind."

Spiro nodded, and Hubbaker, who had been watching from the couch, said, "So you were in the kitchen watching television when the phone rang."

"Hey, Baron," Trace said, "if something comes up about heraldry or falcon-training, pitch right in. Otherwise, I'll do this."

"Sorry," Hubbaker said.

"So you were in the kitchen and the phone rang," Trace said.

"Yeah. So I reached up and grabbed it and said 'hello.' "

"Did you say 'hello' or 'Countess Fallaci's residence' or something like that?"

"No. I just said 'hello' 'cause this isn't the only house phone. The countess's other number, she has a tape machine on it, but if I answered that one, I'd say 'Fallaci residence,' but the phone in the kitchen's like my work phone so I just said 'hello.' "

"Okay. And what then?"

"It was Jarvis and he said—"

"Be exact," Trace said. "Word for word. Try to remember. You said 'hello.' "

"Okay. I said 'hello' and let's see, he said, 'This is Jarvis. Come and get me at the airport. I'm waiting at the middle door of the terminal.' "

"Yeah?" Trace said.

"And that's it?"

"What'd you say?"

"I said, 'Okay, I'll come right now.' "

"And what'd he say?" Trace asked.

"He said, 'And wait for me if I'm in the men's room or something,' and then he said thank you and that was funny 'cause he never said thank you. He didn't have any manners, that man," Spiro said, shaking his head.

"Okay. You left right away?"

"Right away. I went right away."

"Did you lock the front gate when you left?"

"It locks automatically. You open it with a key or a beeper thing, but it's got springs and it closes automatically unless you tie it open. Like now, I got it tied open. I keep it open during the day."

"So you went to the airport. What, then?"

"Jarvis wasn't there. I waited for him and he wasn't there. So I parked and went inside and looked for him, but I didn't see him, so I had him paged."

"Who paged him?"

"I asked at the American Airlines desk. They paged him but he didn't come, but I was afraid to leave, so I waited a long time before I came back here."

"How long?"

"A couple of hours it must've been, because when I got home *Mildred Pierce* was off."

Trace had thought all the while that Spiro was shifty-eyed, unable to look at him, because the young man's eyes seemed to dart left and right. Now he realized that they darted more to the right than to the left, and he glanced out toward the pool and saw why. National Anthem was lying on her back on a kapok mat, with her legs up above her head, pedaling an imaginary bicycle.

"That girl can pedal it all over town," Trace said. "So when you came back, was the gate still closed?"

"Yeah. Like I said, it closes automatic. So I came in and I didn't see anybody or hear anything and I went over to the kitchen and turned on the television. I missed *Mildred Pierce*."

"Then what?"

"Then, later, I decided to go to bed, so I started to walk around the house, just to check, you know, like I always do, and I came in here and I tripped over Jarvis' bag."

"Where was it?"

Spiro turned around and pointed to the steps leading down into the room. "Over there. I nearly broke my neck falling down the stairs. And then I saw the doors was open to the patio and I walked over there, by that switch, and turned on the patio lights and then I seen Jarvis laying over there by the fish pond."

"What'd you do then?"

"I looked at him and touched him, but he didn't move. And I felt for a pulse in his neck but he didn't have one and there was blood all over, it was like a lake, and then I looked real close and I saw his eyes was open and it scared the shit out of me 'cause I knew he was dead. So I came back in here and called the cops."

"When'd you notice the safe was open?"

"I didn't even notice. I went down to the gate to open it for the cops. They came right away and they saw the safe was unlocked. And they asked me all these same questions and that's all I know."

"Okay," Trace said. He turned to Hubbaker. "I forget anything?"

"Aren't you supposed to ask him if he did it?"

"No," Trace said. "Not when I know he didn't do it. Thanks, Spiro."

"Okay, man. Anytime." Spiro got up and walked

toward the exit of the room, but he walked slowly, ogling National Anthem across the pool. Then he shook his head in admiration and left.

"How do you know he didn't do it?" Hubbaker asked.

"I don't. But if I asked him, he'd tell me he didn't, whether he did or not. Now at least he thinks I trust him, so maybe I can get him to drop his guard."

"Very clever."

"Just routine for us fancy detectives," Trace said.

When he went back outside, both parrots were screaming, "Polly want a hit, Polly want a hit." The countess had taken off her bikini bottom and was in the swimming pool.

"You have to go?" she said.

" 'Fraid so."

"Figure out anything yet?" she asked.

Trace noticed that when she stood still in the chest-high water, her breasts floated. Looking down at her from his elevated viewpoint, with her bosom floating that way, Trace thought she looked like something conceived in a Howard Hughes design shop. "Not yet," he said.

"Make them give me my money," she said. "I need it, especially if I'm going to keep supporting all these parasites. Bend down here and give me a kiss."

Trace held onto the ladder, leaned over, and for his effort was tongued by the countess.

"Next time, give me a call first. I'll get rid of this crew and you and I can splash around together."

"Listen. My insurance company is having a hospitality thing tonight. Maybe you and your friends would like to come."

"Is their liquor going to be any different from my liquor?" she asked.

"It'll cost you less 'cause we'll be paying for it. If you can make it. Maybe these folks would like to see how the bourgeois middle class lives. We've got a bank of hospitality rooms at the Araby. Just show up if you want."

"Maybe we will."

"You can try charming Groucho again. That might get you your money," Trace said.

"I'll be there."

8

Trace was in the bathroom, but he came running out when he heard a shriek from Chico.

He found her as he had left her, sitting in a lotus position in the middle of the floor, wearing only a leotard. Except tears were now streaming down her face.

He knelt next to her. "What's the matter?"

She turned her sloe black eyes toward him.

"Eeeeyou," she squealed, and then collapsed backward on the floor, laughing, holding her sides, in such pain from laughing so hard that she rolled from side to side, trying to stop.

She finally did, looked at him, squeaked "Eeee-you" again, and started all over. Trace stood up in disgust and put his foot on her stomach.

She pointed a finger at him. "National Anthem?" she said. Tears rolled down her face. She rolled out from under his foot.

"You're listening to my tapes. I go into the bathroom and you start listening to my tapes. You're not supposed to listen to my tapes."

She was still laughing.

"At least a half-dozen beautiful women threw

themselves at me today," he said. "How are you going to feel when you hear all that on tape?"

"They all mistake you for a donkey?" Chico asked. "Eeeyou." More laughter.

"You really have the capacity to be a hateful little coolie," Trace said. "At least National Anthem was friendly and pleasant. She held my hand for the longest time."

"Probably trying to think of what came after eeeeyou," Chico said. "And stop complaining. I always wind up listening to your tapes anyway because you can't figure out what's going on and I have to listen to them to make sense out of things."

"That was true in the past," Trace conceded. "When I was drinking too much. But now that I'm sobering up, my brain is functioning like a fine Swiss watch. I'll never need your help again."

"That'll be the day," she said. "You really stay sober today?"

"I haven't had a drink," he said. The one in Dan Rosado's office really didn't count because it was forced on him and he didn't finish it all anyway.

"I'm proud of you," she said.

"Too late now after all this abuse. What are you doing home anyway? I thought you're supposed to be a convention hostess?"

"Don't start," she said grimly. "I am a convention hostess. I've been one all day. I baby-sat two surly little snotnoses. I helped some woman who was locked out of her room. I turned down four sexual offers. Why is it only guys named Mel attack me in Las Vegas? Let's see. I told Bob Swenson that I didn't want him to divorce his wife and marry me. Then I told him that I didn't want him to adopt me and try to pass me off to his wife as a Cambodian foundling. I've had my ass pinched and my little tits brushed by more elbows today than I've had in three years of dealing at the Araby. If this is Middle America, give me gambling degenerates every time. I'm exhausted." She looked at him and winked. "Of course, if you were a donkey, I could probably fit you into my schedule. Eeeeyou. *Asses Up.*" And she started laughing again.

"Will you stop? This is serious. You really shouldn't be listening to my tapes."

"You're kidding," she said as she raised herself back to a sitting position and twisted her legs again into a full lotus.

"No, I'm not. You think you've been listening to my tapes other times, but I edit them and launder them and leave some out so I don't upset you. A very important thing. Tapes are private and we've always respected each other's privacy."

"Horse dookie," she said. "Or donkey dookie, if you prefer. Respect privacy? Every time I'm out you want to know where I was and who I was with and did I make any money and was it good for me. Privacy? You don't know the meaning of the word 'privacy.'"

"I never open your mail," he said righteously.

"I never get any. I get a bill for magazines. Two book clubs. That's it."

"Why don't you ever get any mail here?" he said. "Are you getting your mail somewhere else?"

"Sorry," she said. "That's a private matter."

"I don't think that's funny," Trace said. "And I don't appreciate your sitting there showing off, just because you're able to twist your legs into a pretzel."

"Sorry, macho man. You're the one who wanted to play football and wound up with glass knees. Don't blame me."

Trace sat on the couch and tried to look irritated.

"Trace, old buddy," she said, "you can take your tapes and stuff them. You can metamorphose, if you want, into a donkey. You can spend the next six months in rut with National Anthem. Do donkeys rut? Moose rut."

"I think donkeys kong. I think you say spend six months in kong with a donkey."

"That's ridiculous," she said. "Trace, I don't care what you do and what your tapes tell about it. I didn't sign on here for fidelity. I know you: you're about as constant as Old Will's moon. You have screwed half of Las Vegas and the other half is on your schedule. You would sleep with a snake if you were sure it wasn't dead. You are an unregenerate degenerate. You're not faithful, you're not loyal, and you're not even nice."

"And you came all this way home just to tell me that. Isn't that nice?" he said.

"I told you I was exhausted. I came home to exercise."

She said this in a way that convinced Trace that she really believed it was a logical statement and that one thing followed the other. Actually, it probably was. She was a dancer by training, and when her head got fuzzy, she unfuzzed it by making her body work. Her wonderful dancer's body. He looked at her again, taut and trim in her leotards. He approved.

"Get that look out of your eye," she said. "I'm mad at you, for openers, and anyway I've got to shower and get back to the zoo for tonight's reception. Trace, tell me true. Your mother's not going to be there tonight, is she?"

"If the food's free, my mother's going to be there," he said.

"Oh, God," she said. "Someday I'm going to take up your father's offer and run away with him."

"He won't let you listen to his tapes either," Trace said.

"Hey. You're lighting another cigarette," Chico said.

"A necessary prerequisite to smoking it," he said.

"You're smoking too much."

"Listen, I've almost quit drinking for you. Have you been put on earth to harass me?"

"I don't want you to get cancer."

"I don't believe in cancer," he said.

"What do you mean, you don't believe in cancer?"

"Them freaking rats get cancer from everything. Alcohol, tobacco, saccharin, asbestos, blue cheese. Did you ever think that maybe rats are just cancer-prone? Or maybe they're allergic to laboratories? Maybe laboratories give cancer. Call Sloan-Kettering. I've just had a flash."

"Just watch the cigarettes," she said.

"Hai, Michiko-sama," he said.

Still in a lotus position, she put her hands in front of her on the floor, then lowered her head until it rested on the floor between her hands. Slowly she worked her body forward and then moved it upward, until she was balanced in a headstand, her legs still in lotus configuration.

"Can National Anthem do this?" she asked.

"She'd better not. If her boobs fell out of her leotard, she'd crash through into the apartment downstairs," he said.

She rolled forward lightly, onto her feet, and walked to the bathroom. "There you go with the big-jug remarks again," she said. "Got to shower. Duty and lunacy call."

While she was in the shower, Trace went back to reviewing the days' tapes. Sometimes he caught something the second time around that had gone over his head the first time. More often, he didn't.

It was a lousy and a slow way to work, he often thought, but it was the only way he knew. And Chico was right. Making tapes of everything not only let him review them; it let her review them later if he needed help. He usually did.

He had just finished listening to the last of the tapes when Chico came out of the bedroom, cloaked in a floor-length golden gown that intensified the bronze color of her skin.

"God, you look splendid," he said honestly.

"Thank you."

"Hey, I'm sorry I got under your skin," he said. "If this job hostessing is getting to you, just quit it if you want. It's no skin off my nose, you know."

"Thanks, Trace. I appreciate that. But I signed on for the duration and I'll stick with it. You coming over later?"

"After I'm finished with my report," he said.

"Good. You can keep your mother off my back."

She kissed him and left.

When she was gone, he poured himself a glass of vodka, put an operatic tape into the stereo, and placed a fresh tape into his own small recorder.

9

Trace's log:

Tape Recording Number One, 7:15 P.M., Monday, Devlin Tracy in the matter of Early Jarvis et al.

So we've got a murder and a million-dollar jewel heist. Why is my life filled with this kind of trivial bullshit? I'm almost forty. I've got only three more days to live in the thirties and I should be partying with all the other wonderful folks who infest the insurance industry, and Groucho has got me doing this instead.

I should have been born rich instead of handsome and sensitive. Then I could tell Groucho to stick it. I could grab Chico and take her off and buy her her own shogunate somewhere. I'm mad at her. That's the first time she's ever done that, listen to my tapes, just because I left the recorder out while I was going to the bathroom.

My ex-wife, Jaws, used to do that. Not tape recordings. She'd open my mail. When I bitched about it, she stopped opening my mail, but she'd run to the door every day to get the mail and then she'd hand it to me and stand there, shifting her weight from foot to foot, waiting for me to open it. She'd follow me around until I opened my mail.

So I used to make her crazy by going into the bathroom and locking the door behind me. I knew she'd be outside listening, so I'd make a big point of ripping open the envelopes with a lot of noise. It was always some stupid business crap about somebody having reserved a special Visa card just for me, but I'd tear up the envelopes into confetti-size pieces and throw them in the waste-paper basket and hide the letters inside my shoe.

Then, when I'd walk out of the bathroom, Bruno would make believe she was just strolling by and she'd throw her arms around me, as if she was overwhelmed with a sudden feeling of love for me, and she'd frisk me, trying to find out what pocket I was hiding my secret mail in.

I think I was the only American in history who hoped that one day, even in peacetime, he'd get a letter that said, "Greetings, your ass has been drafted." No such luck. Who needed a war anyway? I was surrounded by enemies. Bruno. What's-his-name and the girl. God.

Why am I doing this? What is this lust for reminiscence? I know. Anything is better than working. Come on, Trace, do your duty to God and your country, obey the Scouts' law, keep yourself physically strong, mentally awake, and morally straight.

But first a drink and a cigarette.

Okay, I've vamped till ready and I'm still not ready, but I've got to do this anyway.

Why? Chico says that Walter Marks is up to something. It must be a very short thing for him to be up to it. Haha, Trace, there's been no one wittier than you since Noël Ca'ad. What'd Groucho say? "I've got the bastard now." Chico heard him, and who else could he mean but me? And Swenson told me the same thing when he woke me up today. I don't need this crap.

I think I handled R. J. Roberts beautifully. I didn't hit him. I didn't rip off his plaid shirt and strangle him with it. I didn't grab him by the hair and march him off to a public bath for ablutions.

On the other hand, I didn't get any information out of him either—at least not anything that I couldn't have gotten by reading the papers. But negative information is information in a way. Now I know a thousand things that don't work.

It's nice and consoling to think that even an unprincipled bastard like R. J. Roberts has labor problems. Lip Service, his head hooker, is obviously being eased out. It's got to be tough, hooking, turning forty, watching the wrinkles start to show. What do you do when you reach the end of the line and you still haven't gotten anywhere, especially in a town without one visible stretch mark? Someday I'll point this out to Chico. She's got fourteen years left.

Hell, in fourteen years, that woman will own the western world. As well as me.

Anyway, I didn't think it was possible for Roberts to be embarrassed by anything, and I was right. He wasn't embarrassed at all by Lip Service coming in to bitch at him for getting somebody younger to run his stable of whores. "Stable" might be exactly the right word in this case.

So what does Roberts know? He knows that Jarvis called Spiro from the airport, but he wasn't there when Spiro arrived. And Roberts said he hasn't heard anything about the jewels being fenced, and as a working fence, he'd be in a position to know. So maybe he's right. Maybe it wasn't a local thief who hit the plotzo. The insurance company hasn't heard anything yet either from any thief, and I'll have to ask Groucho to stay in touch with them for me.

How do people like Roberts stay out of jail? I'd suspect that he's got a very large budget item called incidental expenses and it greases a lot of palms.

And then, on that same tape we've got Dan Rosado. Danny's my friend, but he's a lousy detective. I always get this feeling too that he knows that. He can't figure anything out and he's reached a decision in life: he doesn't want to figure anything out. What you don't know won't hurt you. Put in the years, take the pension, and sit home and play opera records.

What's he got? Zilch. The countess got her jewelry as gifts. So what? When you look like she does, it would be very strange not to get a lot of things as gifts.

The Jarvis suitcase: shaving kit, aspirins, airline magazine. A man after my own heart, traveling light.

And Danny's got pictures. Jarvis lying facedown near the goldfish pond in enough blood to make Quincy sick. What the hell was he wearing gloves for? I'd like to publish a book. *Great Police Photos*. Pictures of people lying on railroad tracks with their heads cut off. Disemboweled hookers. Dead junkies with needles still sticking in them. Mangled car-crash victims. Make it coffee-table-size. People sitting around, sucking up a cocktail, and they look at these pictures and upchuck. What the hell. If pictures of cats sell, this ought to be a rumaway. Cats make *me* throw up.

All right. More photos, more blood, overturned

tree, dirt all over the floor, that's what you get for having trees in houses. And Jarvis bled to death. So it might not have been a murder. Technically. No prints anywhere. What did I expect? An easy one?

Jarvis really did travel light. Wallet, couple of bucks, a photo of him and Felicia, driver's license, American Express card. Keys to the house and the rented car. Why the hell did he leave the car on the road and not just drive up to the house?

And where was his passport? Poor Danny didn't even think of that, but how do you get into the country without a passport? I don't know, but at least I thought of it. God, does this mean I'm going to become a good detective? Are people going to come beating a path to my door? Like Banacek. "Our center fielder vanished on a long fly to the outfield. Can you find him before his next turn at bat?" I don't want to be a detective. I'm not one. I piddle around for the insurance company and sometimes for other people, but this is not what I do well. What I do well is be a retired accountant. A formerly married man. Father of two creatures. Maybe *they'll* be detectives. They deserve it, not me.

Now, my father. Sarge would like to be a detective. He'd like to be anything that gets him out of the house, away from my mother. Sarge. Please. The woman's my mother. One bullet in the brain will do. You don't have to make a mess of her. And don't do it right now. They're changing the trapeze act at Circus Circus. The last trapeze act I saw was something where there was this mechanical dummy and it was all alone on the stage, hanging from this bar. The bar went through holes

85

in the dummy's hands. And then, I guess by radio controls or something from offstage, it started to swing and it did handstands and flips and giant slaloms or kips and tucks, whatever they call those things and I never know what they're talking about. Anyway, I'm sitting there with Chico and this stupid audience is applauding. I want to jump up and yell, Why are you applauding a mechanical dummy? You think it'll make it work harder? You think it's listening? Stop it, you morons. Save it for Wayne Newton. But Chico wouldn't let me.

Anyway, my mother likes trapezes and hates Chico and thinks my apartment is ugly and she'd rather be in Miami and she hates me too. I asked Sarge once why that was. He's a very wise man sometimes. He told me that she never forgave me for my divorce. He said she had this big picture of herself, in a flowered apron, being family matriarch at Thanksgiving dinners and like that, with her grandchildren bringing her boxes of chocolate, and I screwed it all up by getting divorced.

To hell with that.

Felicia killed no one. You can't prove a negative; that's one of the rules of science. Prove that there aren't flying saucers. You can't do it. All I can do is prove somebody else killed Jarvis, but I'm not off to much of a start.

I didn't learn anything at Felicia's, except I met some wonderful people, really the salt of the earth. There were Francis and Frances, the nontalking mules who are into shipping and not into insurance. From now on, I think I'm going to be into not being into anything. Paolo Ferrara abuses Willie, the servant, and I don't think that's the only reason I might like to take a slice out of Paolo Ferrara. And then there's our nosey friend, Baron Hubbaker.

His theory sounds right—burglar surprised, burglar cracks head, burglar grabs jewels and runs, Jarvis dies—but I still don't trust him.

I trust National Anthem, though. I'd trust that woman with anything. I mean, can a woman who loves animals be all bad?

Asses Up? It's one movie I will not miss. I've missed every Academy Award–winning film of the last twelve years. I have intentionally missed every Jane Fonda and Shirley MacLaine movie made since they were old enough to open their mouths. I don't want to encourage them. Add Warren Beatty to the list. I mean, how can you plunk down four dollars to go see the history of Communism written and directed by Shirley MacLaine's brother, for Christ's sake?

Visiting the scene of the crime never does any good. I mean, I saw it all on police photos and I never see anything at the scene that isn't in the photos. I could stay home, like Mycroft Holmes, and have them mail me reports and pictures and then solve everything just by the overwhelming power of my intellect. Screw this nose-to-the-ground, tail-up-in-the-air kind of search for the truth. That's for pigs digging up truffles. Give me photos every time.

So I saw where Jarvis' body was found and where he hit his head on that ceramic fish, and I saw the holes in the safe. Hold it. None of the holes ever got through into the safe, so how'd the thief get the safe open? Felicia says that she and Jarvis were the only two with the combination. Every time somebody tells you something like that, they're wrong. Sure, they're the only two. Except one of them wrote it down on the inside cover of the phone book and the other one painted it in nail polish on the bedroom mirror. I know what people are like. They don't have any sense.

Probably somebody from out of town did steal the stuff. Everybody at the place is out of the pool of suspects 'cause they were all in London with Felicia when Jarvis got it. Poor Felicia. She seemed more concerned about her tree getting knocked over than about Jarvis getting knocked off. And her missing ashtray.

Then we've got Spirakos Spirakodopolous, and he makes you realize what a debt we all owe Cassius Clay. What's that, you say? What debt? Well, he changed his name to Muhammad Ali and now all fighters are named Muhammed to imitate him. Suppose he had changed his name to Spirakodopolous? How would you like to hear Howard Cosell broadcast a fight between Willie Spirakodopolous and Tyrone Spirakodopolous? It's truly frightening.

I called the TV station before. The midnight movie that night really was *Mildred Pierce*. But I'd better remember to check Spiro's record. Just in case.

Why, dammit, why was Jarvis wearing gloves? In July. Where is his passport? Felicia doesn't know and neither do I. I wish National Anthem knew. I'd get it out of her, someway. Why didn't Jarvis wait at the airport for Spiro? Why'd he park on the road instead of in the driveway?

So many questions, so few answers. I have been very good all day and I think it's time to go now to an insurance party and see if I can figure out anything else and watch Chico complain and hear my mother whine and watch my father suffer. What a world. Beam me up, Scotty. This one sucks.

Even though this is my home town and I've got my reputation to protect and therefore I should be expected to spend a little extra on tips and stuff to buy information, I'm just going to stick with my usual hundred-and-fifty-dollars-a-day expenses. Until further notice.

10

Trace had just finished dressing and reloading his tape recorder when the telephone rang. It was Dan Rosado.

"Trace, is your father in town?"

"Yes, why?"

"I met him today."

"Oh?"

"Yeah. He came down to headquarters. He said he wanted to register his hands as deadly weapons."

"Was he drinking?"

"I don't think so. I think he just wanted to look around. I think he misses being on the job," Rosado said.

"He misses being out of the house. He's with my mother. Did you meet her?" Trace asked.

"No."

"If you do, register her mouth as a deadly weapon."

"I'll give her a wide berth. Anyway, Trace, I thought you'd just like to know."

"Thanks, Dan."

Trace was at the front door when the telephone rang again.

"Trace, this is Bob," Swenson's voice growled. "Where are you?"

"On my way to that reception."

"Get here fast. There's a woman here that you won't believe."

"I know her," Trace said. "She's into donkeys."

"Hee haw, hee haw," Swenson said. "Will that do?"

"That and maybe your checkbook if you're interested in financing fuck films."

"As long as I don't have to be in them," Swenson said. "Oh, by the way."

"I hate your by-the-ways. They always mean trouble for me," Trace said.

"I think I figured out what Marks is up to," Swenson said.

"What's that?"

"The insurance company that had those jewels insured? I was talking to the president today and he told me they've got a big fancy detective here to investigate the theft."

"So what?" Trace asked.

"I think Marks figures that the guy will show you up and you'll look like an idiot."

"What change would that effect? I always look like an idiot."

"You know that and I know that," Swenson cheerfully agreed. "But I think what Walter has in mind is that if you are really made to look like an imbecile, he can come at me and complain about why I keep you on retainer when, for the same amount of money, we could get somebody really good."

"So this is the way it is," Trace said. "Tossed aside like an old shoe after years of service. Your faithful watchdog. Now I'm old and my teeth are going and my breath is bad, so it's off to the city dump. That's it, huh?"

"Are you rehearsing for the school play or what?" Swenson asked. "How could I ever let you go? You mean too much to me."

"Old friendships are best," Trace said.

"Not really. I just want you around to introduce me to this blonde with the knockers."

"What about Flamma?"

"Next to this one? Flamma could incinerate herself in my fireplace and I wouldn't bother getting a cup of water from the kitchen."

"I'll be over in a little bit," Trace said. "By the way, what's the guy's name?"

"What guy?"

"The big insurance detective who's going to make me look bad."

"That's an interesting part," Swenson said. "Nobody knows. He works in secret for a lot of companies but no one knows his name or who he is. They say he's bagged a lot of jewel thieves in Europe. Just gives the information to the cops and then splits, and no one knows anything about him."

"When's he coming? Maybe I can get done fast," Trace said.

"I'm told he's already here in town. Hurry up over."

It didn't really matter, Trace told himself as he walked from his condominium down the broad Las Vegas Strip toward the Araby Casino and Hotel four blocks away. What did he care if the ghost of Sherlock Holmes was trudging the Las Vegas streets right now, ready to swoop down on the jewel thief and murderer? No skin off his nose.

Right?

Definitely not right, he admitted to himself. Screw Groucho. He was just not about to be shown up, not by Sherlock Holmes, not by anybody. It didn't have anything to do with any longing for justice or any overriding sense that murderers and jewel thieves should be brought to the bar.

What it had to do with was pride. Trace might be the most reluctant detective who ever lived, but right now he was a detective and this was his case, and if anybody was going to solve it, it would be him. Not R. J. Grundge or Sherlock Holmes or Groucho or even Dan Rosado. Him. Devlin Tracy. Nobody else. Case closed.

He was musing about this when a young girl planted herself in front of him on the sidewalk. She wore a short white skirt and sweater and looked like a high-school cheerleader.

"Mister, excuse me," she said. "I need change of a twenty."

Trace looked around. Sure enough, about eight feet away, casually lighting a cigarette, was a young man, about eighteen, trying very hard not to watch them.

"Sure thing, Sweetie Pie," Trace said. "Anything for a pretty little girl like you."

He pulled some bills out of his pocket and found two tens. The girl started to hand him the twenty and he put forth the two tens when the youth with the cigarette made his move, running forward, ready to clip all forty dollars from their hands and race off down the street.

He was too slow. Trace swallowed up the youth's hand in his and squeezed. Hard.

"What are two nice children like you doing, trying to run a stupid stunt like this?" Trace said.

The girl started to back away. "I don't know him," she told Trace. "I never saw him before."

"Sure. And everybody who believes in fairies should clap."

The young man was squirming, trying to pull his hand free from Trace's.

"Sonny," Trace said, "spend some time in the minors before you try to make it in the bigs." He released the youth's hand.

The youth backed off about ten feet and snarled, "Prick."

"That just cost you twenty dollars," Trace said. He pocketed his own bills and the girl's twenty and walked up the drive toward the Araby.

He was feeling good. Let Sherlock Holmes come to town. He might find out pretty quickly that Las Vegas had very little in common with foggy streets in London Town.

The Garrison Fidelity hospitality suite spread out over three connecting rooms on one of the upstairs floors of the hotel. The bar was situated in the center of the three rooms, manned by a uniformed bartender whom Trace recognized because he worked generally in the casino lounge bar downstairs.

"Hi, Trace. Usual?"

"Just Perrier, Richie. I'm tapering off. Seen Chico?"

"Wandering off in that direction with some greasegun in hot pursuit," Richie said.

"Thanks." Trace took his drink, sipped it, hated it, and tipped Richie his twenty dollars of stolen money. He stood by the bar and looked to see who was in the room. He didn't recognize anyone. They were mostly men with a sprinkling of women who had the happy part-of-it look of convention wives. The insurance men traveling alone would be in the other two rooms, trying to engage whatever passable-looking woman they could find in conversation.

Trace let the conversation in the room sort of wash over him and in thirty seconds he had heard the phrase "sales quota" four times and decided to leave. He nodded to Richie, then wandered off in Chico's direction.

Compared to the bar room, the side room was almost empty. He saw Chico in a corner. Paolo Ferrara was leaning his arm against the wall on one side of her. His body blocked her escape on the other side. She was smiling, but Trace knew the smile well. It was the kind of tolerant mouth-wrinkle she gave to high-spending but personally obnoxious gamblers at her blackjack table downstairs. Polite enough so no one could complain; cold enough so no one could think they were going to win the dealer. Nobody did that. Not unless Chico wanted them to.

Ferrara was being very continental. He had enough gold chains around his neck to get a sixteen-wheeler up Pikes Peak in a blizzard. He was flashing a lot of white teeth in a very tan face, and when he glanced over and saw Trace, he didn't even acknowledge him. No, Trace decided, he didn't like Paolo Ferrara very much, and if the opportunity arose sometime during the evening, he might try explaining that to the young man.

Trace looked around the rest of the room. He saw Felicia Fallaci. She was dressed in modish tight blue jeans and cowboy boots with a fancy embroidered silk shirt that was tightly tailored to display her bosom. She was talking to a man who had his back to Trace, and when she saw him, she nodded and winked. He winked back.

Past the countess he saw why the room was less crowded than the other two rooms. Bob Swenson was sitting on the windowsill, and salesmen, until they were drunker, would just as soon stay out of the way of the president of the company. Later, fortified by demon rum, they would stop in to brag about their sales exploits, but it would do them no good because, by that time, Swenson would have been drinking all night, would care nothing about insurance, and would play drunk so that they would have to go away.

He wasn't playing drunk now. He was talking very earnestly to National Anthem. Trace waited but didn't hear her squeal once. Swenson seemed very serious and she was very serious right back. He was a wonder to watch, Trace thought. Some people had to work to figure out the right things to say to different people, but Swenson did it on automatic pilot; instinctively, he seemed to know who wanted to be treated seriously and who wanted to be looked at like Hard-hearted Hannah, the Vamp of Savannah.

National Anthem, Trace figured, would like very much to be treated like Sarah Bernhardt.

Walter Marks was in the room too. He was sitting on a sofa in the corner, tied up in a tight conversation with Baron Hubbaker. Another sofa was given over to the Neddlemans, who sat side by side, each holding a drink, neither talking nor stirring, just staring straight ahead. Trace wondered if they walked side by side, in lockstep. They'd be a great team to bet on in a sack race.

The countess had brought her entire retinue, except . . . There he was. Willie Parmenter was by himself in a corner of the room, looking out a window toward the Las Vegas Strip, nondescript and small in a dark-blue suit. Even as Trace noticed him, he heard Ferrara bellow, "Willie."

The small man almost trotted toward his employer, who did not take his eyes off Chico. Instead, he just held out his empty glass, a king not deigning to look at a commoner, and kept jawing at Chico. No, Trace didn't like Ferrara at all.

Parmenter took the glass and turned away, looking around the room. Was he embarrassed in case anyone had noticed his treatment at Ferrara's hands? No. He was just looking to see if anyone else wanted a drink.

Hubbaker waved to him and Parmenter nodded and approached.

"Hello, Mr. Tracy," he said.

"Hello, Parmenter." Trace couldn't bring himself to call the man Willie. "If you ever want to hit that boss of yours, I'll hold him while you do it."

Parmenter flashed a nervous little smile. His eyes looked lost behind the big lenses of his eyeglasses. "He's really all right," Parmenter said.

"Sure," Trace said. "So is rain, if you don't have it every day."

Parmenter smiled again and walked toward the baron, with Trace following him.

"Willie, if you please, would you freshen this?" the baron said politely.

"Of course."

Marks held out his glass too. "Fill mine too," he snapped. He was speaking without looking at Parmenter. "And last time you made it too sweet. Don't make it too sweet this time, if you can manage that."

"Sorry," Parmenter mumbled.

Marks grunted. Trust Groucho, Trace thought, to be a bully when he thought he could get away with it. A tiny tyrant. Walter Marks, the midget king of Misanthrope.

After Willie had walked away, Trace said, "I see you're as pleasant to the help as you always are, Groucho."

Marks looked at him in disgust and turned back to the baron, who nodded at Tracy, smiled, and said to Marks, "But of course your man here is the expert on crime."

"He's not my man," Marks snapped.

"Oh . . ." The baron seemed confused. "I thought you two worked for the same company."

"No," Marks said. "*I* work for the company. Tracy here avoids working for the company. He just collects an inflated check from us once in a while."

"I was watching Mr. Tracy today," the baron said. "He seems to know what he's doing." He looked up at Trace and said, "We were discussing Felicia's jewel robbery."

"Come up with any new theories?"

"Maybe all the good theories are taken," Hubbaker said. "And of course we amateurs shouldn't really interfere with professionals."

"Professional?" Marks said. "Tracy's an accountant."

"No, no," Trace said. "I'm a former accountant. I worked my way down through gambling degenerate and alcoholic until now I've reached the absolute bottom of the line. I draw checks from an insurance company." He sat in an easy chair near the baron. "Anyway," Trace said, "I thought your theory this afternoon was pretty good."

"You would," Marks said. "It might give you something to work on."

"Are you having your period, Groucho? Why are you so cranky tonight?"

"We'll see," Marks said. "We'll see just how good you are. You've been lucky once in a while and you've got Mr. Swenson snowed, but I know what you are."

"At last. The metaphysical explanation to the big question. What am I?"

"You're a faker. You get lucky once in a while, but you don't fool me. Now if you don't mind, the baron and I were discussing the robbery and I wanted to hear his theory."

"Just amateur stuff, you understand," Hubbaker said. Marks snorted. Trace nodded.

"One of the questions that needs answering," Hubbaker said, "has to be why didn't Jarvis wait at the airport for Spiro to pick him up."

"My question exactly," Trace said.

"Suppose he met somebody at the airport. Somebody that he knew who offered to drive him back to the house. Then he tried to call Spiro and tell him not to pick him up, but Spiro had already left. So Jarvis said, 'Oh, well,' and left with this person he recognized, and then that person came into the house with Jarvis and he's the one that looted the safe and killed him." Hubbaker paused. "Just a theory, you understand."

Marks looked as proud as if his wife had just delivered a full-grown child, Trace thought.

"Good theory," Trace said.

Hubbaker nodded. Marks had a what-else-would-you-expect look.

"Only one thing wrong with it," Trace said. "Maybe two."

"What's that?" the baron asked.

"Yeah. What's wrong with it?" Marks said.

"Jarvis rented a car at the airport. If he met somebody he knew who had a car, he would have driven in that person's car. And if he met somebody who didn't have a car, they'd probably have waited for Spiro to pick them up. Either way they wouldn't have rented a car to drive into town. And why did Jarvis park on the road and not in Felicia's driveway? But it's not a bad theory. It just needs a little work."

Marks looked as if he had swallowed a rat tailfirst, but Hubbaker merely shrugged. "That's the blessing of being an amateur. We can postulate anything we want and we bear no responsibility if it doesn't work out."

They were interrupted by Willie Parmenter returning with the drinks, napkins carefully wrapped around their bases. Hubbaker thanked him. Marks sipped his and grumbled, "It's still too sweet."

Parmenter said, "Sorry. Should I have another one made?"

"No. I'll get my own the next time. I guess it's the only way to get it right."

Parmenter walked away and Trace looked to the far corner of the room. Paolo Ferrara, a fresh drink in his hand now, still had Chico trapped, and her smile, thin to start with, was now as finely drawn as a line from a freshly sharpened pencil.

Trace put his glass down on an end table and started to stroll over to her, but he was intercepted in midroom by the countess.

"She'll survive," Felicia said, nodding toward Chico. "She could handle four like him before lunch."

Trace nodded but started to move away and

Felicia caught him by the arm. "I couldn't find that passport. It occurs to me that maybe the jewel thief stole it," she said. "Passports are worth something on the black market or wherever you sell stolen stuff, aren't they?"

"So is cash," Trace said. "But the thief didn't take Jarvis's wallet."

"I guess you're right."

"And if I had a million dollars' worth of jewelry stuffed in my pockets, I don't think I'd stop for either a wallet or a passport," Trace said. "Excuse me, Felicia. Something needs doing."

11

Chico saw him coming and gave a tiny little shake "no" of her head. It was obviously not noticed by Ferrara, who kept oozing snake oil over her and who didn't notice Trace, even when he stopped alongside them.

"Hello, Miss Mangini," Trace said.

"Hello, Trace. Do you know Mr. Ferrara?"

"We've met," Trace said.

"Not really a high point of my trip to America," Ferrara said. He pointedly turned his back a little more on Trace, inviting him out of the corner conversation.

Trace tapped him on the shoulder. "I think you've monopolized our hostess's time long enough," he said.

"I think that's for her to say," Ferrara said.

"She can't."

"Why not?"

"She has a fatal weakness. She can't tell bores to shove off."

"I can," Ferrara said. "Shove off."

He turned away from Trace again and Trace picked up Ferrara's drink, which the Italian had set down on a small end table. Slowly he began to pour a thin stream of the vodka over Ferrara's jacket sleeve.

It took a full second and a half of spilled highball before Ferrara realized something was happening. He turned, looked at Trace, and then at his wet sleeve.

"You bastard," he said, rubbing his sleeve. "I'm going to punch your face."

"I'm afraid that's not the way it's going to happen," Trace said calmly.

Ferrara swung anyway and Trace slid to the side and the punch moved harmlessly past his right ear. Trace grabbed the man's right wrist in his own right hand, moved it down, and then twisted it up behind Ferrara's back. He reached around in front of the man with his left hand and handed him his glass.

"You forgot your drink." He suggested strongly that Ferrara take it by forcing the right wrist up higher behind the man's back. Ferrara took the glass in his left hand and Trace released him.

"Go away now," Trace said.

Ferrara stood there momentarily, his back still toward Trace, then rubbed his sleeve again, bellowed "Willie," and set off across the room to his hapless assistant. Trace looked around the room. No one had seemed to notice what had happened, except the countess, who smiled at him. Everybody else was still talking.

"You're really a vile-tempered thing," Chico told him.

"I think alcohol deprivation is ruining my ability to tolerate people. How are you?" Trace asked.

"All right, until this guy. I mean, I figured I'd be fighting Swenson off, but Bob's in love."

"He's in love every day with somebody different," Trace said. "You're one of the few constants."

"Frozen out now, though," she said. "I think National Anthem there has him by the nose."

"One of the most inappropriate figures of speech I ever heard," Trace said.

"She is something, though, isn't she?" Chico said. She was looking across the room at the porn actress. Trace turned to see National Anthem with her hands together, both of them held in Bob Swenson's big hands. "Trace, if you decide to take a run at her, I'll understand," Chico said.

"I'm sorry. I'm not her species," Trace said.

Chico giggled and said, "Come on, big boy. You can buy me a drink."

Trace knew that meant soda. Some Oriental gene, common among Japanese, had made it impossible for Chico to drink alcohol. Any liquor at all brought on a flushed face, a quickened pulse, and if the drink was strong enough, a pass-out.

Trace got them both tonic waters so they could at least look like drinkers, and they stood in a corner of the bar room by themselves.

"Remember you thought that Marks was up to something?" he said.

"Yup. Congratulations by the way on not drinking."

"Don't remind me. Anyway, Groucho's waiting for me to fall on my face. There's some big insurance detective in town to check out the jewel robbery."

"Do you know him?" she asked.

"Nope. Nobody does. He's a big mystery man. Wears a mask and a cloak when he works, I think."

"How'd you find out?"

"Bob found out from one of his drunken cronies and told me."

Chico nodded. "That must be what Marks was talking about last night. Remember, I told you, he said something about enough rope to hang himself. He was talking about you. Oh, Trace, it'd be wonderful if you could figure this one out. What a kick in the ass for that surly little Munchkin."

"Did you see him abusing that other guy inside?" Trace asked.

"What guy?"

"Willie. Your boyfriend's assistant."

"Yeah. I was watching. Don't give a small person power," Chico said.

"Not a chance," Trace said. "I gave you power and look what it's gotten me. A sober, dull, ill-tempered miserable life."

"Speaking of which, here's your mother. You'll forgive me. I'm going forth to commit *seppuku*."

"And leave me to suffer through by myself? Not a chance. Stay alive." He grabbed Chico's arm and held her by his side.

"Hello, Mother. You remember Michiko? The woman I live with?"

"Devlin, I played the machines by the casino door just like you told me. I lost another ten dollars."

"Maybe it wasn't your lucky day. Where's Sarge?"

"Maybe everything in this casino is crooked," she said, finally looking at Chico. "You work here, Miss Manzano. Would you think so?"

"Mangini's the name," Chico said. "Actually, I wouldn't know. I deal blackjack and a lot of people win at blackjack. We don't really think about slot-machine players because there's a saying in casinos."

"Oh? What's that saying?"

"People who play slot machines are imbeciles," Chico said. "Excuse me, Trace." She walked away.

"Really," his mother said. "I don't know how you can stand that woman."

"She makes good shrimp tempura. Where's Sarge?"

"He had a drink in his hand. He went out there, I think. I swear, he's enough to make me crazy. Every time I turn around, he's vanished."

"I can't imagine why, Mother. Except maybe he doesn't like watching you lose your inheritance in the slot machines."

"What else would he do except get into trouble?" she said.

"Walter Marks is inside," Trace said. "He asked me if you were coming tonight. Why don't you go say hello? He's with a real baron."

"Oh. Well, of course."

Trace found his father sitting in the first room on a sofa, holding a glass of liquor in his outsized mitt, staring at the floor, looking glum.

"I never saw anybody in Las Vegas look that forlorn," Trace said.

"It's that woman," his father said. "I never realized how comfortable my house is. Somehow, when we're there, I tune her out. She goes to the bedroom, I go to the kitchen. She goes to the kitchen, I go to the cellar. She goes to sleep and I go to the saloon. Here, I can't get out of her sight."

"You vanished long enough today to get to police headquarters," Trace said.

"Oh, you heard. Well, I just wanted to look around and see how they work. Nice fellow, that Rosado." He looked at Trace for a moment as if measuring his reaction. "Don't think he's much of a detective, though."

"Why not?" Trace asked.

"Not mean enough. He's got the look of the kind of person who trusts people."

"Yeah, Sarge, that old demon trust. It'll get you in trouble every time."

"It will if you're a detective," the old man said. "I never trusted anybody. Not partners, not superiors, not suspects, lawyers, prosecutors, anybody. Twenty-five years and I was never indicted."

Trace thought to himself that not having been indicted was a pretty small merit badge to wear for twenty-five years of policework.

But instead, Trace said, "Listen. Suppose I got Mom a lover. What would you think about that? Some dancer or something. Maybe an acrobat."

"Well, for a couple of days I think it'd be wonderful. Get her off my back. I'd have to kill him, of course, before I left town."

"Hell, I don't think I can get anybody to do it if he knows he has to die," Trace said.

"Try," his father urged, then looked glum again. "No. Never mind. I'm just doomed. Thanks for thinking of me."

"Your father's drinking too much," Chico said.

"Funny. I'm the one who's going to be forty and he's the one who's got the midlife crisis."

"That's now. Wait until Thursday when the big four-oh comes. I'll tell you how it'll be. First, you won't be able to get out of bed. What for? Another dismal day like all the rest? So you'll stay in bed. Your body will ache and you'll think of a cup of tea. With lemon. And honey. I'll parade through the room naked, but I won't get any response because you know if you use it all up right away, it'll be another week before you can do it again. You'll start riding buses, instead of walking, and you'll think about answering ads in the sex columns. 'Beautiful horny young woman looking for generous elderly bachelor. Please write Lulu LaTour. Send photo. All letters answered.' I tell you, Trace, I don't envy you. Your pop's all right. He's just depressed, but he'll get better when he gets home. For you, it's the end of the line."

"The only thing that keeps me going is knowing that you'll be there with me in my sunset years," Trace said.

"Hah. All these years you've been abusing me?" Chico said. "Now it's my turn. From now on I flaunt my lovers in front of you. Eighteen-year-old bellhops. Valet parking attendants. Carry-out boys from the supermarket."

"You don't go to a supermarket," he said.

"I'm going to start. I'm going to all the supermarkets. A different one each day. And I'm going to have them all deliver. You can lie in bed rusting and hear the squeals of pleasure from the living room. We'll be on the rug."

"It's nylon. I hope it scratches your butt and he gets knee burns. If he turns his back, I'll club him with my cane."

Chico didn't answer. She was looking from the doorway toward the sofa where Trace's father sat, still looking at his drink. Mrs. Tracy was next to him, her jaw moving continuously. "Your father's quite a man to have let her live," Chico said.

"I know. I wish there was some way to bail him out. You know, that's what my marriage was turning into?" He stopped as Bob Swenson came into the room, holding two glasses. He saw Chico and

Trace, gave the bartender the glasses to fill, and walked over.

"How's it going?" Trace asked.

"I've got her now. I've got her convinced that she's Ingrid Bergman, Pola Negri, and Lillian Gish all rolled up into one."

"Even better than them," Trace said. "She does an animal act."

"That was in the past. A youthful indiscretion," Swenson said. "From here on in, it's only serious acting. She and I are discussing her career plans right now. She needs an older, wiser man to rely on. A mentor. I shall be her mentor."

"You're really a disgusting vulture," Chico said with a smile.

"You've driven me to it," Swenson said, "by rejecting me all these years." He glanced over his shoulder. "Sorry, got to go back before someone tries to make a move on her."

As he walked away, Chico said, "I love him. I really love him. He's the quintessential male animal. You never have to wonder where he's coming from 'cause he's always coming from the same place. Love letters straight from the groin."

Trace saw his father nod his head and stand up alongside his wife, and he thought they should take a picture of his parents and post it in every marriage-license bureau in America and force every applicant to look at it and initial it first. The marriage rate would drop 50 percent. You wanted zero population growth? That picture'd give you a minus expectation.

Sarge and his wife met them near the door.

"Well, it's about that time," Trace's father said with a sigh. "Hilda's getting tired."

"What's on the schedule for tomorrow?" Trace asked.

His mother answered. "I think we ought to keep trying those slot machines near the door. After all, you promised."

"And probably Circus Circus," Sarge said wearily.

"Not tomorrow," Trace said suddenly.

"What do you mean?"

"I need your help, Sarge," he said. "I've got this case and there's just too much legwork for me to do alone. I need you to help me. I know it's imposing on you, you being on vacation and all—"

"It certainly is," Trace's mother said.

"Quiet, woman," Sarge snapped. "What are you dealing with, son?"

"A murder and a million-dollar jewel heist. I think I'm in over my head. Can you help?"

His father stroked his square jaw. "Well, I hate to miss Circus Circus. I think they're changing their trapeze act tomorrow. But, well, you're my kid. What else could I do?"

"Thanks, Sarge. I appreciate it," Trace said.

"And what will I do?" his mother whined.

Trace and his father looked at each other. Both had a good answer and neither wanted to say it, so they smiled.

"You'll think of something," Trace said. "Sarge, come on up to my place in the morning, maybe tennish, and we'll go over what I've got so far."

"I'll be there. Come on, Hildie. I've got to get some sleep. If I'm going to be sharp tomorrow, I can't party all night. 'Night, son. 'Night, Chico."

"Good night, Sarge. Good night, Mrs. Tracy," Chico said.

Mrs. Tracy sniffed and her husband pulled her

through the door. After they were gone, Chico said, "Trace, I love you."

"Aaaah, you're just saying that to torment my aging body."

"No. Really. Love you. You're such an asshole most of the time and then you can do something like that. It's the only reason I hang out with you, why I've turned down fame, fortune, and young men with good bodies. Just because, once in a while, you can do something really nice."

"I guess I'm just my mother's son, after all," Trace said.

Trace and Chico were in bed and she said, "I'm extending your option for another month." In the dimly lit bedroom, she lit a cigarette and handed it to him. "Here. A reward. For services rendered."

"Oh, God, have I come to this? Tricking for cigarettes?"

"Quiet, I'm thinking."

Trace smoked silently, blowing large billows of barely visible smoke up toward the ceiling. The ceiling of the room had started out like the walls, white, three years before, but a four-packs-a-day habit, only now being corrected, had coated the entire apartment with a thin, sticky yellow film. He was only aware of it when Chico took down a painting and he could see how white the wall was underneath it. It was one of the nice things about her. She didn't smoke, but she didn't squawk either. If she complained about his smoking, it was not because of its effect on the walls, ceiling, or furniture. Only about what it might be doing to his lungs.

"You know," she said, "that insurance detective. Nobody knows who he is."

"Right."

"I bet Walter Marks knows."

"I think he would," Trace said.

"So why do you think he was cozying up to that baron all night long? You said they were talking about the case."

"Yeah." A light was starting to glimmer in his head.

"And the insurance detective was supposed to just arrive, and that Baron Humbug or whatever his name is, he just arrived. Wouldn't being a baron be a wonderful cover for some insurance snoop who works on jewel thefts?"

"Sure would. And it would also explain a lot of inquisitiveness on his part," Trace said.

"Think about it. He may be your man," Chico said.

"I don't have to think about it. He is."

"I didn't say that, remember. Just a possibility. But Marks *was* all over him."

"Yeah, he was doing everything but shine his shoes. When he wasn't abusing Willie."

"My secret Italian lover's valet?" Chico said.

"The same."

"I was talking to him. He's nice. And very funny."

" 'Funny' is never a word I would have applied to Willie," Trace said.

"He did an impersonation of Marks while I was talking to him. You know how Marks curls up his lip when he tries to sound important and winds up sounding like a constipated Richard Nixon?"

"God, do I know. I hear it all the time. In my sleep I hear it."

"Willie did him to an absolute T. And he's cute. He never said he was doing him, but he was watching my eyes, and when he knew that I knew, we both laughed."

"Good for him," Trace said. "The next time you're chitter-chattering with him, tell him to keep his eyes open for Jarvis' passport. Felicia couldn't find it."

"Maybe Sarge can help," Chico said.

"Maybe. Quiet now. It's time for my thinking cigarette. No more talk."

"Who'd want to talk to you anyway?" Chico said.

12

Sober, well-rested, Trace woke up at eight-thirty and panicked. God, he thought, I'm sober and well-rested. I don't even feel like throwing up. This can't be allowed to continue.

"What do you want for breakfast?" Chico yelled from the kitchen.

"A glass of ipecac. A big glass. Get me back to normal fast."

"Stay as you are. Your father will be over in a while."

"Oh oh. Now I've got to think of something for him to do."

"Stop worrying."

Trace showered and brushed his teeth and went into the kitchen, where he answered the phone on the first ring. Chico was already at the table eating. She was always eating, it seemed. The tiny woman seemed to have the determination of a picnic ant and Trace sometimes wondered if she actually ate all the food that she made disappear or if she buried some of it for the winter.

Bob Swenson was on the telephone.

"How'd it go last night?" Trace asked.

"Awful. The worst night of my life."

"I don't believe it. You had her eating out of your hand," Trace said.

"I overplayed my hand," Swenson said. "I got her head so filled with dog dust, I didn't know she was going to believe it. I'm cursed. I slept with a woman who makes her living balling donkeys and I didn't get in. If this gets out, it'll be the end of me."

"There, there. I'll never tell," Trace said consolingly.

Swenson grumbled on for a while and then admitted he had forgotten why he called. "Tell Chico I'll see her at the sales workshop."

Trace hung up. "Swenson," he said.

"How is he?" Chico asked, and put more food in her face without waiting for an answer.

"He's not happy," Trace said as he sat down, sipped at his coffee, and looked without enthusiasm at his plate. It held one egg, one piece of bacon, a half-slice of toast, and a dollop of jam. He nibbled at the edge of the toast like a mouse on a diet.

"He was doing all right," Trace said. "National Anthem thought that he was warm and wise and wonderful. She was really impressed by his plans for her career. She should go straight, make people regard her as a serious actress. How long can one screw donkeys before the public begins to regard it as a shallow gimmick?"

"It's hard to have a relationship with a donkey and have anyone think it's meaningful," Chico mumbled with a full mouth. "God knows I've tried."

"Silence, woman. So he spirits her off to his room, still talking his nonsense. Be the part. Let your good heart shine through. Drop your drawers. They were thinking out parts for her to make her career on. Swenson had in mind Cleopatra. Did you know that she blew the whole Roman Senate?"

"I didn't know that," Chico said.

"Well, Swenson said that she did and he knows things like that. Anyway, he's thinking Cleopatra or Catherine the Great—she was kind of strange too—but somehow Nash gets in her head Joan of Arc, the Virgin of Orleans. And then she's got to be Stanislavsky and live her part. No touchie, no feelie. Her womanhood is assault-proof. She puts her hands over her crotch and falls asleep. And she snores. This morning, she gets up and dresses and kisses Bob like he's her pastor and tells him that he's a very special man to her and leaves and he's yelling at the door, 'I don't want to be a special man in your life. I want to fuck you like everybody else does.' But she's gone and he's miserable. Watch out for him today."

"I'll wear my chain-mail knickers," Chico said. "He should have stuck with Flamma. First rule of wing-walking."

"What's that?"

"Don't let go of what you got until you're damn sure you've got hold of something else," Chico said.

Trace nibbled another crumb from his toast. "You know, eating is good sometimes."

"All the time," Chico agreed, and stole his single piece of bacon.

She had already left, looking very professional and very lovely in a dark-blue suit with a red blouse and a red handkerchief in her jacket pocket, when the doorbell rang and Trace let Sarge in.

"Sergeant Tracy reporting as ordered, sir," his father said, and tossed off a snappy military salute. He was wearing a gray business suit. His shoes

116

were thick-soled, highly shined, and very practical-looking. Under his arm, he carried a red-covered spiral-bound notebook.

"Have some coffee, Sarge. Where's Mother?"

"I left her in the coffee shop playing Keno. It's a new game for her. She likes the idea of maybe winning twenty-five thousand for only seventy cents."

"Good. Keep her busy."

"Just what is it you want me to do?" Sarge asked.

They sat at the small table in the kitchen and Trace poured coffee.

"What's the notebook for?" he said.

"For notes."

"Good," Trace said. "The first thing you have to do is keep accurate records. That's really important."

"Accurate records of what?"

"Your expenses, of course. But now, don't give them to anybody or talk to anybody about them except me. Well, you can talk to Chico if you want, but mostly me. And what I'll do is I'll be very creative with them and I'll send them in to Groucho, and then when he and I are finished negotiating over them, you'll probably get all your money back and maybe show a small profit."

Trace sipped more coffee and sat back with a satisfied look, as if he had just solved the mystery of existence. "That's all there is to it," he said.

"I think I ought to know a little bit about how I'm supposed to run up these expenses," Sarge said. "Like maybe, what is this case all about?"

"Okay. Let me tell you what's going on." Trace quickly and carefully explained the jewel theft and the murder of Early Jarvis. Before he could even

117

sum up, his father said, "Where was this Jarvis' passport?"

"That's good, Sarge," Trace said. "That's what I'm wondering too. He needed a passport to get back into the country. But he didn't have one on him and Felicia told me last night that she couldn't find it."

"Felicia?"

"The countess."

"Oh, the redhead who was here. I didn't know you had friends who were countesses," Sarge said.

"To know me is to love me. Anyway, the passport. I'd like to know where it is. Did he lose it? Did he put it in a locker at the airport? What the hell for, if he did? What's that all about? You got any ideas?"

"Some," Sarge said. "But I'd like to nose around first."

"How do you start?" Trace asked.

"You have a picture of Jarvis?"

Trace shook his head.

"Your first mistake. All right. I'll go down and see your friend Rosado at headquarters. He should have a picture of him and I'll borrow it. Then I'm going out to the airport and start talking around, see if anybody saw him, the usual. I know how to do all this stuff, son." While he talked, he was making a neat list in his notebook of things to do. Trace thought of suggesting to him that he keep one page free for his grocery list.

He said, "I know you know how to do this stuff, but this isn't New York."

"What do you mean?"

"In New York, everybody talks. Hell, you can't buy a newspaper without getting somebody's whole life story. But that's New York. This town's dif-

118

ferent. Everybody's a smart guy or thinks he's a smart guy. Keeping your mouth shut around here is a way of life. Nobody talks in Vegas, nobody tells you a thing. If you give them money, then, maybe. But they're all just afraid that if they wind up saying the wrong thing to the wrong person, they're going to be found the next day buried in the desert with a canary sewn inside their mouth."

"They'll talk to me," Sarge said confidently.

"How's that?"

"Because I'll reason with them. I'll be very polite. I'll explain how it's incumbent on a citizen to cooperate with a police investigation because if one man isn't safe, then no man is safe. I'll talk, movingly, about the responsibilities of good citizenship. And then, if they still won't talk to me, I'll punch the piss out of them. You got a gun?"

For a moment, Trace envisioned the Las Vegas Airport laid waste, strewn with dead bodies, and Sarge standing atop the Golden West Airlines counter, shooting his gun into the air and screaming, "Talk. Damn your eyes, talk."

"I don't think we actually need a gun yet. Not until we get closer to something. If you need a deadly weapon, use your hands."

"Don't be smart."

"You're not licensed to carry a gun around here anyway," Trace said.

"Devlin, my boy, I may be retired but I'm not senile. Everybody in this town carries a gun. Or else there's a helluvan outbreak of goiter under the left armpit."

"That's why we'll do it without guns. It adds a touch of challenge to it. Another thing. Remember that guy you met last night, the baron?"

"What's his name? Hubbell?"

119

"Hubbaker. I think he's a secret agent for the insurance company that insured the jewels. Let me know if you run across him today."

"Got it."

"And there's a private eye in town named Roberts who's on this case too. He's a hairball. Watch out for him."

"Got it," said Sarge.

"Good. Go get 'em, Tiger."

His father drained his coffee, wrote down the names of Hubbaker and Roberts in his notebook, snapped it shut, and rose from the table.

"Maybe this'll be the start of a new career," Sarge said. He clapped a big heavy hand on Trace's shoulder. "You and me, fighting crime. Patrick and Devlin Tracy. Confidential investigations. We never sleep. Crooks'll tremble at the mere mention of our names."

"Or we could work the other side of the street," Trace said. "Open an accounting firm. And steal."

"I'll do that too. I'll do anything to get out of the house. I'm off to see Rosado."

"All right. If you've got any messages for me, filter them through Chico at the convention. Otherwise, I'll see you back there, maybe around five. I think they have cocktails today at five."

After Sarge left, Trace called police headquarters and spoke to Rosado.

"Dan, my father's on his way down to see you. He's working with me on this Jarvis case. I'd appreciate it if you'd help him out with anything he needs."

"I'm not going to give him a gun permit," Rosado said.

"No, God, no. Don't give him a gun permit."

"Anything else he can have. Who's going to argue with a man whose hands are deadly weapons?"

"Thanks, Dan. He used to be pretty good, you know. He might still help."

"We're dead-ended. We can use all the help we can get."

"It'll be good to give him a chance to work again too," Trace said.

"Trace, it's all right. This is your friend you're talking to. I met him yesterday, remember? I know he's going stir-nuts hanging around this town playing slot machines. It's a nice thing for you to let him work."

"Don't let on you know," Trace said. "This is one I owe you."

"You can buy me a Bjoerling record for my collection. I don't have *Trovatore*."

"I refuse to promulgate mediocrity in the world," Trace said.

"Go screw yourself."

Trace heard a voice inside Roberts' office, so he waited across the hall where Roberts couldn't see his outline through the frosted-glass windows that overlooked the hallway.

"I don't care, dammit, that's the way things are," he heard Roberts say. He was talking on the telephone; there was no answering voice.

Then Roberts said, louder, "Just do what she says," and Trace heard the receiver slam down.

He waited a few seconds, then began to whistle loudly and stepped toward the door. He rapped once, hard, and walked inside.

Roberts looked up from behind his dirty desk.

"Hello, Tracy."

"How's it going, R. J.?" Trace said with unfelt warmth.

"Win a couple, lose a couple. Sit down. You want a drink or something?"

"No, thanks. I was just wondering if you'd heard anything on the street yet about the countess's jewels?"

Roberts shook his head, and folded his hands on his notebook. "Like they vanished," he said. "I've got lines out all over and I haven't felt a quiver. I'm telling you, Tracy, this is out-of-town work. You find out anything?"

"Nothing yet. I was up at the plotzo yesterday and looked around. Nothing."

"You talk to Spiro?" Roberts asked.

"Yeah."

"What'd you think of him? I figured, maybe an inside job," Roberts said.

"I don't know," Trace said. "Little thieves are always little thieves. The way they make more money is to do more little thefts, not one big theft. They deal in quantity, not quality."

"How'd you know he's a thief?" Roberts asked.

"Just a guess," Trace said.

"He's got a little record. Nickel-and-dime stuff. Did six months about four years ago, then started hopping cars and keeping clean. He's a Greek. Greeks never steal anything big."

This was a breakthrough in crime detection that Trace had never heard before, but he decided to let it slide.

"You hear anything about another detective in town?" he asked.

"No. Who?"

"I don't know. I hear the insurance company's

got some hotshot jewel detective in town. I thought you might have run into him."

"Those bastards. They got me on this, what do they need anybody else for? Those bastards."

"That's the insurance business for you," Trace said cheerily. "Swine of the earth."

"What's his name?" Roberts asked.

"Nobody knows. He's the Secret Avenger, right out of the Saturday-morning television cartoons."

"I'll Secret Avenge him. You find out who he is, Tracy, you let me know."

"Sure will," Trace lied. "And I'll keep you posted on anything else I come up with."

The clerk was very pretty and very young, and her eyes were very wary. It was the kind of look that came naturally to people who worked in businesses with a high armed-robbery rate. It came extra easily to girls who were voted the prettiest in their high-school class and came to Las Vegas to take the town by storm and wound up working, a few months later, in a side-street jewelry shop.

"I want to see Herman," he told her.

"May I tell him your name?"

"Tell him Trace is here, please."

She nodded but gave him a smile that suggested he was a loan shark coming for an overdue payment, and went into a back room. A moment later, she came out and the smile was real. "You can go right in."

Herman was a man with no discernible bones in his body. His face looked like a water-filled baloon. His body was round, his arms were short thick ovals, his fingers overstuffed little sausages. He had a jeweler's loupe in his eye and he grunted when Trace entered the small back-room office.

There was a piece of black velvet on the work counter in front of Herman and it glittered with the jagged flashing of a few dozen diamonds.

Trace walked to a file cabinet in the far corner of the room, opened the top drawer, and removed a chess set. He walked back to the work counter, cleared aside the IN basket, and set up the board.

He moved one of the white pieces and called out, "Pawn king four."

Herman was holding a diamond between narrow little tweezers, turning it back and forth under his glass. Without looking away, he said, "Pawn queen bishop four."

Trace made Herman's move on the board for him, and then his own. "Knight king bishop three."

Herman put the diamond to one side and picked up another. Still without looking at the board, he said "Pawn queen three."

Herman was sorting the diamonds into two piles. Playing both sides of the chess board, Trace called out each move he had made, and the jeweler, without even a glance at the board, would instantly call out his response, which Trace entered on the board.

It took Herman eight minutes to finish examining the diamonds. He had separated four from the rest. He pushed the black velvet aside and said, "Crap, all crap. You'd be amazed at the crap we get. Hello, Trace."

"Hello, Herman. I thought diamonds were forever."

"No. Crap is forever," Herman said. "Now what have we here?"

He looked down at the chessboard, where Trace had just launched a queen, knight, and rook attack on Herman's castled king. He grunted to himself and, after Trace's next move, sacrificed a bishop to check Trace's own king, and three moves later had won Trace's queen.

Trace turned his king over in the traditional gesture of surrender. "You're slipping," he said. "You had to look at the board this time."

"The ravages of age," Herman said. He was still looking at the chessboard. "You always attack too soon. You play like an Irishman."

"The old argument," Trace said. "Nature versus nurture. What's wrong with the stones?"

"All dreck," Herman said. "They come from the same rotten armpit of the world, they're all umpty-ump million years old, and lately, all I get is bort. Stuff you should put in drills, not in rings."

"That's what you get for making your living in a controlled marketplace," Trace said. "Diamonds are off, so the geniuses who run the industry push out junk because junk always draws junk prices. When the market goes up, good stones go up more, and that's when you'll see them."

"You're very smart, Trace. It took me half a lifetime to figure it out."

"That's because you're Jewish and I'm only half a Jew. The Irish half of me figures out plots and conspiracies, things we're good at. Most of the time we don't make any sense at all, but if we luck into a real conspiracy, then, hell, you came to the right place. You know why I'm here?"

"Actually, I thought you came in for your bi-weekly drubbing," Herman said.

"Not this time. Felicia Fallaci."

"I heard that that was Roberts' case," Herman said.

"It is, kind of. I'm checking out the murder that

125

went with it, but since the two of them are connected, I've got to check the jewels too."

"What can I do for you?"

"Roberts tells me there's no sign of the jewels on the street. Is that right?"

"Yes."

"I thought he might be lying to me," Trace said.

"Not this time."

"He talk to you?" Trace asked.

"There you are, being Irish again. No conspiracy. Ever since that business with young Jack, you're my friend. Sure, Roberts talked to me. He asked me to keep an eye open for him, even promised me a piece of a reward if he gets one. So I'm keeping my eyes open for him. Nothing going on in town and nothing in California either."

"How the hell can anybody tell that?" Trace asked. "So many jewelers, so many diamond dealers."

"And so many big mouths," Herman said. "One guy makes a buy and he's got to tell his brother-in-law, but his brother-in-law hates him, so he tells everybody else and before you know it, the whole world knows about it. It's rotten, but it's the way our business works. It's why we can make deals with handshakes, 'cause everybody knows everybody else's business. If someone ran across a lot of good stuff, everybody'd know about it and so would I. Nobody. Nothing."

"New York?" Trace said.

Herman threw his hands up into the air. The motion set the fat on the backs of his arms to jiggling.

"New York is different. It's . . . well, it's New York. People change so fast, so much money changes hands. There's a million dollars changing hands

126

on Forty-seventh Street every five minutes. Another million would just get lost in the shuffle. Nobody hears anything out of New York."

"If Felicia's jewels wound up there, they could just vanish?"

"Off the face of the earth," Herman said.

"Why doesn't every thief go to New York, then?" Trace asked.

"The good ones do. The rest panic. They're afraid their luggage will rip open and somebody will find the stones. Or that they'll get mugged. Or who knows what. Most thieves aren't very smart."

"So far, you can't prove it by me," Trace said. "I don't have an inkling on this one."

"It'll come," Herman said confidently. "Time for another?"

"Where were you when mercy was handed out?" Trace asked, but he began setting up the chessboard again.

"Am I on tape?" Herman asked.

"Yes. Should I turn it off?"

"Leave it on," Herman said. "Later you can play back your screams of anguish."

13

Spiro lived in a two-family house on a tired old street a half-mile from the downtown business district.

Trace leaned on his door bell and, when he got no answer, pushed the lower bell on the assumption that the owner lived on the first floor. If the woman who answered the bell was the owner, she wasn't exactly thrilled by her status as a real-estate mogul.

She was short and fat and aggressively packed into pedal pushers and a pink sweater. Her hair gave new dimension to the description "lifeless," and she had a cigarette hung from her mouth that kept curling smoke into her eyes and causing her to squint.

"What do you want?" she said.

"Just in time," Trace said. He took the cigarette from her mouth and threw it out onto the broken-cement walk.

"Hey. Hey. What's that for?"

"I'm from the gas company," Trace said. "Mr. Spirakodopolous called and said he had a gas leak."

"He ain't home," the woman said. It hadn't been

the smoke that made her eyes squint. She was still squinting.

"Probably fled before everything blows up," Trace said. "I've got to look around. If you've got a gas leak, it can be very serious."

"I told you, he ain't home."

"And, lady, I thought I just told you that if I don't check this out, this house might blow up around your ears. Is this your house?"

"Naturally it's my house."

"And where's Mr. Spirakodopolous's apartment?"

"Upstairs, but he ain't home."

"His gas leak's still home. Get me the key. Hurry, woman, before we're all incinerated."

"Who are you?"

"I told you, I'm from the gas company."

"You got any identification?"

"Yes. My name's Reddy Kilowatt and you might want to stand here chatting, but I don't want to blow up. I'm leaving."

"All right. Wait a minute." She lumbered off and came back a few seconds later with a key. She handed it to Trace.

"Now, listen, ma'am. This is very important. While I look around, please step outside and wait on the sidewalk. No point in both of us dying."

She had finally started to believe him. She pushed by him and walked out onto the sidewalk.

"Wait there for me," Trace said.

He went quickly up the steps and unlocked the door to Spiro's apartment. He just looked inside and knew he was too late. The apartment was two rooms: a small kitchen and an all-purpose living room—dining room with a pull-out bed. The entire place had been turned upside down. Drawers had been pulled out and their contents emptied. Magazines were tossed all over the floor. A large closet in the living room had been ransacked. Clothes were piled in a heap on the floor.

Somebody had gotten the idea to search Spiro's apartment before Trace did. Score one for Sherlock Holmes. He looked around and decided there was no point in looking for anything. If there had been something in the apartment, either it had been found already, or he wouldn't be able to find it either.

He closed the door and made sure it was locked, then walked down the stairs, whistling. Outside, he gave the landlady her key back.

"It's all A-okay," he said. "No danger."

"What was it?"

"It's hard to tell sometimes since the Alaska pipeline opened. But it's perfectly safe. Tell me, has anybody else been here today?"

"From the gas company? No."

"From anywhere? Anybody come in to see Mr. Spirakodopolous?"

"No."

"You been home all day?"

"Yeah. Well, except this morning, when I went to get my hair done."

"And done very well it is, too, ma'am," Trace said.

"Your father called," Chico said.

"What'd he say?"

"He said he's made a major breakthrough in this case. He said that he wants half your fee."

"What'd you tell him?"

"To hold out for two-thirds. I've got expensive habits and it's going to cost him to take me away from all this."

"Is he still at the airport?"

"He told me he was, but that was about an hour ago. He said he wants to meet you at four o'clock. He said pick a cops' bar."

"There aren't any cops' bars in Vegas. This isn't New York. In New York, you can't go near Third Avenue and Twenty-third Street without tripping over cops. Did he say what he found?"

"No. He's going to call back. What should I tell him?"

"Tell him to meet me at Boggle's."

"That's a mob bar," Chico said.

"Only difference is that the clientele dresses better in a mob bar. Boggle's. At four."

"I'll tell him when he calls."

"You see my mother?"

"Not today," Chico said. She turned back to the cocktail lounge bar and waved to the bartender for another Coke.

"Not even for lunch?" Trace asked.

"Nope."

"My mother passed up a free lunch?"

"Maybe she's on a hot streak at the slot machines."

"I hope so," Trace said. "If she loses another ten dollars, I'm never going to hear the end of it. The next thing will be the gas pipe."

"She can take Bob Swenson with her," Chico said. "He's had this look on his face all day."

"Just because National Anthem wouldn't play?"

"He's been wandering around, I think they call it mumbling darkly, about some people born to be unlucky in love."

"You've got to admit it must have been tough for him. Sleeping next to her and having her imitate Little Goody Two-Shoes."

131

"You'd really like to give her a go, wouldn't you?" Chico said.

"Stop it, will you? I'm sober. I'm watching my cigarettes. What more do you want from me?"

"Total loyalty and unremitting faithfulness. You'd really like to take a run at that big cow, wouldn't you? Just because she's got a big chest."

"Not just because she's got a big chest. It's the challenge. To boldly go where only donkeys have gone before."

"Tell the truth. The chest has something to do with it, doesn't it?"

"Yes. Actually, yes," Trace said.

"I hate you when you get fixated on other women's bosoms. Here I am, working my little tits off for your insurance company and—"

"No, thank you, that dog won't hunt. You're working your reasonably sized, nice, beautiful knockers off for two thousand dollars. And how do you figure I'm fixated on chests when you're the one who's always talking about them?"

"You think I'd be doing this if it weren't for you?" she asked.

"For two thousand dollars? Sure."

"You're hateful, Trace."

"Last night you told me I was lovable."

"Last night you *were* lovable. Now you're the same hateful no-good that I've come to know and despise."

"Only a fool is loved by everyone."

"And what about somebody who's loved by no one? What do you call him?" she snapped.

"An insurance man, I guess," said Trace. "And right on cue, here comes Walter Marks, sprightly of step, clear of eye."

"And empty of mind," Chico mumbled, then

turned her dazzling smile on Marks. "Good afternoon, sir," she said.

"Yes. Well, Tracy, what's going on? I mean, it's nice that you're able to sit here on company time, drinking . . . I guess it's nice that the two of you can do that, but I was wondering what gives with the Jarvis case."

"We're getting close to a breakthrough," Trace said.

"Oh?"

"I think it was a ritual killing. All the signs are there. The gloves on his hands. The blow to the skull with a blunt instrument. The overturned tree, the dirt scattered all over the living-room floor. Even the missing jewels and the ashtray. It has all the earmarks of another killing done by the Rustinayle Terrorist Society of Upper Egypt. Don't confuse that with Lower Egypt. If you look at a map, you'll see that Upper Egypt is at the bottom of Egypt and Lower Egypt is at the top. This is what we call in the trade a paradox."

"Don't talk to me about Egypt," Marks said. "What is this society?"

"The Rustinayles. After the Thuggees in India, they were the most fearsome of all the groups. Lately, they've been financing their nefarious activities by jewel theft. But trust me, Groucho. I'll bring those towel-heads to justice if it's the last thing I do. It'll be a great feather in our caps. Well, maybe a smaller feather for your cap."

"The Rustinayles, you say?"

"None other," Trace said.

Marks nodded, then strolled away as if he had just remembered an appointment. Chico had been sitting with her back to them, and when she turned, Trace saw that she had a cocktail napkin stuffed into her mouth. She pulled it out and said, "You are a terrible person, Trace."

"We'll see. If he goes right to a telephone, then we know he's calling the fancy insurance detective to warn him to get right on the trail of those Egyptians."

"The Rusty Nails. You're awful," she said.

"Stay here." Trace walked away and was back a minute later. "Groucho went right to a phone booth in the lobby. He knows who the insurance detective is."

"If the guy's got any sense at all, he's going to know you're jerking Marks around."

"One never know, do one?"

Chico finished her Coke and started to excuse herself when Marks returned.

He tried to chuckle. "That was a good one, Trace. The Rusty Nails. Heh, heh. Sorry I had to run off like that. Now, tell me the truth. Any breaks in the case?"

"Excuse me, you two," Chico said. "I have to run."

Trace kissed her cheek. "Tell Sarge Boggle's." She nodded and smiled at Marks, who ignored her.

Trace turned back to him. "I wasn't kidding, Walter. You know I'm serious when I call you Walter."

"Come on. You can't expect me to believe that nonsense."

"When I have the perpetrator incarcerated, you'll see," Trace said. "A great feat of detection. I'm thinking of having my brain registered with the police as a deadly weapon."

"Or another victim of alcohol abuse," Marks snapped.

"That too," Trace said.

"I don't know," Sarge said. "An awful lot of Italians in here for this to be a cop's bar."

He was sitting with Trace at a table in a dark corner of Boggle's, a cocktail lounge on Desert Inn Road, but far off the usual tourist paths that tended toward excess in both prices and air-conditioning.

"I don't see an Irishman in here, except us," Sarge said. "All cops in Vegas are Italians?"

"These aren't really cops, Sarge."

"Mobsters, right? Gunsels? I could smell it when I came in. All that cheap cologne. Ten Nights on a Pepper Farm. A dollar a gallon. Why don't we roust the joint?"

"Because they haven't really done anything wrong. And because most of them are friends of mine."

"I guess we'll let it go, then," Sarge said grudgingly.

"So let me in on your big discovery today," Trace said.

"No job for amateurs, son," Sarge said.

A man sitting at the bar glanced in their direction. His eyes lingered a shade too long on Trace's father, and Sarge started to rise to his feet, a scowl on his face. The man at the bar turned away and Sarge settled down, nodding in satisfaction. "Got to teach these people to keep in their places," he said.

"Today. The airport. What happened?"

"Nobody at American Airlines remembered seeing Jarvis the other night. I talked to a couple of people who were working then and there's a couple more to go. I'm going back tonight to talk to them."

"That's the big revelation?"

"I'm coming to it. You've got some good friends out there at the airport," Sarge said. "That Sergeant Murray, the redheaded guy, he said he owes you."

"I did a favor for him once."

"More than just a favor, the way he told it. You kept his kid out of jail."

"They had the wrong kid. Just a mistake. What did Murray do?"

"The two of us sneaked around checking lockers with a master key. No passport. Who do you have to know to get a drink around here?"

"Just me," Trace said. He waved to a cocktail waitress in a skirted sailor suit, who came quickly to their table.

"Debbie, this is my father."

"What will you have, sir?" she asked.

"Whatever he has," Sarge said.

"I'll have Perrier water," Trace said.

"Hold it," Sarge said. "I'll have beer."

Sarge waited until she had left, then opened his big red notebook and brought out a photo of Jarvis, an enlargment of a typical but clear backyard snapshot. "I showed this around," he said.

"And?"

"Your man Jarvis was quite a traveler," Sarge said.

Trace realized that his father was relishing this and was going to tell the story in his own good time. So, let him. He lit a cigarette and sat silently, waiting for Sarge to continue.

"Yup, quite a traveler," Sarge said.

"I didn't know that."

"I bet you didn't. And I bet you didn't know that for three weeks in a row before he got killed, he flew to New York every Thursday. Three weeks in a row."

"No, I didn't know that either."

136

"I found a girl at the ticket counter. That's her regular shift and she sold him his tickets. She recognized his picture. But you know what?" He stopped as Debbie approached. "Hold it until she goes. She might be on the earie, you know."

He waited as Debbie put down their drinks, smiled, and left.

"You were saying," Trace prompted.

"The name 'Jarvis' didn't ring any bell with this girl at the airport. She recognized the face from the picture but not the name. So I had her dig out the manifests from those flights. There was only one name on all three of them: Edward Stark. Mean anything to you?"

"No."

"Me neither," Sarge said, "but I'm going to check it out. So why'd he go to New York three Thursdays in a row and why'd he go under a different name?"

"A girlfriend? Maybe he was in love? Business? I don't know."

"Funny kind of business because the girl told me that he came back the same day. He'd go to New York and it was like he turned around and came right back the same day. Does that make any sense?"

"Well, it rules out a girlfriend, unless Jarvis was into quickies. You got any ideas?"

"I'm thinking about it," Sarge said.

"Sure as hell complicates things, doesn't it?"

"Life is complicated, son. The more you check things, the more you find out they're complicated. Easy answers are almost always wrong in our line of work. I think that guy over there is staring at us." He cracked his knuckles. It sounded like sticks breaking in the dark, quiet bar.

Trace glanced at the bar, saw a man who was indeed staring at them, and waved to the man "Don't worry about him, Sarge. He's my bookie."

"I thought we were going to have to fight our way out of here," Sarge said.

"No. Just pay the bill, the way we do in most places."

"So I didn't get anything on the missing passport, but I think that's a big lead about Jarvis flying to New York."

Trace nodded. "I'll talk to the countess about it. That's good work, Sarge."

"So how was your day? You learn anything?"

"Just that those jewels aren't on the street. Whoever lifted them hasn't dumped them around here."

"You're the one who told me this is a town of smart guys," Sarge said. "A lot of people could have bought up that stuff and you'd never know."

"Somebody would know. That's a lot of money and money always talks. Roberts hasn't heard anything either."

"Who's Roberts?"

"The p.i. I told you about. He's got lines out in the street, but he hasn't heard anything either."

"Do you believe him?"

"I double-checked him, Sarge, with somebody I do believe. No sign of the jewels yet."

"When you going to question that countess?" Sarge asked.

"I don't know. Today I guess."

"I never questioned a countess before," Sarge said wistfully.

"Your life's not over yet either," Trace said. "I've got something else I want to talk to her about."

"Okay, I'll leave it to you. I'm going back to the

airport tonight. Check the late-night people, see if they saw Jarvis."

Trace looked at his watch. "Sounds good to me. I wonder how Mother is."

"You really know how to ruin an afternoon," Sarge said. "She's always fine, that woman." Suddenly he asked, "You going to marry Chico?"

"I don't know. Probably not," Trace said. "Why?"

"Don't," Sarge said.

"Not even if I love her?" Trace asked.

"Especially then," Sarge said. "You know, before we got married, your mother and I were friends, like you and Chico are. But then we got married, and I don't know, somehow your mother put her friend's head away and put on her wife's head."

"She loves you, Pop. You know that."

"Sure. She loves me. Like a wife. But she doesn't even like me. Not like a friend. Trust me, Devlin. Make a woman your wife, make an enemy for life."

"I don't know if Chico's got a wife's head to wear," Trace said. "And I don't have any husband's head at all. I proved that already in my last marriage."

"If that's true about Chico, don't let her get away," Sarge said.

"Sarge, you know how she makes her living. Even despite that?"

"Even despite anything," Sarge said.

"Felicia, this is Trace."

"Hello, darling. Where's my money?"

"I'm working on it. Did Jarvis have a regular day off?"

"Yes. He was off on Thursday."

"What did he do on his day off?"

"I don't know. We didn't talk about it. Are you playing *cherchez la femme*? A jilted lover killed him? What's going on?"

"What if I told you that he flew to New York and back every Thursday?"

"I'd say I'll be damned."

"He did. Why do you think he did that?"

"I don't know. A girlfriend?"

"He never stayed overnight," Trace said. "Just flew in and out."

"Platonic," she said. "Plato lives."

"Yeah, but I'm told he's in retreat. Does the name 'Edward Stark' mean anything to you?"

"No. Should it?"

"That was the name he flew to New York under."

"Trace, I don't know what it's all about." Then she laughed.

"What's so funny?"

"Jarvis was with me for years. I've learned more about him in the few weeks he's been dead than I did in all those years."

"How long was Jarvis with you?" Trace asked.

"Fifteen years. I met him in Italy right after I broke up with my husband, the count. I needed somebody and Jarvis needed work."

"You didn't know anything about him when you hired him?"

"I still don't know anything about him," Felicia said. "Jarvis never talked. He said he didn't have a family, but I don't know his home town or where he went to school or whatever. I didn't even know that he had insurance, or that I was the beneficiary, until that insurance agent in town who wrote the policy called me. And now you're telling me he's hopping all over on airplanes. Why that name, Stark? Why Stark? Why New York?"

"I don't know. I wish I did," Trace said.

"So do I, if it'd get me my money from your company."

"I want to come out and look at Jarvis' room. I forgot it the last time I was there," Trace said.

"Come tomorrow. I'll get rid of everybody and we can roll around in the hay."

"Thanks, but no thanks. I'll come tonight."

"Are you rejecting me again?" she asked.

"No. I'm just trying to get you your money," Trace said.

"Come whenever you want," she said. "Bring a check."

14

Driving back to his condominium, Trace felt satisfied. He hadn't seen his father looking so happy in a long time, and finding out that Jarvis made it a practice to fly to New York every week was a good beat. It had to mean something, and it didn't bother him that right now he had no idea what it meant.

He had always regarded figuring out a case as a bone-chew. Take the smallest dog, give him the biggest bone, and if you gave him time enough, he would chew his way through it. Trace had time, and if he kept nibbling and scratching, sooner or later the bone that was the Jarvis murder mystery would break. It had always worked that way before and he was sure it would again.

So everything was going well and he felt reasonably good.

Until he got back to his apartment.

"Look at this place," Chico said. She was waiting for him, inside the door, her hands on her hips, her black eyes flashing. He had never seen a real person express anger before by putting hands on hips. He had thought that was done only in cartoons and in movies.

"What in the hell's gone on here?" Trace asked.

"What do you think's gone on here?"

"We were either burgled or we've been victimized by an interior decorator run amok."

He looked around the large living room. Their twin couches, which had formed a cozy conversational L in the middle of the floor, were now side by side against a wall. Coffee tables were placed squarely in front of them, so precisely centered that they might have been moved by an engineer. They were also so close to the couches that no one could sit down without scraping a knee.

Their lamps had been moved and now stood side by side in a far corner of the room where they illuminated each other. The formal dining table, which had been at one end of the long room, was now in the center of the floor. It might have been a viable idea, except that for anyone to sit at one side of the table they would have to move the cocktail tables that were behind their chairs. That, in turn, would mean that anyone sitting on the couch would have to get up.

The apartment had been turned into a series of accidents waiting to happen. Chico pointed with a quivering finger toward a far wall.

One of their paintings, a lithograph of an aged monk, numbered and signed by Ivan Le Lorraine Albright, the artist, had been removed from a wall. In its place now hung some kind of white glazed lavabo, a make-believe pot holding make-believe water so that make-believe people could wash their make-believe hands.

"What is that fucking thing?" Chico demanded.

"A lavabo. From the Latin. I will wash."

"Don't give me any of your erudition bullshit. I've forgotten more Latin than you ever knew. I

143

know it's a goddamn lavabo, what I don't know is what the hell it's doing on our wall."

"Who did this?"

"Three guesses," she said.

Trace had a sinking feeling in his stomach. "No, not her. Not that sweet old lady. She couldn't have."

"She did. She left clues all over the place. Her cloven hoofmarks are all over my fucking kitchen. I want a knife, I've got to go searching for knives now. She didn't like my knife drawer. You want a blender? I'll tell you where the blender is. It's in the back, under the sink, where only fucking E.T. can reach it. The glasses are now stacked by size. Small ones in front. This probably makes a lot of sense to that woman, except we use only the big glasses. You can't get a big glass now without knocking over eight small ones."

"How'd she get in here?" Trace asked.

"The way she does everything. She bullied her way past the concierge. Not only that, she got him to bring her up and open the door for her because she said she had misplaced her key. If you give that woman a key, Trace, you'll find your clothes in the hall. And then she went cheerfully about her day's activity, wrecking my fucking house. Look at this place. It looks like a religious mission in the goddamn Australian outback. Who could live like this?"

Trace opened his mouth but Chico wasn't finished yet.

"You think she didn't leave clues? I'll give you a clue. Come here." She grabbed his right wrist and jerked him toward the bedroom.

"Good idea," he said. "We'll hold each other until the hurt passes away."

"Shut your face," she said. "There. Look."

Trace looked. On the bed were four two-inch squares of wallpaper samples, ranging from atrocious to hideous without even a moment's hesitation at passable. And there was a note. It read:

I think your white painted walls are terrible. They're very ugly and they're all stained yellow with cigarette smoke. I will wallpaper this room for you before I go. With your father busy, I don't have anything else to do because I am not made of money and can't keep throwing ten dollarses into slot machines that never pay off, despite promises to the contrary. Besides, I think you should have a nice house to live in and it is obvious that this place needs a woman's touch. Please pick out which one of these samples you like best.

She had signed the note "Hilda Tracy."

Trace held the note up to the light from the window.

"It's her handwriting, all right. I can tell by the pinched way she makes the loops in her e's."

"So what are you going to do about it?"

"I'll talk to her," Trace said.

"If talking to her would help, I'd talk to her," Chico said. "You can't talk to that woman. It's like talking to an obelisk with a hat."

"She'll listen to me," Trace promised. He knew she would never listen to him.

"She won't listen to you," Chico said. "All that woman understands is force. All right, she wants force, I'll give her force."

She picked up the telephone and dialed a three-digit number.

"Hello, Harold? Okay, this is Miss Mangini in

three-seventeen. If that woman comes back to-morrow, these are our instructions. Shoot her on sight. Right between the eyes. . . . Don't worry, I'll get you a gun. . . .You can't shoot her? You never shot anybody? Okay. Slice her Achilles tendons with a sharp knife. People have been known to linger for weeks that way before dying. She'll have time to crawl off to the elephant graveyard. . . . No? Okay. If she bullies past you, you call the cops and have her arrested for trespassing and illegal entry. Try burglary if you want. Theft. I think she lifted a pair of my ornamental chopsticks. . . . Of course, I'll press the charges. So will Trace. I'm warning you. If she gets by you tomorrow, she dies and I report you to the tenants' management board. . . . You think you've got troubles now? I'll give you troubles. You'll be happy to die when I'm done with you."

She slammed down the telephone.

Trace tossed the wallpaper samples into a waste-paper basket in the corner and flopped down onto the bed. He put his hands behind his head.

"So how you doing?" he said brightly. "Have a nice day?"

"Go fuck yourself," Chico said. "I'm not forgetting your culpability in this."

"What culpability?" he demanded.

"You could have been an orphan." She stomped out of the room and a few seconds later Trace heard her grunting, and he knew it was time now to choose sides or be marked rotten forever. He rose from the bed and went inside to help her move the furniture back where it belonged.

"Do you know, I dream about that woman?" she said as she grunted, lugging a corner of the heavy sofa.

"I never dream," he said.

"You're lucky. I dream. She comes up to me in a dream, I always know it's a dream because she's talking to me and she doesn't talk to me in real life. She says, 'I've got a piano for my son's apartment.' I say, 'We've got a piano.' She says, 'How much did you pay for it?' I say, 'Six thousand dollars.' She goes, 'Hah! Fifteen hundred dollars, a beauty.'"

"What happens then?" Trace asked.

"I don't know. I always wake up in a cold sweat. You know your mother. Fifteen hundred dollars. She got it in Piano City and it's got yellow flowers painted on it. She gets everything at some kind of city. Food City. Shoe City. Embalming at Funeral City. She's making me into Crazy City."

"A little more to the front on your end," Trace directed. "That's good. You shouldn't let her bother you. She'll be gone in a couple more days. You can do a couple more days' standing on your head."

"Yeah? That's what you think. Try telling that sometime to somebody who's really standing on her head. The blood pools in your head after just three hours and your feet start to die. Your toes fall off in a couple of days. I'll never dance again. Your father will have to take me around dancing. Your mother can carry me in a pack on her back."

"You can go to Ankle City dancing," Trace said. "My mother's got a discount pass."

"We can all go to Nuthouse City," Chico said. "We can go together. Rent a bus from Bus City, me, your father, and that woman. She can drive. We can bibble our lips—"

"Bibble? Bibble our lips?"

"You know. Bibibibibibibibble," Chico said, running her fingers up and down over her lower lip.

"We can all bibble our lips and slobber and wet our pants. We can get a room together at the Ha-ha House. Your mother can decorate it. She can smear dirt on the walls."

They finished moving the other couch and Trace pushed Chico down onto it. "Sit there," he said. He kissed her on the mouth. "I don't know how a nice girl like you ever got hooked up with this traveling circus anyway," he said.

She sat and he put the cocktail tables back where they belonged. He heard Chico giggling, so he knew the worst was over.

"The nerve of her," Chico said. "Trace, the woman's a wonder. Just when I think she's figured out every way to make me nuts, she finds a new one. How'd you manage to escape quasi-sane?"

" 'Twaren't easy, little girl." He sat alongside her and she put her arms around his neck and kissed his forehead.

"You poor thing," she said. "Remind me to show you some compassion in the future."

"I will. You can count on it."

"You know," Chico said, "my mother wanders around like a geisha, wearing kimonos, with her hands hidden inside the sleeves. But all she ever did was threaten suicide if she thought my skirt was too short. Nothing like this. It's like being violated."

"Speaking of which," he said.

"Sorry, pal. Duty calls," she said.

"I could be quick," he said.

"I couldn't." She started to laugh again.

"What's so funny?" he asked.

"We forgot something."

She pointed toward the white lavabo. Trace nodded, got up, and took the wretched thing down from the wall and carried it into the bedroom. In the closet there, he found the print that had been on the wall and he brought it back out and hung it up again.

He sat back down.

"What'd you do with it?" she asked.

"Circular File City," he said.

15

There was nothing to see in Jarvis' room except neatly hung clothing and sparkling clean furniture.

"I cleaned it for you," Felicia said brightly.

"I didn't want you to clean it for me," Trace said. "I wanted to root around in the dirt and grime myself. Rubbish can be very informative. Ask Henry Kissinger."

"I've got four garbage pails outside the kitchen," she said. "You can root around in there. Find out what we had for breakfast. I didn't throw anything out. I just straightened things up in here to make it easier for you."

"He didn't have anything? No phone books? No notes? No papers?"

"No nothing," the countess said. "I didn't find anything either."

"This whole trip out here was a waste," Trace said. "I could've stayed home."

"I resent being called a waste. If you had stayed home, could you grab my wrist and drag me kicking and screaming up off to my bedroom—it's two doors over—and toss me on the bed and rip off my clothes and punish my body? Huh? Could you do that at home?"

"Felicia, someday I'm going to take you up on your offer and you're going to be the most surprised person in town."

"Uh huh," she said. "You will. When you find out what you've been missing, you'll mourn for time wasted, never to be found again."

"Didn't he even have a checkbook? Everybody's got a checkbook," Trace said.

"If he had one, I don't know where he kept it. It wasn't in here," she said. "Come on, Trace. Let's go over my room and trick."

Trace looked at her. She was wearing shorts made from cut-off white jeans, and they showed off her long tan legs and a little north of that. A man's shirt was tied around her waist, exposing her navel and her flat little belly. The shirt buttons were open, and as she moved, her breasts moved, sweetly, independently, bouncily.

He walked to where she stood in the doorway, put his arms around her, and kissed her hard. Her tongue slid into his mouth as easily as a family car rolling into the house garage.

"Keep a civil tongue in your head," he said. "Two doors over in what direction?"

"You serious?" she said.

"I never joke about important things," he said.

"Then let's make this a very important thing," she said as she led him into the hallway and toward her room.

While she slipped out of her clothes, Trace reached under his shirt and yanked the tape recorder and the surgical tape from his waist and stuck the machine in his jacket pocket. He hung his tie over the door so that the microphone was aimed at Felicia's bed.

She was beautiful, silhouetted against the dying

light from outside, as she turned and walked toward him.

"Let me help you undress," she said.

"Yes."

They lay side by side in bed. Through the open window, Trace could hear the sounds of her house guests, talking, tinkling glasses, punctuated occasionally by the lunatic squawk of one of her parrots: "Polly want a hit, Polly want a hit."

"Well?" she said.

"I like a woman who keeps her promises," Trace said. "It was a very important thing."

And it was a lie. The sex had been routine acrobatics, a highly polished practiced routine that had all the emotional significance of scratching one's neck to get rid of an itch. The only thing it needed right now, to round it off, he thought, was for someone to jump into the room and hold up two signs: 9.9 for technical merit, 9.1 for artistic achievement.

"I knew I'd get you in this bed someday," she said. "It's just strange that it took a murder for it to happen."

"Things are complicated sometimes," Trace said meaninglessly, and waited to see if she were going to pump him.

She was.

She curled her head onto his shoulder and kissed his neck.

"Have you found out anything yet?" she asked softly.

"No. Nothing really. No leads, no trace of the jewels, nothing."

"And that detective, Roberts? He's got nothing either?"

"No. I don't think so."

"It's strange," she said. "I would have thought someone would contact me by now."

"Why you?" Trace asked.

"Oh, I don't know. I just thought, I don't know, maybe the thief, I don't know."

"But no one's contacted you," he said.

"No. Except you." She laughed softly in the darkened room. "I think we've just gotten into very close contact."

"The closest," he said, and wondered how long he would have to lie there to be considered civil, before he could get up and dress.

Felicia seemed content to stay in his arms. "Do you think you'll catch Jarvis' killer?" she asked.

"Probably," he said. "I'm smarter than I look."

"And the jewels?"

"They're not really my concern," Trace said. "If I had to guess, I'd say they're long gone."

"Do you think Spiro had anything to do with it?" she asked.

"No."

"But who'd know where the safe was? Who'd know I had jewels?" she asked.

"You'd be surprised. All your friends. One piece of chitchat leads to another piece of chitchat. Everybody gossips, and before you know it, somebody you don't even know knows everything about your house and its layout and your schedule."

"I try to avoid that," she said. "I stay off charity boards and I don't go and join fund-raising organizations. I've been in this town a year and I don't think I've gone to anything formal yet. I turn down all those invitations just because I don't want a lot of strangers hanging around here, finding out things."

"Well, somebody found out something," Trace said.

He waited, holding her, for another ten minutes and then he rose and tripped over something in the dark.

"What the hell's that?" he growled.

"Oh. My luggage. I haven't unpacked yet. I'm hiring a maid. Throw me my clothes from the chair," she said.

They dressed and went down to join Felicia's guests, who were sitting around, under smoky oil lamps, near the pool.

Felicia went to fix Trace a drink and he sat on a chaise next to Baron Hubbaker, who was wearing a white polo shirt and white trousers.

"I take it you didn't think much of my theory about the Rustinayles," Trace said.

"Excuse me?"

"When Walter Marks called you today. After I told him that I thought Jarvis was a ritual murder."

"Oh. Having a bit of fun tweaking his nose, weren't you?"

"Yeah," Trace said. "That nose was made for tweaking."

"You had him believing it," Hubbaker said.

"Why'd he call you?"

"Damned if I know," the baron said. "I think maybe he's a little crazy. I like to play detective as much as the next fellow, but Walter Marks is obsessive."

Ferrara was sitting on the other corner of the pool. He roared, "Willie," and Parmenter came to him from out of the house. "Let's get out of here," Ferrara said. "I don't like the direction this neighborhood is taking."

He glared pointedly toward Trace, who said, "Don't be nasty. Life's too short to hold grudges."

"In your case, I hope that would be true," Ferrara said as he walked toward the house.

"Not exactly a new warm friend, is he?" Hubbaker said.

"I wouldn't call him if my car broke down late at night," Trace said. "What do you think about Spiro?"

"He's a terrible cook," Hubbaker said. "He made a thing tonight with peppers and rice that should be used to patch stucco."

"I meant involved in this case."

"The jewels? Jarvis? I don't know. I think he's harmless. Why do you ask?"

"I just wondered if you had an opinion," Trace said.

"None at all," Hubbaker said.

Felicia joined them and handed Trace a tall vodka and tonic. He drank it quickly, then went into the kitchen to get a refill.

Spiro was doing dishes. The television set played softly in a corner of the room.

"Hello, Mr. Tracy."

"How's it going, Spiro?"

"Okay."

"Anything strange happening to you lately?" Trace asked.

"No." He shrugged. "What do you mean?"

"I don't know," Trace said. "I've heard a couple people drop your name in this investigation. I wondered if you had anything, like detectives trailing you or like that."

Spiro shook his head. "Jesus Christ, I don't think so. Nobody's going to try to pin this on me, are they, Mr. Tracy?"

"You didn't do it?"

"I swear to God. I only know what I told you."

"Then don't worry about anything," Trace said.

"Easy for you to say," Spiro said as he turned back to the dishes.

Chico was already home when Trace got there. As he feared, she was in bed with a look in her eye that made come-hither sound wishy-washy.

"Climb in here and feel me up a little," she said.

How do women get such insanely bad timing? he wondered. He had been pure for weeks and Chico had looked at him with not much more interest than if he had been an advertisement for lawn mowers. One night he goes out tipping on her, and she picks that night to be horny, and aggressive about it.

"Absolutely," he said. "My idea exactly."

"Don't talk about it. Do it," she said.

"I'm going to," he said. "I'm going to pound your body flat. I'm going to make you sorry for all the times you've rejected me. You're going to be nothing but a repository for my stored-up passion."

"You got laid tonight, didn't you?"

"You're disgusting," he said. "Honest, you are. I come home, exhausted from working, and you're lying there with your filthy little Oriental-Sicilian mind filled with disgusting fantasies."

"Who was it? I bet you hit that big-uddered cow."

"I'm not even going to dignify that with a comment," he said.

It was good that she picked the wrong woman. Now he could spar with her and let her get herself all worked up about his bagging National Anthem, and then he could tell her, with honesty and sincerity just oozing out of his every word, that, no, he had not slept with National Anthem and he was really tired of her sick suspicions. If he did it right, maybe he could even make her feel guilty. Timing was everything. The trick was not to deny it now, but first let her get it firmly implanted in her mind that National Anthem was the woman in the piece.

"Was she good? Was she as good as I am?"

"Nobody could be as good as you are," he said. Very clever, he thought. Just the right kind of answer. An all-purpose nondenial.

"I thought she was only into donkeys," Chico said.

"So I'm told," he said blandly.

"Of course. Of course, you qualify. You're more of a mule than a donkey, but I'm sure she couldn't tell the difference."

"I really would rather not discuss this with you," he said righteously. "You're getting yourself all worked up over nothing."

"Nothing? You call that amazon, that bovine, a nothing? Where did you do it?"

"I don't really know what you're talking about. Honestly, I hate it when you get this way."

"Does she do it in bed like normal women? A motel room? Or did you have to rent a stable? Tell me, you Irish-Jewish half-breed bastard. Confess your sins."

"I have nothing to confess. How come you're home so early?"

"Don't change the subject, you son of a bitch. I came home early because I got tired of all those insurance people. I wanted to spend part of an evening with you. I hungered—no, I yearned for your body. I wanted to make love to you. And what's he do? He's out porking some nitwit. I'm ashamed of you."

"The day will come when you'll apologize to me for this," he said.

"I'll die before I apologize. You are beneath contempt. A hundred generations of Japanese ancestors curse your name."

"That may be true, but I'm nevertheless innocent of all charges."

"I want you to come to bed and tell me all about it. I want to know how she did it. Describe it in great detail. Maybe I can learn something I can use on the job."

"That is a low blow," he said. "Totally uncalled for. I refuse to stand here and listen to you degrade yourself."

He went out into the living room, very pleased with himself. She was convinced now that he had made love to National Anthem. Now, at the right moment, he could be very honest and very sincere and tell her the absolute, totally acquitting truth: he had not slept with National Anthem. He would make her believe him because truth and justice were on his side.

"Did you tape it?" she called out from the bedroom. "I want to hear the tape. Does she go eeeeyou when you stick it in?"

"I'm sure I wouldn't know," he called back. "Please go to sleep. There's nothing worse in the world than an accusing woman who has her mind made up in total disregard of the facts."

"I insist that you play me the tape of her. I absolutely insist."

"It's obvious that I'm never going to get any peace, isn't it? You want to talk about this. Okay, we'll discuss it when I come back in. Then we'll talk about it as much as you want, but I've got things to do first."

"I hope dying is one of them. Die, you bastard. Rust, then die. I hope she gave you donkey fever. Your ears are going to grow and then your balls will explode."

"See how little you know. It's a well-known fact that porn stars are the cleanest people in the world," he said. He took the tape recording of Felicia from his recorder and hid it behind a book.

"A well-known fact," she scoffed. "How come you're the only person in the world who knows that well-known fact?"

"Just think about it. Who's going to hire somebody for a pornographic epic if she's going to give a dose to everybody?"

"Including the livestock," Chico screamed.

"It'd ruin the industry. I tell you, cleanliness is their stock-in-trade. Of course, I don't know this personally, since I do not associate with such types, but it has been told to me by people in a position to know."

"You lie, you bastard."

"We'll discuss it when I come in there," he said. "I have no desire to be accused by you long-distance, with you baying in full throat. I will not entertain another word you say. Meanwhile, consider this. I am clothed in rectitude." He felt better having hidden the tape.

The telephone rang and Trace answered it before Chico could. It was his father.

"How's it going, Sarge?"

"Some ups, some downs, mostly downs. I couldn't find out anything about his passport, so that's a dead end. But I found the woman who was working at the car-rental desk that night. She remembered Jarvis when I showed her the picture. I got a copy of the contract."

"Okay. That's all right."

"How's your night been?" Sarge asked.

"Pretty much a blank. There wasn't anything in Jarvis' room and the countess doesn't know anything about why he was flying in and out of New York like that."

"Let me work on that some," Sarge said. "I've got some ideas."

"Good."

"I'll be over at ten?" Sarge asked.

"Sure. Get some sleep. I'll see you then. By the way, have you talked to Mother?"

"Not all day."

"If the right occasion arises," Trace said, "you might tell her that I don't want her redecorating my apartment."

"That occasion will never arise," his father said.

Trace had barely hung up the telephone when it rang again. This time it was Bob Swenson.

"Trace, I'm in trouble."

"What happened?"

"It's all your fault for getting me near that National Anthem."

"What has she got to do with it?" Trace asked.

"Everything. It's her fault and yours."

"You'd better explain yourself," Trace said. "I'm losing my tolerance tonight for being wrongfully accused."

"Hah," he heard Chico chortle from the bedroom.

Swenson said, "I told you how I spent last night, virginal and pure, lying next to that woman."

"I envied you your restraint," Trace said.

"Sure. But I wasn't going to make that same

mistake tonight. So I picked up this hooker at the lounge downstairs and I brought her up here."

"How much did she get?" Trace asked.

"Three thousand dollars in casino chips. All in hundreds. I had them in a sock and she stole the sock. I was in the bathroom and she lifted the sock and beat it out the door."

"Do you know her name?" Trace asked. "What was she wearing? What'd she look like?"

"She was wearing this zebra outfit, tight pants and top. She was a big blonde. I went downstairs and asked the bartender, but he played mummy on me and said he never saw her before."

"It's all right," Trace said. "I have."

"Good," Swenson said.

"And you want your three thousand dollars back," Trace said.

"No, I want my sock back. It's a particularly beautiful argyle, handwoven by Scottish peasants out of peat moss. Of course I want my three thousand back."

"You haven't called the cops or done anything dopey, have you?"

"Trace, I'd rather be broke than dead. I get my name in the paper, right? Insurance-company president swindled by hooker. Swell, my wife sees that, I'm a dead man. Of course, I trust your discretion."

"Leave it with me," Trace said.

"Thank you. I knew I could count on you. I just want you to know that no matter how badly Walter Marks' foreign detective embarrasses you, you'll always have a job with Garrison Fidelity . . . if you get my money back for me."

"I'll try my best."

"That won't do," Swenson said. "You must succeed."

"Bob?" Trace said.

"What?"

"Please stay away from hookers at the bar."

"You have my word. I'm going to bed now. Alone."

Trace pressed down the phone button and got out the telephone book. There was only an office address listed for R. J. Roberts, so he called it, expecting a tape machine or an answering service. Instead, Roberts answered.

"R. J. Roberts," he announced.

"This is Devlin Tracy. Are you in the office?"

"Did you call the office number?" Roberts asked.

"Yes."

"Then naturally I'm in the office. I answered the phone, didn't I?"

"Why is everybody so full of glib repartee to-night?" Trace said. "Wait there. I'm coming right down. I have to talk to you."

"It sounds important," Roberts said.

"It is. Wait for me."

Trace hung up and went into the bedroom.

"I'm ignoring you," Chico said.

"Why?"

"When I was a kid, I was always afraid that there were ghosts in the room. When I told my mother, she said if I ignored them, they'd go away."

"Did it work?"

"It didn't work with the ghosts, but I'm hoping it works with you," she said.

"You want me to leave, I'm leaving," Trace said.

"Good."

He put on his jacket.

"Where are you going? That cow need another milking?"

"No. I have to see Roberts and it's all your fault," Trace said.

"Why me?"

"If you had stayed on the job tonight instead of surrendering to your base animal desires, you might have been around to keep Swenson out of trouble. But, no, you had to come home here to harass me, and that left him free to get in trouble with a hooker and she clipped him for three grand."

"Oh, crap," Chico said. "Do you know who it was?"

"Yeah. One of Roberts' girls. I'll be back as soon as I get the money. Then we'll talk."

"I'll be asleep. Don't wake me. We've got nothing to talk about," Chico said.

"Then you'll never know, will you?"

"I hate you, Trace."

"I love you, Chico."

"You don't look happy," Roberts said.

"Maybe you like working these hours, but I don't. I like to get some sleep," Trace said.

"Go to sleep. Who's stopping you?"

"You are. Now just listen, Roberts. I'm going to go through this just once. I'm not going to negotiate and I'm not going to play cat and mouse. I'm just going to tell you what I want and you're going to give it to me."

"I don't think I like your tone," Roberts said.

"Wait until you hear the content," Trace said. "It's even worse. Here it is. Your hooker, Lip Service, nabbed a John tonight at the Araby. She clipped three thousand dollars in casino chips from his room. He's a very important man and I want his money back now. I don't want any blackmail

163

threats, or any hints that we'll tell the wife, or any of that. All I want is three thousand dollars."

"What do you mean, my—"

"See," Trace interrupted. "There you go. You're going to want to deny that you're running hookers. You're going to try to play games with my head. You're going to waste my time and I'm going to get mad and fry your ass. Three thousand dollars. That concludes this unfortunate piece of business."

"I don't—"

"No. You're going to do it again, aren't you? Three thousand. No conversation, please. I'm very tired. I've had a rough day."

Roberts looked at him for a full five seconds before answering. "You think I keep three thousand in cash around here?"

"R. J., old buddy, your check's good enough for me. Because I know where to find you."

Roberts looked at him some more, then nodded and drew a checkbook from a drawer.

"All right," he said. "Who do I make this to?"

"Make it to me. Devlin Tracy. I'll see that my man gets the money."

Roberts wrote the check and handed it to Trace.

"Thank you."

"Now will you get out of here?" Roberts said.

"Consider it done," Trace said.

Chico was making believe she was asleep when Trace climbed into the bed and slid under the light cover.

He rolled toward her and whispered in her ear as if he believed she was asleep.

"Good night, Chico. I love you very much."

"You know I'm awake, don't you?"

"I thought you were asleep. Honest."

"Tell me the truth, Trace. Purely professional interest, since I know we've got nothing and we're going nowhere. Was she good?"

"Who?"

"Miss Stars and Stripes Forever," Chico said.

"Chico, I want you to know how much you hurt me tonight. I want to tell you one thing: I didn't make love to National Anthem. I didn't go near that woman. I didn't so much as touch her."

Chico rolled over toward him and seemed to examine his face in the dark, then said, "Hey, you're telling the truth, aren't you?"

"I've never been more truthful," he said.

"I'm sorry, Trace."

"It's all right. Forget it."

"I can't just forget it. How can I make it up to you?"

"You'll think of something," he said.

16

Tape Recording Number Two, 5:30 A.M., Wednesday, in the matter of Early Jarvis, late of Las Vegas. I, Devlin Tracy, am becoming a conglomerate. I have added an assistant. My father. So, if I'm so smart and now so thoroughly staffed, why am I up at 5:30 in the morning talking to this stupid machine while Chico sleeps?

I know why and I'm not saying, but tomorrow I'll bring Chico flowers. Women are suckers for flowers. Give me enough flowers and I can get over on the world. Maybe I'll send some to National Anthem.

Or maybe straw.

I had to put Pop on this job. Christ, going to police headquarters just to talk to cops. You know you're desperate when you want to talk to cops.

I've spent a lot of time today and wasted a lot of tape and I don't know any more, I guess, than when I started. Well, maybe a couple of things. Like when I told Groucho that nonsense about the ritual murder, he went right to a phone to call Hubbaker. So there's my insurance detective, the baron, sneaking around. And probably burgling

Spiro's apartment while that landlady was out having her hair fried.

Roberts said there was nothing on the street about the jewels and Herman backed him up. I trust Herman. How can you not trust a chess player? But he's right: if those jewels wind up in New York, they're gone forever. They'll sink without a trace.

Well, that's not my problem. My problem is murder. I wish I knew where Jarvis' passport is. Felicia couldn't find it and maybe, reluctantly, I'm going to have to agree with her point that maybe the killer stole it. But it just doesn't jell. If I had a million in jewels in my hand, would I stop to steal a passport? And an ashtray too? No sense.

I wonder. I wonder if the baron is back at the plotzo right now, talking to a tape recorder, asking the same stupid questions that I always ask.

Aaaah, screw the baron. Back to business. So I got Roberts on tape and he checked out Spiro's police record and he's definitely the petty-thief kind, so scratch him. Anyway, his place was burgled, and that's got to mean the baron looking for the jewels. When I talked to Spiro tonight at Felicia's, he wasn't lying to me. He doesn't know anything more than he said he does. I know; I'm an expert on lying. Except I don't think he was home to find out yet that his place had been looted. Maybe he'll think it was the landlady cleaning.

So Jarvis went to New York every Thursday before he died, and he traveled under the name of Edward Stark. Now, why is that? That was, by the way, a good find for Sarge. Whatever I wind up paying him, he'll have earned it right there. Anyway, Jarvis goes to New York and comes back the same day. Why?

And Sarge found the woman at the car counter who rented Jarvis the car. It's not really anything new, but at least he nailed it down. So Jarvis calls Spiro and says, 'Pick me up,' and then rents a car. Why? Another illogical loose end. Why isn't the world as logical as I am?

There was nothing in Jarvis' room. Felicia said she cleaned it up for me and that was stupid. I wish she'd clean up her own room 'cause my toe hurts where I stubbed it on that goddamn unpacked luggage of hers. Get a maid and clean your room, Countess. Why did Felicia expect the jewel thief to be calling her? That doesn't ring quite right, but I don't know why.

There's a lot of things I don't know, except Jarvis ought to have had a checking account. Everybody does.

So that's that. Except for what Sarge found out, today was pretty much of a blank, and I did a personal thing for Bob Swenson that I'm not going to talk about in case anybody ever hears this tape and I've got to remember to go to the bank in the morning.

Anyway, that was my day. I'm not going to make one single comment about my mother trying to redecorate our apartment. All it did was put Chico in a bad mood and she was unjustly on my case all night because of that bad mood. Are you listening, Chico? Feel guilty. You ought to.

Expenses. My usual one hundred and fifty dollars. I'll be adding Sarge's expenses in when I get done, but that'll wait until later. I'm glad I got him away from my mother. Now if only I can get me away from my mother. Jesus, one more day and I'm forty.

I'm going back to bed.

17

Trace slept late and was awakened by a buzz from the doorman.

Naked, he padded to the speaker box in the kitchen.

"A man here says he's your father."

"He's my father. Send him up."

"I just didn't want to take any chances after yesterday," the doorman said.

"Look again. It's not my mother in disguise, is it?"

"No. It's a man."

"Send him up."

He tossed on his bathrobe and found a note on Chico's pillow. "Dear Trace, Sorry for not trusting you. Love you, Chico."

Great. Just what he needed to start the day. More guilt.

Chico had already loaded the electric coffeepot. He pressed the ON switch, then opened his front door so his father could just walk in, then went to the bathroom to shower. One nagging problem, he realized, was that he had nothing today for his father to do. Actually he had nothing today for himself to do. Sarge had done well yesterday at the airport, but what was left for him to bird-dog?

"Dev, I'm here," he heard Sarge call.

"Coffee's on. I'm taking a shower."

Later, he sat with his father over coffee in the kitchen and Sarge handed him a copy of the rental agreement Jarvis had signed for the airport car. "His own American Express card," Sarge said. "And I'm getting the flight manifest for the night he came into town. American Airlines. But his name won't be on it."

"You sure of that?"

"Yeah," Sarge said. "I think he was flying incognito. And you've got to ask yourself why."

"I've already been asking myself that."

"Only one reason why somebody would fly under a false name. So if somebody checks the records, they won't find his name. I think we'll find Edward Stark listed in the passengers but no Jarvis."

"Why wouldn't he want anybody to know he flew into Vegas?" Trace asked. "He lived here. No big secret about going home, is there?"

"I don't have an inkling, son," Sarge said.

Sarge had his big red notebook on the kitchen table, and when he looked at it, Trace remembered that Roberts had a similar notebook on his desk, and it gave him an idea.

"I want you to go see that detective named Roberts today," Trace said. "Find out if he's holding anything back from us."

"Can I lean into him?" Sarge asked.

"Well, not to excess. I don't want him squawking to anybody. Don't expect him to be too happy with us, though."

"Why's that?"

"You know, he's a detective, but he's more of a thief. He's a pimp and he runs hookers. Last night one of them clipped a friend of mine for three grand. I made him give it back."

"I can see why he might be annoyed with you," Sarge said. "I'll make him first stop, then I've got some other stuff that I want to do."

"Okay. Did you get a chance to talk to Mother about the apartment here?"

Sarge looked around. "She said she came up here just to straighten up. I don't see anything that she did."

"We put it all back," Trace said.

"Oh. Anyway, I told her I didn't think you wanted her straightening up."

"What'd she say?"

"She said, 'Nonsense, what are mothers for?' "

"What, indeed?" Trace said.

Sarge had another cup of coffee, then left to see Roberts. Trace glanced at the rental agreement Jarvis had signed at the airport.

In there somewhere there ought to be a key. Why did Jarvis call Spiro and then rent a car and drive to the house himself? Okay. Simple. He wanted Spiro out of the house. But why? What was the point of all of it? And why had he parked on the road instead of going into the driveway and up to the house?

Trace took his time dressing and hooking up his tape recorder, and before he left the house, the telephone rang.

Sarge's voice sounded crackly and excited.

"I guess you really got that guy's money back last night, didn't you?" he said.

"What are you talking about?"

"You don't think you went a little off the deep end?"

"I don't think so. Why?"

" 'Cause Roberts is dead. Somebody cut his throat," Sarge said. "You didn't do it?"

"Of course not. What'd you do?"

"I got here and I knocked. There wasn't any answer, but the light was on, so I opened the door. It was unlocked and he was at the desk, with his head forward. I thought he was sleeping, but then I saw the blood on the blotter. Ear to ear."

"Did you call the cops yet?"

"No."

"Good. Wait till I get there. Lock the door and wait for me. Don't touch anything."

"Son, you're talking to me. How long will you be?"

"Ten minutes."

"Okay," Sarge said.

"No, make it fifteen. I have to go to the bank first to deposit a check."

Trace didn't often deal with the freshly dead. Most of his work involved people who'd been dead for some time and it was up to him to figure out how they died. So his stomach did an unusual nip-up when Sarge let him into Roberts' office and he saw the investigator's blood-soaked throat-cut body slouched forward over his desk blotter.

Sarge, for his part, looked as if he could put death on bread and make a sandwich of it.

"You didn't touch anything, did you?"

"No. What's the matter? Your face is a funny color."

"Sarge, you sent me to accounting school. You

didn't raise your boy to be a soldier. Blood in the morning doesn't exactly thrill me."

"You'll get used to it," Sarge said.

"God, I hope not."

Trace looked around on Roberts' desk, carefully not touching the body, but he saw nothing significant. What was he looking for anyway? A message written with a bloody fingernail? "The killer is . . ."

"I didn't see anything either," Sarge said.

"No weapon around?"

"No."

Trace saw the red notebook on the desk and opened it, after first wrapping a handkerchief around his hand. It contained only one page of numbers with dates along side them, but no names. The numbers were in the three-hundred and four-hundred range, all divisible by ten, and Trace suspected that they may have been a listing of the night's receipts from Roberts' small squad of prostitutes. The last date was the previous day's.

The detective had probably never left the office after Trace had seen him. At least he had not gone anywhere to change his clothes. Still using the handkerchief, Trace opened the file cabinet and found a folder marked Jarvis.

He opened it and looked inside. It still contained the two yellow pieces of paper that it had on the first day Roberts had shown it to him. And the clipping showing Felicia wearing some of her jewelry. In the bottom of the file, though, was another piece of paper, small and white. On it was penciled one word: "Records."

What the hell did that mean?

"Anything there?" Sarge asked. "What are you looking for?"

"His Jarvis file. It's the same as it was the other

day, except for this." He showed Sarge the piece of paper.

"Records. What does that mean?" Sarge asked.

"Got me." Trace returned the papers to the folder and put it back in the cabinet. "I guess we'd better call Rosado," he said.

"We don't have to, you know," Sarge said.

"What do you mean?"

"We could just leave here and forget about it. No one's ever got to know that we found the body. Let the cleaning lady find it." He looked around the dingy office. "I think she's due for another pass-through in December. Meanwhile, we can go wherever this guy lives . . . used to live . . . and ransack his place. See if we find anything."

"Can't do that," Trace said. "With my luck, it'd go wrong."

"Just a thought," Sarge said.

Trace used his handkerchief to lift the telephone. "Sarge, you call me from here?"

"Yeah."

"Did you get prints on the phone?"

"I used a handkerchief, dummy, like you're doing."

"Okay."

Trace called Dan Rosado at police headquarters.

"Hello, Trace. How's it by you?"

"By me, okay. By R. J. Roberts, not so good."

"Why not?"

"I'm at his office. Somebody cut his throat."

"Is he dead?"

"Yeah."

"I'll be right over. Don't touch anything."

Trace hung up the phone and said to his father, "Let's make it simple, Sarge. They come and we tell them the truth. You came here to talk to Roberts, you found the body, you called me, I came and called the cops."

"They're gonna be pissed. I should have called them right away."

"Tell them I told you not to. You're a stranger in town. I'll tell them I thought you were having a senile delusion. If they get mad, they'll get mad at me. And Dan doesn't stay mad long."

"You rotten Irish bastard, Trace, what do you mean you didn't call us right away?" Rosado's face was red and the veins in his neck were pulsating, like living snakes he was somehow in the process of swallowing.

"See, Sarge," Trace said. "I told you he wouldn't get mad."

"You ought to be ashamed of yourself, Mr. Tracy," Rosado said. "Trace doesn't know any better because he doesn't have a brain in his head, but you used to be a cop. You should know how to act."

"Instead of yelling at my son, you ought to be catching the killer," Sarge said.

"Give me his name and address and I'll have my men pick him up on their way back from lunch."

"Give me some time, maybe I'll do just that," Sarge snapped.

"I'll give you some time. I'd like to give you both some time. Three to five years for meddling, no time off."

"Dan, I think you're in danger now of overreacting," Trace said.

"You really think so?"

"Yes."

"All right. Let me get a grip on myself." Rosado gazed off into the distance as if summoning up some mystic spiritual energy. "There we are," he said calmly. "All together now."

"Good," said Trace.

"I should still book your ass," Rosado screamed.

18

"All right, Trace. You know I'm your friend. You know I'd like not to have to file charges against you."

"I know that, Dan. Your friendship is one of the few constants in my life. I just wish you'd stop yelling at me."

"I'm trying not to yell. I'm really trying. But it's difficult sometimes when someone you've come to know and trust and regard almost as a brother is so obviously lying to you."

"Come on, Dan. You know I didn't kill anybody."

"I know it and you know. Probably everybody who knows you knows it. But will the district attorney know it? Will the grand jury know it? See, there are a lot of imponderables in this kind of business. So why did Roberts write you a three-thousand-dollar check?"

"Because he owed me the money," Trace said. "I told you that."

"And you went to see him at what time?"

"At one A.M. I lent him the money in cash on Monday. He said that he wanted it just for the day, something about possibly buying information in the Jarvis case. He said he would have it back for me Monday night. But he didn't call Monday night, so I called him yesterday and caught him in the office and I went down there at one o'clock. He said he didn't have the money in cash and I told him I'd take a check, so I took it and left."

"You don't know what he used the money for?"

"No," Trace said.

"Wouldn't that have been a question you'd ask him? Here you are, you're both working on the same case and he's going to buy three thousand dollars' worth of information. Doesn't it seem logical that you'd at least ask him, 'What'd you get with the three thousand dollars I lent you?'" Rosado asked.

"It probably would have been logical," Trace said, "but I wasn't into logic last night. I was fighting with Chico. I was not at my emotional best. I think my biorhythms must be at a critical point. You don't have a biorhythm calculator, do you? We could check."

"Dammit, Trace, I'm not interested in your biorhythms."

"I bet yours are bad too. I wouldn't be surprised if we have the same chart. This is definitely not one of your emotional up days."

"So he wrote you a check and you left?"

"That's right."

"Where's the check?"

"I deposited it this morning."

"Before or after you knew he was dead?" Rosado asked.

"After. Sarge told me and I stopped at the bank on my way downtown. Then I went to Roberts' office and called you immediately. I didn't even waste a single second lifting up that telephone to call you, as all good citizens should."

"That is the single dumbest stupid story I ever heard in my life," Rosado said.

"That's because you didn't give me much of a chance to prepare. I mean, I could really have given you a good story if I had a lot of time to think about it. I could have given you dark hints from Roberts to me, chuckles over the telephone in late-night conversations. Meaningful chuckles, naturally. Suggestions that maybe people were lurking in hallways when I walked toward his office. I don't know. I could have given you a lot of things. Instead, I've just given you the simple unadorned truth."

Rosado turned off the tape recorder on the desk. They were in his office, facing each other across the desk, each drinking coffee.

"Okay. You don't know what Roberts was working on with the Jarvis case?" Rosado said.

"Technically, Dan, the murder wasn't any of his business. He was working for the insurance company on the jewel theft. Basically, he was trying to trace the stones if they came on the market. He told me that they hadn't yet."

"You believed him?"

"He didn't have any reason to lie. I told him I wasn't trying to cut him out of his fee," Trace said.

Rosado pushed a manila file folder across his desk and Trace opened it.

"That's Roberts' file on the Jarvis case," Rosado said. Trace nodded and looked at the familiar pieces of paper.

"The yellow sheets are just facts, dates, places, et cetera. What did he mean by that little white slip? It reads 'Records,'"

Trace shook his head. "I don't know."

"He never mentioned that to you? Never told

179

you what kind of records that meant? Nothing like that?"

"No," Trace said honestly.

"All right," the policeman said with a sigh. "I'm going to try to keep your ass out of a sling, Trace. I'm going to try. There's no reason to slap you with murder and I'm going to try to convince the district attorney that you didn't mean anything wrong by not telling your father to report the murder right away. Just a lapse of judgment."

"He'll buy it," Trace said. "Lawyers are always having lapses of judgment."

"But I hope we get the killer quick anyway. It'll take off a lot of heat. You know how attorneys are. You get somebody putting heat on them and they'll indict anything that moves. I don't want you to get caught up in that kind of mess."

"Thanks, Dan. I know you wish only the best for me," Trace said. "Can I go now?"

"Yes. If you figure this one out, you let me know right away."

"You got it, Dan," Trace said. Slowly. With feeling.

Trace wondered where Sarge might be, but his father was waiting for him outside police headquarters in his rented car. The August heat wave was still boiling, and when Trace got into the car, he winced and said, "Ouch."

"Don't complain about hot seats," Sarge said. "You're the one who wants to live here."

"It's not the weather," Trace said. "The car company took you. They always give you out-of-towners the cars with black upholstery. It absorbs all the heat. Next time, get white seats."

"Those dirty dogs," Sarge said. "How'd it go inside?"

"Well, let's just say I want a drink," Trace said.

"The three thousand?"

"That's what was on his mind."

"What'd you tell him?" Sarge asked.

"That I lent it to Roberts and he paid me back by check. I couldn't hand up Swenson, could I?" Trace said.

"Guess not. I told those other detectives that I didn't know anything about any three thousand. That I just came to see Roberts 'cause you wanted me to work with him on the robbery case. Then, when I found the body, I got confused because I'm scared of the sight of blood. Everybody knows I'm senile almost and I called you by mistake instead of them. I told them that probably you didn't call the cops right away because you thought I might have been dreaming and you wanted to be sure I was telling you the truth about the body."

"Pretty good lies," Trace said. "They should do."

"I was a cop for twenty-five years. I spent most of my time being lied to. I learned something from it."

Trace noticed that Sarge had a grin on his face as he pulled the car away from the curb and into downtown's afternoon traffic.

"You look very happy, considering that your only son has just escaped booking by the skin of his teeth. Why the smirk?"

"Do you really think I'm senile?" his father asked.

"Sure. You. Me and Chico too. All of us. We'll all be ready to go to Happydale and make pot holders out of cigarette butts. Why are you smirking?"

"Because I think I got the killer," Sarge said.

"Who is?"

"I think it's the baron, whatever his name is."

"Hubbaker?"

"Yeah. Him," Sarge said.

They were sitting in Boggle's. Sarge was giving a good workout to a giant cheeseburger and a bottle of beer, and Trace was sipping from a double vodka and eyeing the pickles on Sarge's plate.

"This is a sick town," Sarge said. "Unhand that pickle."

"Sorry. Of course it is. It was created by criminals for degenerates. What'd you expect, a choir on the corner singing the Hallelujah chorus?"

"You've got hookers on the street all the time. Like most places have hookers only at night. Reasonable hours. Here, you've got them marching around even in the morning. You know how they must sweat?"

"People gamble twenty-four hours a day. When they're finished gambling, they get horny. Particularly if they win," Trace said. "It must have something to do with power. Now you've stalled long enough. Tell me about the baron."

"There's that all-night restaurant across the street from Roberts' place," Sarge said.

"Don't eat there. They have a special recipe for making coffee. A spoon of coffee and a pound of lard."

"Eat there? I didn't even want to breathe there. Anyway, I got the name of the night people from the manager. Bolling Widentsky. You know him?"

"No."

"He's the night cashier. You know, the cashier just sits by the window there and he can look right out at Roberts' building. So, anyway, this Widentsky. I got a whole bunch of names but I didn't need them, because this Widentsky lives right nearby the place and I went and talked to him."

"Yeah?"

"So we talked awhile and he finally remembered that he saw a guy coming into Roberts' building at around four A.M. He described him and it was that Hubbaker. Tall, skinny as a pencil. Beard. Does he drive a Jeep?"

"I don't know," Trace said. "Wait. There's a Jeep out at the countess's place. Why?"

"Okay. Widentsky remembered this guy because he saw him pull up and park out in front in this white Jeep, he said it was."

"Felicia's Jeep is white."

"Good. So he parked out in front and went inside. Widentsky said he was inside just a couple of minutes and then he came out. He said he wasn't running, but he was hurrying, kind of, and he got into the Jeep and rode away fast."

"Around four o'clock, you say?"

"That's what he says," Sarge said.

"Didn't the cops talk to Widentsky? Are Rosado's cops so bad that they wouldn't check that out?"

"They talked to him. They got there before me, but he didn't tell them that."

"Why not?"

"He didn't remember it."

"How come he remembered it for you?" Trace asked.

"He didn't really want to."

"No? Hold on, Sarge. You didn't— What did you do?"

"Don't worry. I didn't hit him or anything like that. God, you're getting squeamish."

"What did you do?"

"I told him I was Roberts' uncle. And if he didn't

talk to me, I was going to blow his brains out. It's a wonder how that'll often improve somebody's memory right away. Go ahead, eat the pickle. I don't want it."

"I've changed my mind. Hubbaker. I don't understand it."

"Don't you read English detective stories?" Sarge said. "Those barons are always phoneys. They're always the killer. Usually they don't use knives, though."

"He's a detective," Trace said. "Why the hell would he be killing another detective who was working on the same case?"

"Nobody ever told you this work was going to be easy, son. If it was easy, anybody could do it. That's one of the questions we've got to answer."

"I don't know any better way to do it," Trace said. "Let's go talk to the baron."

"Good," Sarge said. "I've never been to a countess's palace. Don't tell your mother."

"This is it?" Sarge said. They were driving up the long road to the countess's house and he sounded disgusted. "This is her palace?"

"Afraid so."

"This ain't no palace. It looks like Long Island, except with more sand. I've seen bigger houses in Queens."

"It's pretty big for around here," Trace said. "Now listen, Sarge. These people are a little strange."

"How strange?"

"They're druggies, kind of. They keep parrots. Don't get upset if they're sniffing, snorting, smoking, or swallowing."

"You think I live in a hothouse? If they're into

Better Living Through Chemistry, that's their business."

They parked the car and walked through the ever-open front door, passing back toward the pool section where they heard voices.

Sarge whispered, "You didn't tell me they weren't going to have any clothes on."

"Try to ignore it," Trace said.

"Oh, to be sixty again."

"Please. I'm going to be forty tomorrow. No talk about age."

National Anthem was doing her exercises naked on the far side of the pool, and as usual, Willie Parmenter was sitting on a lounge chair near her.

The Neddlemans were in their accustomed spot, side by side, silent and unmoving, on a chaise longue, and the countess and Ferrara were sitting at a small umbrella-shielded table at the far end of the pool. Felicia, bare-breasted, saw Trace and waved. Ferrara was wearing a long-sleeved white shirt and trousers, and his face clouded over when he saw Trace.

They walked toward Felicia, and Trace saw that Ferrara was mashing between his fingers an inch-and-a-half-square lump of something that looked like black tar.

"Felicia, this is my father. You probably bumped into each other the other night," Trace said.

She nodded and Sarge leaned forward and kissed her hand.

"Good manners will get you everywhere," Felicia said with a warm smile.

"Hopefully out of that family," Ferrara mumbled, then looked at Sarge and extended the black lump toward him. "Want some hash?"

"No, thanks. We just ate lunch," Sarge said.

"Very funny."

"He wasn't being funny," Trace said.

"It's funny turning down Afghan hash. I mean, look at this stuff. Have you ever seen anything like it?" Ferrara said.

"I used to have a dog who couldn't be house-broken," Sarge said. "He'd leave me presents like that all over."

"Not like this. Do you know they use opium for a binder to hold this stuff together?" Ferrara said. "Raw opium. Processed opium gets too crystalline, but the raw stuff holds this like gum."

"I thought they used lamb's fat," Sarge said.

Ferrara raised his eyebrows in surprise. "Very good," he said. "Knowledge is everywhere around us."

"Oh, get off it, Paolo, will you?" Felicia said. "You're being obnoxious."

"Sarge, what do you know about this?" Trace asked.

"I know what I know. The Afghans use lamb's fat to bind their hash."

"That's why this is special," Ferrara said. "Even the binder's a kick. Oh, beauty, thy name is cannabis."

"Ferrara, thy name is bullshit," Trace said. "Felicia, we have to talk to the baron. Is he around?"

"I just heard him inside taking a shower. He should be out any minute. Want a drink?"

"No, thanks, we'll pass. Mind if I show Sarge the safe?"

"Go ahead. Anything to get me my money," she said.

Trace and Sarge walked back toward the house.

National Anthem saw them and waved, and Parmenter nodded to them.

Sarge said, "Boy, can that woman wave. Who are all these people? I saw them the other night but none of them registered."

"The two statues on the lounge chairs are the Neddlemans. They say they're into shipping, but I think they just ship their bodies around to anyone who'll have them. Ferrara there is some kind of Italian drug dealer, and the mousy guy across the way is his valet. Felicia, you know. The girl with the jugs is National Anthem. She makes porn movies."

"Disgusting," Sarge said. "Where are they playing?"

"Her first isn't out yet," Trace said. "I'll let you know when. We'll go together."

"And these are all house guests?"

"Them and the baron," Trace said. "Felicia says they're a bunch of parasites."

"I believe it."

"Where did you learn so much about drugs?" Trace asked.

"I don't know. I read a lot. He's the guy you almost hit the other night?"

"Yeah."

"You should have," Sarge said.

"I probably will before he leaves town. This is where Jarvis' body was found. Did Rosado show you the pictures?"

"Yeah," Sarge said. "Christ, that water's filthy. How can goldfish live in it?"

"God knows."

"Remember that aquarium you had when you were a kid?" Sarge asked.

"Yeah. The fish were always dying."

"It was my fault. I always killed them," Sarge said. "I'd be sneaking a drink around the house and your mother'd catch me and I'd dump the drink into the fish tank so she didn't find me with it, and the damn alcohol would kill the fish."

"There's a great lesson in there somewhere," Trace said.

"Yeah. Fish shouldn't drink," Sarge said.

"This is where the coroner said he hit his head," Trace said, touching the ceramic fish statue with his toe. Then he led his father into the living room and showed him the panel that popped out to reveal the safe.

"How'd the thief get into the safe?" Sarge asked after looking at the front cover.

"I don't know. He was drilling, then changed his mind."

"He must have opened it with the combination," Sarge said.

"Right. But if he had the combination to begin with, he wouldn't have started drilling, would he?"

"No," Sarge said. "So he starts drilling and then he gets the combination. And the only change is that Jarvis came home."

"So he got it from Jarvis," Trace said. "But why would Jarvis give him the combination?"

"Were they working together? Or maybe he had a gun and he forced it out of him?"

"Maybe," Trace said. "I don't know."

The baron bounded through the open patio doors into the living room.

"Felicia said you were looking for me?"

"Hello, Baron," Trace said. "We wanted to talk to you. This is my father. Patrick Tracy, Baron Hubbaker."

"Call me Ed," the baron said.

His father stepped forward, shook hands warmly with the tall lean man, and then, almost casually, strolled behind him.

"This isn't official," Trace said.

"Well, I'm glad of that, whatever it is," Hubbaker said with a small smile. "Mind if I sit down? That way, your father won't have to tackle me from behind."

"Help yourself," Trace said.

The baron sprawled casually on the sofa, facing the fireplace.

"R. J. Roberts."

The smile vanished from Hubbaker's face.

"You know?" he said.

"Yeah," Trace said. "We found witnesses who saw you going in and coming out early this morning."

"The man in the diner across the street?"

Trace nodded.

"I thought he saw me. I was hoping he wouldn't have, but I thought he did."

"He did. Want to tell us what happened?"

"Sure. Hold on. Wait. You think I killed him?"

"It's as reasonable as anything else I've heard," Trace said.

"No, no, no, no, no. He was dead when I got there. Somebody slit his throat open."

"We saw the body," Trace said. "Maybe you ought to start from the top and tell us what happened. How did you know Roberts?"

"I didn't. I never even met the man," Hubbaker said.

"Come on, you're at his office at four A.M. and you don't even know him?"

"This is the way it was," Hubbaker said. "Right after you left here last night, Roberts called. We were sitting around watching sex movies. I didn't

189

even know who he was. He told me he had to talk to me about the jewels. Something that he said was important to me and he wanted to see me. Initially, I thought he was crazy, but he was very insistent. Vague but insistent, and finally I said okay, I'd meet him."

"Who picked the time?" Trace asked.

"He didn't really pick it. He told me he was going to be out of his office most of the night, but I should try him really late. I told him that I could just as easily see him tomorrow, that's today, but he said no, it wouldn't wait. The cheek of the man."

"So why'd you go at four o'clock?" Trace asked.

"I fell asleep. I had a little too much to drink. When I woke up, it was almost three. I called him and he said I should come over and he'd wait for me. I did. By now, I was intrigued by what he wanted. When I got there, his office door was open and he was dead."

"Why didn't you call the police?"

Hubbaker shrugged. "It was stupid, I guess. But I thought for a minute and I thought how dumb it was that I was there at all. Would the police believe me? I mean, going to a four-A.M. meeting with a man I'd never met? Did that sound believable?"

"No," Trace said. "Actually, it still doesn't."

"That's why I didn't call the police. I hadn't touched anything. I just walked in and saw the body. I don't know what he wanted to talk to me about. The police, well, I couldn't be any help to them. So I left and I came back here and went to sleep. I don't mind telling you, I didn't sleep well at all."

"Roberts slept like a dead man," Trace said.

"You can't believe I had anything to—"

"It's not for me to believe or disbelieve," Trace

said. "That's for the cops. When they find out your background, I'm sure—"

Hubbaker interrupted him back. "What do you mean, my background?"

"Your work with the insurance companies," Trace said. "You had a perfect right to talk to Roberts."

"Will someone please explain to me what you're talking about?" He looked at Trace, then at Sarge as if for help. Sarge shrugged. Hubbaker said, "Everybody's talking as if I've got something to do with insurance. You, that ridiculous dwarf you work for. What is going on here?"

"Don't you work for an insurance company?"

"Of course not. Actually, I don't work at all," Hubbaker said. "Is that what this is all about? Does Marks think I work for an insurance company? Is that why he called me the other day to tell me that idiotic theory of yours?"

Trace nodded.

"Well, I don't," Hubbaker said.

"Too bad," Trace said.

"Why?"

"Cops'd be less likely to think you were a killer if you were a detective."

"I guess you have to tell them I was there?" Hubbaker said.

"You guess right. Withholding information from the police is a very serious matter. One I could not countenance in any way," Trace said.

"Amen," Sarge said.

19

"Tell me," Trace asked Hubbaker. "Anybody here know you were going to see Roberts? Did you tell anybody?"

Hubbaker thought a moment, then said slowly, "Yes. Actually I told everybody."

"Everybody in the house?"

"Yes. And, let's see, Spiro. He was serving drinks. He would have heard too."

"All right," Trace said. "I've got to call Dan Rosado. You're not going to try to leave or anything, are you, Baron?"

"Where would I go? Out into the desert and live like a prospector? Suck water from the roots of cactus? Of course I'm not going anywhere."

Trace walked around to the kitchen telephone, leaving his father to watch Hubbaker. He dialed Rosado.

"This is Trace. You still mad at me?"

"You bet your ass I'm mad at you," Rosado said. "What do you want?"

"I want to make amends for all my failures as a human being in the past."

"It'll take too long. What do you want now?"

"Sarge and I found a witness who saw somebody leaving Roberts' office at four o'clock this morning."

"You did? Who was that?"

"I'll tell you all about it when you get here," Trace said.

"Where's here?"

"I'm at Felicia Fallaci's place."

"What are you doing there?"

"We found the guy that was seen leaving."

"And you went to talk to him yourself first?" Rosado snapped. "You're doing it again."

"No, I'm not. We came here to make sure it was the same guy. We thought we recognized the description, but we didn't want to accuse an innocent man. He admits it."

"He admit the killing too?" Rosado asked.

"No."

"I'll be right there," Rosado said. "You know, Trace?"

"What?"

"I used to like you better when you weren't involved in my business."

"I know. This is the last time. I'll never get in your way again."

"I'll be right there. And you better tell me who the hell that witness was too. I don't know how my men missed him."

"Your men didn't miss him. It's just that Sarge was more persuasive," Trace said.

"The police will be here in a few minutes," Trace told Hubbaker.

"You know, this is quite terrible," the baron said. "They are going to try to put the blame for this murder on me and I didn't do it."

"Then they won't pin it on you," Trace said.

193

"I wish I were as confident as you are," Hubbaker said. "Can the condemned man have a final swim?"

"Be my guest. Just don't try to swim out of town," Trace said.

The baron got up, peeled off his shorts and shirt, then walked past them and dived into the pool. He was a powerful swimmer and he coursed up and down the pool in solid, steady strokes, leaving only a thin wake behind him.

"I guess I ought to protect Felicia," Trace said. Sarge looked quizzical, and Trace said, "The drugs."

He walked to the end of the pool where Felicia was still talking to Ferrara. National Anthem was sprawled out naked in the sun on the far side, and if eyes could satisfy hunger, Willie Parmenter would never have to worry about another meal.

"Felicia, the police are on their way here. They want to talk to the baron."

"Oh? Anytning I should know about?" she asked Trace.

"Not really. I just thought it might be wise if you stashed all your goodies before they arrive."

"You mean to say the police are busting in here without a warrant," Ferrara said. "Sniffing around like watchdogs. That's not legal."

"Talk legal, talk from jail," Trace said. "I just thought I'd tell you."

"Thanks, Trace," Felicia said.

Ferrara curled a lip. "Police are really stupid things," he said. He was fondling his stick of Afghan hashish. "All detectives are, actually."

Sarge tapped Trace on the shoulder. "Why didn't you hit him when you had a chance?"

"My better nature showing through," Trace said. "Besides, I thought it was be-kind-to-assholes week."

"I won't make that mistake," Sarge said. He

reached toward the table, yanked the lump of hash from Ferrara's hands, and threw it into the pool.

"Why, you . . ." Ferrara jumped to his feet. He seemed to make a quick judgment about the inevitable outcome of mixing it with Sarge, because he suddenly bellowed, "Willie, get that."

"Get it yourself," Sarge said. He grabbed Ferrara by the neck and the seat of the pants and tossed him into the pool too.

"Bad form," Trace said.

"I'm out of practice," Sarge said.

Ferrara was splashing around, yelling for Parmenter to help. Felicia was laughing aloud. "He's the only one with drugs," she said. "Cops take him away, who cares?"

"I just hope he doesn't leave an oil slick in your pool," Trace said.

Ferrara clambered up the ladder on the far side of the pool. Parmenter gave him a hand up and Ferrara said, "Get my hash."

"Yes, sir," Parmenter said.

Ferrara, squishing water from his shoes, stomped off toward the house. Parmenter looked at the black lump in the pool for a few seconds, then went to a small utility shed and brought back a net to try to scoop it out. But the baron, powering by in the water above it, dived down, brought up the hashish, and dropped it on the deck in front of Parmenter.

"Thanks," Willie said.

Hubbaker nodded, then dragged himself out onto the deck near Felicia's chair and let out a big sigh.

"What have you done to get the police interested in you?" she asked.

"Wrong place at the wrong time. It's all a mistake. Not to worry," Hubbaker said.

"Felicia," said Trace, "don't you think that maybe you and Nash might put on some clothing?"

"Oh, yes. Good idea. I don't know if Nash owns any, but maybe I can lend her something." She walked into the house, followed by National Anthem, who looked confused.

They came back a few minutes later, wearing long terry-cloth robes. Sarge said, "I liked it better when they didn't know the cops were coming."

"Quiet, you dirty old man. Don't you know you're supposed to be a role model for me?" Trace said.

When Rosado arrived, Trace met him in front of the house and explained to him quickly about the eyewitness who had seen Hubbaker. "Of course, it's not any positive identification yet," Trace said, "but he admits he was there. He's all yours now."

"Trace, keep out of my face."

Rosado talked for a while to Hubbaker, then asked him to accompany him downtown for formal questioning. When he left, the police officer said to Sarge, "That was good work, Mr. Tracy."

"What are you going to do with him?" Sarge asked.

"Question him, then see," Rosado said.

"We've got a saying in the N.Y.P.D.," Sarge said.

"What's that?"

"Fuck him, book him," Sarge said.

When Trace and Sarge were leaving, Felicia invited Sarge to come back some night for dinner before he left town, and in the car driving back to Las Vegas Sarge said he might take the offer.

"It'll just get you into trouble," Trace said.

"Only if you drop a dime on me," Sarge said.

"Not me. You know, I'm really confused about Hubbaker."

"Why's that?"

"I would have sworn he was the insurance detective," Trace said.

"You told me the detective was a mystery man. Worked in secret?"

"That's right."

"Maybe Hubbaker is the guy and just didn't want to tell us because it'd blow his cover. Maybe he'll tell Rosado if he has to."

"That's possible," Trace admitted, and the more he thought about it, the more sense he made.

Sarge let out a big sigh when he dropped Trace downtown in the parking lot where his son had left his white Mazda.

"You going back to your hotel now?" Trace asked.

"Not yet. I've got some things to do first."

"There's another cocktail reception at the Araby for Gone Fishing. I thought I'd stop in there and see how Chico's holding up. Why don't you come over when you're done? Bring Mother. They're serving free food."

"Maybe I'll do that. She'd be upset with me if I make her miss a free meal."

"She'll be upset with you anyway," Trace said. "By the way, Sarge, good work today." When he saw his father's eyes glow, he added, "I didn't know how good you really were."

"I used to be all right, son," Sarge said.

"Still are," Trace said. "You can work with me anytime. Maybe we will start that agency. You can handle the East Coast and I'll take the West."

"I'd like it better the other way around. It'd get me out of the house more."

"We'll work on it," Trace promised. He clapped the older man on the shoulder and got out of the car. His father was whistling as he drove off.

*   *   *

"So what's the latest report from the front?" Trace asked. He was talking to Chico in the hospitality suite of Garrison Fidelity. The suite had just been opened, but already it was fuller than it had been the previous night. And there were more and better-looking women, which meant that some of the bachelors at the convention were in the process of getting lucky, Trace realized.

"Reasonably peaceful today," Chico said. "No lockouts, no lost wives, nobody roughed up by hookers or crooked dealers. Did you get my note?"

"Apology accepted. Forget about it. I have," he said.

"You're very gracious today," she said. "What happened to you?"

"Well, Sarge found a body and it was downhill after that."

"Good for him," she said. He was surprised at her reaction. "It must have made his day. Anybody I know?" she asked.

"R. J. Roberts," Trace said. Briefly he recapped the day's events for her, but when he finished, she was giggling.

"Honestly, Chico, I don't think the day was a laughing matter. Murder. Questioned by the cops. Dan mad at me. I don't find even a snicker there, much less a sustained giggle."

"I'm just thinking of poor Walter Marks," she said. "His big detective has his butt in the hoosegow. It's going to ruin his week. When will you tell him?"

"Let him find out himself."

"Good for you," she said. "Have a drink."

"I don't believe you said that."

"What would the end of the day's work be if you

couldn't have a pop? Help yourself. I've got to be charming hostess. Cio-Cio-San, number-one lady helping all Melicans visiting our stlange city." She steepled her hands in front of her and rocked her head from side to side in imitation of a geisha.

"Later, remind me to tell you how Sarge threw your Italian lover boy into the swimming pool."

"I love it," she said. "I absolutely love it."

While Trace was getting a drink at the bar, Bob Swenson sidled up to him.

"I expected you to call this morning," he said.

"What for?"

"To tell me mission accomplished," Swenson said.

"I only call to say mission not accomplished."

"Good. You've got my three grand back?"

"As soon as the check clears the bank," Trace said.

"You took a check from a hooker?" Swenson said.

"No, it's complicated. I took it from the guy who ran the hookers."

"If the check doesn't clear, we'll sue the bastard. Can you sue a pimp?"

"Actually," Trace said, "this wasn't a pimp. It was a private detective, and you can't sue him."

"Why not?"

"His throat got cut," Trace said.

"You didn't have to do that. Not even for three thousand dollars."

"I didn't do it," Trace said, "but the cops took some convincing. They wanted to know why he had just written me a check for three K and then was killed."

"What'd you tell them?"

"That I lent him the money and he was paying it back."

"Trace, you're an absolute gem. No way I'm going to be involved?"

"No way."

"Remind me to give you a raise."

"I'll remind you when you're sober. Just do me a favor," Trace said. "Don't pick up hookers in the bar. Ask me. Or a pit boss. Get a newspaper on the street and call a service. Not a hooker in the bar."

"A temporary moment of madness, Trace. I won't do it again."

"No?" Trace said.

"No. National Velvet—"

"Anthem," Trace corrected.

"Right. National Anthem and I are having dinner tonight. Tonight, I will not fail. Where donkeys have succeeded, can I do less?"

" 'There is no glory in outdoing donkeys,' " Trace said.

"I know that's some obscure literary reference from your wasted youth."

"Martial, Roman poet."

"Screw him, what'd he know? He never saw National Anthem," Swenson said.

At a little after six o'clock, Chico said, "The Good Ship *Dreadnought* has arrived." Trace saw Sarge and Mrs. Tracy standing in the doorway. His mother had a tight set to her lips.

"From the looks of her, I think she might have tried to get into our apartment," Trace said.

"Oh, didn't I tell you?" Chico said sweetly. "She did try. I thought I told you."

"No, you didn't tell me. What happened?"

"The concierge turned her away."

"How do you know that?"

"She came here for lunch. She hoped she'd see you."

"Sorry I missed her," Trace said.

"I didn't," Chico said. "You could tell how desperate she was because she even deigned to talk to me, rittle chopstick girl."

"What did you tell her?"

"I told her that we had planted land mines inside our front door, and no, we did not appreciate her attempts to redo our apartment. That's what she calls it. Redo. And if she tried to bust in one more time, I'd have her arrested for breaking and entry and you'd cosign the complaint."

Trace chuckled. "Always the kidder," he said. "What'd you really tell her?"

"Sorry, sport. That's what I really told her. That and other things."

"What other things?"

"That you personally threw her lavabo in the garbage. Lavabo. I shall wash. Her lavabo. I shall puke. That she put up that cheap nine-dollar piece of glazed crap over a thousand-dollar print that you personally bought at Christie's. Are you paying attention to this?"

"I'm hanging on every word. Really hanging."

"I just wanted to be sure I had your attention," she said. "I told her further that putting that white monstrosity on our wall was the equivalent of hanging a bank calendar on the ceiling of the Sistine Chapel."

"What did she sputter to all this?"

"She was almost civil. She said that she had once taken a correspondence course in decorating and that I had no taste."

"And?" Trace asked.

"I told her that I didn't know that Bette Midler ran a decorating school."

Trace said, "Chico, I don't think my mother's ever going to welcome you into the family with open arms."

"I'll settle for closed arms and mouth to match," she said.

"Hello, Chico," Sarge said.

"Hi, Sarge. Heard you had a big day today."

"Kind of. Son, Mother wants to speak to you."

"I gather she wants to talk to just me and not to me and Chico."

"I'd say you have gathered a very accurate gather," Sarge said. "And when you get finished defusing her, we ought to talk business. I want to tell you what I'm up to."

"Hang tough. It may take a while," Trace said, and walked into the next room, where his mother stood belligerently in a corner, surveying the room like a farmer counting locusts.

"Hello, Mother, I've got to talk to you."

"I didn't think you had time to talk to me, Devlin. After all, why should you? I'm just your mother, and you and your father are so busy running all over this city, playing cops and Indians."

"That's what I wanted to talk to you about. Mom, he's driving me crazy. I can't get any work done with him hanging around. My professional life is suffering, my personal life is in a shambles. If I don't get him back to you, I don't know what will become of me."

"He seems to enjoy being with you," she said warily.

"Why shouldn't he? He makes a mess and I've got to clean it up after him," Trace said. "I don't know how you put up with him year after year. It's . . . Well, it's just more than I could tolerate."

"It's not been easy sometimes," she allowed.

"You've the patience of a saint. But you've got to take him back."

"You know, this is the first vacation I've had in years where I haven't had to play nursemaid to him all the time," she said. "Don't you think I deserve some consideration too?"

"Oh, Mom. I—"

"No. You're always thinking of yourself. Sure, you want him back with me. So that you and that woman can . . . well, do whatever it is you want. The trouble with you, Devlin, is that you've never understood family obligations. You have an obligation to me. Just like you have to your wife and children."

"I'm pleading with you."

"I think it's nice that Patrick has a chance to be with you. Of course, he *is* a terrible pain. He is to me all the time, but don't you think for just a few days a year, you could put up with it? I have to."

Trace sighed. "I guess you're right," he said.

"You know I'm right. Just like I was right trying to do something about that hideous apartment of yours. It's like living inside an ashtray."

"You know what was wrong, Mother?"

"I'm sure you'll tell me."

"You know my apartment's hideous and I know it's hideous. It's just that I couldn't, for the longest time, convince Chico it was hideous. And then, just last week, I finally got her to agree to have a decorator come in and redo the place. It was hard getting her to do that. And when you started redoing it, well, she just snapped. It was more than she could take. It was so hard to get her to accept Moe Ginzburg."

"Moe Ginzburg?"

"Moe Ginzburg. Interior designer to the stars. He did Wayne Newton's stable area. He's one of the great decorators in America and he's coming next week. You see, Mother, once we pay for it, then Chico will just have to go along with what he says. It's just delicate sometimes, well, because she's Oriental, you know. They can be very stubborn."

"Don't I know it?" his mother said. "Did you really throw away that lavabo?"

"Of course not," Trace said. "I made believe I threw it away. I hid it in the closet. I'm sure it's just what Moe will want to make my place perfect. And when *he* puts it up, why, Chico won't be able to say a word."

"I really don't know why you have her around," Mrs. Tracy said.

"It may not be for too much longer," he said. "Her behavior today may just be the last straw."

"It's about time."

"You know me, Mother. I'm not as good as you are about making quick judgments, but I'm coming around to your way of thinking. I mean, you're right, after all."

"I want your father to keep working with you."

Trace sighed. "All right," he said. "You know tomorrow's my birthday?"

"I wouldn't forget *your* birthday."

"You know what I'm doing for my birthday?" he asked.

"No. What?"

"I'm coming over to pick you up in the morning

and I'm going to show you a slot machine that pays off," he said.

"I lost another ten dollars today," she said.

"We're all set," Trace said. "You, Sarge, you keep working with me. Chico. She won't be around to redo our apartment anymore. Now, what's on your mind, Sarge?"

Chico made a T out of her fingers. "Time out," she said. "How'd you work that miracle?"

"I reasoned with her," Trace said.

Chico looked at him, then asked Sarge, "Do you believe him?"

"Him and the tooth fairy," Sarge said.

"When you two are finished picking me apart, maybe we can discuss some business," Trace said.

"Okay. I'm going to the airport tonight to try to get the manifest from Jarvis' flight in. My guess is he'll be on there under a phony name," Sarge said.

"We talked about that," Trace said. "Anything else?"

"And I made some calls to New York today. I may have something interesting pretty soon."

"What kind of calls did you make?"

"I'll tell you if they pan out," Sarge said.

"I hate secrets," Trace said.

"I love them," Chico said.

"You two deserve each other," Trace said.

"We both know it," Chico said.

20

Trace spoke to Walter Marks before they left the cocktail party.

"Hello, Groucho. You look particularly dapper this evening. You borrow the suit from Tattoo?"

"Can the cute talk. What's happening on the Jarvis case?"

"Things are breaking loose all the time. It's probably just a matter of hours before the investigation roars to a successful conclusion. Pity, though."

"What pity? What's a pity?" Marks asked.

"That poor R. J. Roberts won't be here to share in the glory."

"Why not?"

"You haven't heard?" Trace said. "You mean, you really haven't heard? You mean, I've been here making small talk all evening with people I don't even care about and you haven't heard?"

"Heard? Heard what? Dammit, Trace, talk to me."

"Roberts is dead."

"How'd that happen?" Marks asked.

"Murdered. Somebody filleted his gullet from earlobe to earlobe."

"That's a particularly disgusting way of putting it. Who did it?"

"We're not sure yet," Trace said.

"Is it involved with the jewel case?"

"Indubitably."

"When'd this happen?" Marks asked.

"During the night."

"Wow," Marks said. "This is really turning into a big case. Thanks for telling me about it."

"You're very welcome," Trace said. He walked a few steps away, then came back.

"Oh. By the way. If you're planning on calling your friend, the baron, don't bother. He's not home."

"No? Where is he?"

"He's at police headquarters. They're questioning him in the Roberts murder," Trace said. He walked away again and this time did not come back.

In the hallway to the suite, he and Chico met Bob Swenson. With the insurance-company president was National Anthem, wearing a red satin gown cut almost to the navel.

The two couples greeted each other and Nash said to Trace, "Did I see you at the house?"

"Yes. And I, you. Chico, I don't believe you've met Miss Anthem. National, this is Chico."

"Eeeeyou," Chico said. "What a beautiful name. Pleased to meetcha." She snapped her cheeks as if she were chewing gum.

"Thank you, dolling," National said in a grisly rendition of Tallulah Bankhead.

"Nash and I are going to discuss her career tonight," Swenson said with a leering wink at Trace. "I've got this idea for a film. She'd be a natural for it."

"*Mule Train?*" Chico said sweetly.

"No. *Great Sex Goddesses of the Silver Screen*," Swenson said.

"Eeeeyou," Chico squeaked. "You'll be a natural for the part, for shurr, for shurr."

Trace pinched her behind. "Sounds wonderful," he said.

"Yes," Swenson agreed. "We've discussed various kinds of films Nash might do. We talked about religious dramas the other night, but I don't think she can afford to be limited that way. She's got to show her versatility."

"Eeeeyou," Chico agreed. "I think Miss Anthem will be wonderful at showing her versatility."

"Yes, dolling," Nash said. "One has to be versatile, don't one?"

"Well, we don't want to hold you up," Swenson said.

"You're not holding us up," Chico said. "We'd love to stay and chat with you. Maybe all night." Trace pinched her butt again and she squeaked, "Eeeeyou."

"We were just leaving," Trace said. "Have a nice night."

The two couples passed in the hall, and as they walked away, Trace heard Nash say to Swenson, "Doesn't that little woman talk funny, dolling?"

Chico giggled and Trace told her, "You are hateful, woman."

"Trace, I take it all back. I told you once if you wanted to hit her, you could. You can't. I refuse to let you have anything to do with a woman that dumb."

"What would I need with her when I have you?" he said.

"You'll pay for that," she said. "Dolling."

* * *

From his apartment, Trace called Dan Rosado at home.

"What's happening with the baron?" Trace asked.

"Nothing," Rosado said. "I booked him on a technical charge of impeding a police investigation. Just to hold him for a while. Same thing I should have booked you on."

"What do you think?"

"I think he's telling the truth," Rosado said.

"So do I. No inkling of why Roberts wanted to talk to him?"

"None at all," Rosado said. "That's the part of his story I don't believe: that somehow he'd go at four in the morning to meet a guy he never met, without knowing what for. He must have known. But we couldn't crack him."

"Maybe you ought to let Sarge work him over," Trace said. "He squeezed that eyewitness out of the bushes for you. Did Hubbaker say he's an insurance detective?"

"No," Rosado said. "Is he?"

"I don't think so now," Trace said.

After he hung up, Trace called the pit boss at the Araby Casino.

"Armando, this is Trace."

"What's up, champ?" the pit boss said.

"Is your slot-machine mechanic around?"

"Yup."

"I need a favor."

"Name it," the pit boss said.

"I've got my mother in town and all she's doing is bitch that she's supporting your casino. I think she dropped twenty dollars in the slots."

"I'll give her the twenty back. Tell her to see me," the pit boss said.

"That won't do. And she's making my life miserable."

"I know what you want," Armando said.

"I figured you would."

"A nickel slot, no doubt?"

"Yeah," Trace said.

"Okay. I'll have Jerry jigger up the second nickel machine on the right bank inside the door. Good advertising for the house. How about a hundred and ten percent?"

"That sounds good," Trace said. "It'll keep her busy all day and it won't cost me a fortune."

"All right. He'll set it up to pay a hundred and ten. We'll turn the machine off and put out-of-order on it. When you come in, see the day boss. He'll know about it and he'll turn it on. Just make sure that when she's done, we know about it so we can set the machine back."

"Armando, if I were there, I'd kiss you."

"Kiss Chico instead. She likes you."

Chico stuck her head into the living room.

"Trace, I'm going to bed."

"Okay. I just want to go over a tape or two and I'll be in."

"Don't stay up too late."

"I won't," he promised.

She closed the bedroom door behind her and he sat on the sofa with his tape machine and tapes around him, and the telephone rang.

"Mr. Tracy, this is Spiro. From the countess's?"

"Sure. How are you doing, Spiro?"

"Not too good. I just got home from work and my apartment was torn apart."

"Oh. Was anything taken?"

"There wasn't anything to take," Spiro said.

"Any idea who did it?" Trace asked.

"I talked to my landlady. She said a big guy, made believe he was from the gas company, he came and she let him in."

"She get his name?"

"She thought it was something like Kilowatt but that was stupid. He must have been talking about kilowatts or something. My landlady ain't too bright. What should I do, Mr. Tracy?"

"Clean your apartment," Trace said. "I don't think he'll be back."

"Who could that guy be?" Spiro asked.

"We just may never know," Trace said.

21

Trace's log:

Tape Recording Number Three, Devlin Tracy in the matter of Early Jarvis. Eleven P.M. Wednesday and our one murder has now become two, and I still don't have clue number one. Am I getting stupid now that I'm getting old?

I didn't care much for R. J. Roberts, but I don't like people practicing their carving on detectives' throats. Today Germany, tomorrow the world. Screw the world, maybe tomorrow me. I don't need that. Sarge won't always be here to protect me.

Well, the good news first. I got Roberts' check in the bank and I didn't get arrested over it and I didn't have to hand up Swenson. End of the good-news report.

I'm talking softly because Chico's sleeping and I don't want to wake her up. I mean, she went into the cave to wrestle with the Great Earth Mother today and that would tire anybody out. You have to have affection for a woman who tells your mother that she's put land mines inside your front door to keep your mother out.

Sarge was going to get the manifest from Jarvis' flight into Las Vegas. I don't think it's going to tell us a damned thing, except maybe Jarvis was flying under a different name. What else Sarge has in mind, I don't know. And I've got Jarvis' car-rental agreement. So he rented a car at 11:46 P.M. and drove to the house and got killed. Why, dammit? By whom?

All I did today was get Dan Rosado mad at me for not calling the cops right away about Roberts' death. But I wanted to look around the office. Nothing except his pimp receipts, which don't concern me, and that little note in the Jarvis file. "Records." What records? Maybe he was joining the Columbia Record Club and wanted to remember Joan Jett and the Blackhearts.

It was good we redeemed ourself by Sarge finding that witness and giving Rosado the baron. I don't think he killed anybody, but don't count on it. I'm the same genius who was sure Hubbaker was Groucho's big insurance detective.

Aaaah, life's not all that bad. How bad can a day be when Sarge throws Ferrara into a swimming pool? Along with his Afghan hashish.

The thief probably got the combination from Jarvis. Sarge figured it out. That's why he stopped drilling the holes in the safe. Were they working together? Some kind of scheme to rip off Felicia? Okay, let's try that. The thief's supposed to meet Jarvis at the house.

But Jarvis is late, so the thief starts drilling the safe. Then Jarvis arrives and gives him the combination. They open the safe and swipe the jewels. Then the thief gets greedy and hits Jarvis over the head. They struggled some. They knock over a tree. The thief gets away. Jarvis dies from bleeding.

What's wrong with that? I don't know. Everything. Nothing. Why'd Jarvis call from the airport and not wait? Okay. He wants to get Spiro out of the house. Fine. Except when the place was found robbed, the first thing Spiro would tell the cops was that Jarvis called him from the airport. Jarvis couldn't get away with that.

Jarvis had keys to the house. It doesn't make any sense. Wait till Spiro's asleep. Let yourself in with keys. Bop Spiro on the head, blindfold him, and tie him up. Take your own sweet time about opening the safe and then leave. No complications.

I give up.

Hubbaker says he found Roberts dead. Did Roberts find out something between the time I left him and when Hubbaker arrived? Something that got his throat cut?

Couldn't be. He called Hubbaker in the evening, before I saw him.

Hubbaker says everybody at the house knew he was going to see Roberts. Maybe I can find out who left the house besides Hubbaker. And probably the same guy who looted Spiro's apartment.

Oh, well. At least I calmed my mother down and got her off Sarge's case for a while. And tomorrow that rigged machine will keep her busy. That's good. And the look on Marks' face when I told him the baron was in jail, that was good too.

Enough, I'm tired. This day has been long and complicated, and who needs it. Usual expenses, one hundred and fifty dollars. Sarge is keeping his own, I hope, in that big notebook he keeps carrying around with him. He looks like a guest host on *Sesame Street*.

Good night, all. I wish somebody would solve

this thing for me. Brace up, Trace. Remember. When the going gets tough. . . .

Yeah, the scared get scareder and the dumb get dumber. *Auf Wiedersehen*, world of my youth.

22

As he got up from the couch, Trace heard the alarm go off in the bedroom. It rang just a moment, then stopped.

Chico called, "Trace, come in here."

He walked into the darkened bedroom. "What, little girl?" he said.

"Come over here."

He walked to the side of the bed and sat down next to her. "What happened with the alarm?" he asked.

"I set it," she said. She put her arms around his neck and kissed him. "Happy birthday. You're now officially too old for me."

"What are you giving me for my birthday?"

"You have to ask?" she said.

23

"Sorry, son, but this was important enough to wake you up for."

"Wake me up? Surely you jest. I've been awake for hours. I'm always up at dawn."

"It's not dawn and I'm sorry to hear it. You know what they say?"

"What do they say?"

"They say, 'Early to rise and early to bed makes a man healthy, wealthy, and dead,'" Sarge said.

"So why'd you call?" Trace asked.

"Just to let you know I'm on my way over."

Trace hung up the telephone, rolled over, lifted the sheet, and kissed Chico's naked belly.

"Mmmmm." She smiled a perfect little smile. "Make bigger circles," she mumbled.

"You're a disgusting little thing," he said.

"At your age, what else are you good for?"

"Oh, my God," he said. "My age. I'm forty. Quick. Look. Do I have wattles yet?"

"What's a wattle?" Chico asked.

"I don't know. What's a wattle with you?" Trace said. "Fast, check my butt. Do I have cellulite?"

"The only way you'll have orange skin is with

vodka. Why did you wake me up in the middle of the night if not to ravish me?"

"It's not the middle of the night. It's the middle of the morning on the first day of the rest of your life. And mine too, the few days I have left to me."

She squeezed open one eye. "No, you look the same as you always look. But I think I'm going to get a delivery boy just in case."

"See if he's got a sister. A young one. I want to take her bicycle seat to bed with me. Remember my days of triumph."

Trace put his arms around her and held her close. She fit. Some women just didn't fit. They always seemed to have an elbow or a knee or some other part out of place, and holding them was like trying to put ten pounds of potatoes into a five-pound bag; something always spilled out. But Chico fit as if she had been machined; she molded herself to his body and all her right places touched all his right places and her body was always warm and smooth to his touch.

Trace closed his eyes. "Call me when I'm forty-one," he said.

"Who was on the phone?"

"Sarge. Oh, hell, he's on his way over."

"Do you think he'll mind if we stay in here and shout to him out in the living room?" Chico asked.

"Do you think he knows we sleep together?" Trace asked.

"Better not take the chance," she said. "He might tell your mother. You ought to get up and make coffee."

"Wait. Wait. Hold, woman. *I* should get up and make coffee? Whatever happened to equality? Long live the ERA. Hanoi Hannah too."

"I made coffee yesterday," Chico said. "And breakfast, too, as I recall."

"Yes, " he said. "And the day before that?"

"I made coffee and breakfast then too," she said.

"Exactly what I mean. From each according to his abilities, to each according to his needs. I need coffee, that's my need. You make good coffee; that's your ability. *You* make the coffee."

"I never knew anybody before who could use Marxism as an excuse for staying in bed," Chico said.

"There's enough in Marx for all of us. He's a giant ocean in which all may swim."

"Very pretty," Chico said. "But what's *your* ability?"

"I don't know. What's your need?"

"I told you before. Make bigger circles," she said.

"Monumentally disgusting," he said.

The three sat around the kitchen table with coffee mugs. Sarge carefully opened his notebook in front of him, extracted a piece of paper, and handed it to Trace.

"That's the manifest from the American flight into town. No Jarvis on it, but if you look, there's Edward Stark. He was flying under his fake name."

"You expected that," Chico told Trace.

Trace glanced at the sheet and nodded. "It doesn't tell us anything, but it's nice to know we guess right once in a while. You didn't wake me up for this, Sarge."

"No. For this." He cleared his throat and looked down at some scrawled notes in his book. "Your friend? Hubbaker?"

"Yeah?"

"He's a jewel thief," Sarge said.

"Holy moley," Trace said.

"He was bagged once in Amsterdam. In 1977. They had to let him go for lack of evidence."

"How'd you find that out?"

"You know, your mother's always complaining that I wouldn't take the lieutenant's test. But all my friends did. And now they're inspectors and chiefs and all over the N.Y.P.D. They ran him through Interpol for me. Some private contacts."

"Dammit, though," Trace said. "All it does is confuse things. He couldn't steal Felicia's jewels 'cause he was in Europe. And even if he was involved in it somehow, why the hell would he come back here and take the chance of getting into trouble?" He paused a moment. "Anyway, now we know what Roberts meant with that note in his files. 'Records.' He must have found out about Hubbaker's record."

"I'm not done yet," Sarge said.

"Listen to your father, Trace. There's a twinkle in his eye. I love it when there's a twinkle in his eye."

"All right, Twinkie, shoot," Trace said.

"Jarvis was a thief too. Edward Stark was his real name. He was from Elmira, New York. I had New York run him through and he had a long record: burglary, auto theft, fencing, what have you. And then, for the last fifteen years, nothing."

"That's all the time he was working for Felicia," Trace said.

"Ah, yes, the countess," Sarge said. "You want to know what Interpol has to say about her?"

"Oh, no," Trace said.

"Oh, yes." Sarge began to read. "Felicia Fallaci, who calls herself a countess on the basis of some unrecorded marriage to a destitute Italian count, is considered by Interpol to be one of the major international jewel thieves working today. She and her constant companion, Early Jarvis, have over the past dozen years been on the scene of many events where large jewel thefts have occurred. Although no direct evidence has been uncovered linking Fallaci and Jarvis to these thefts, the circumstantial links seem quite strong and compelling to Interpol. Interpol would appreciate any updated information regarding the activities of these two suspected thieves."

Trace brought the coffeepot back to the table and poured for all of them. "I give up," he said. "Now I don't even know which end is up. Felicia may be a thief, yet she gets her own stuff stolen." He shook his head. "Maybe there's some sense in here but I don't know what it is."

Chico was looking out their window toward the Las Vegas Strip below. "Maybe I do," she said softly.

"Well, tell me. Tell me."

"Not quite yet," she said. "I've got to think about it some more. Excuse me." She left the table and went into the bedroom, and Trace sat back down.

"Well, at least we know for sure now that the baron isn't the insurance detective," he said.

"Guess not," Sarge agreed.

"Then, who is?"

The question hung in the air and the two men sat silently, sipping their coffee. Chico came back into the kitchen and said, "I've got your birthday present, Trace."

"What's that?"

"Me."

"Please, woman. This is my father. Are you trying to embarrass me?"

"I mean I'm taking the day off and I'm going to help you figure this out."

"What about the convention?"

"I just called Flamma. She's going to do it for me."

"Flamma? She'll have half the convention in bed before lunch."

"It'll make for a memorable convention, won't it?" Chico said. "She promised to be on her best behavior. And I promised to give her four hundred dollars. That's what your birthday present's costing me, four hundred beans. When my birthday comes, I don't want another sweat shirt."

She sat back down and Trace said, "So talk. What is it you think you know?"

"I think Jarvis came to town to steal the countess's jewelry," she said as she bit into a piece of toast.

"Does that make any sense? He was devoted to her. You know that."

"Sure. And now we know that both of them were probably jewel thieves. Maybe this time, instead of stealing jewelry from somebody else, they were going to steal it from themselves for the insurance money. The big score, kid."

Trace thought about that for a few moments. "I don't know," he said.

"Of course not. I'm just getting started and I don't have everything put together yet. But think about Jarvis sneaking into town, traveling under a phony name. He was avoiding leaving a track so that when the safe wound up empty, nobody could blame it on him."

"I still don't know."

"Try this. You wondered why his bag had so

222

damned little in it? Because he wasn't staying. He was going to boost the jewelry and get back on the next plane."

"Listen to her," Sarge said admiringly. " 'Boost the jewelry.' Where'd you learn to talk like that?"

"*Charlie's Angels* reruns," she said.

"Still too many holes," Trace said. "Why an accomplice? Why the rented car? Why the call from the airport?"

"Give me your tapes," Chico said. "I've got some ideas and I can go over them. Sarge, you want to come out and play with me today?"

"Actually, I've got this long string of beautiful women who've been begging me to spend time with them, but I'll pass them all up for you."

"You'll never regret it," Chico said.

"Hey, can I get in on this?" Trace asked.

"Sure," Chico said. "What do you have to say?"

"Do anything you want."

"Thanks, old-timer," she said.

"Hey, I forgot," Sarge said. "Happy birthday, son."

"Thank you."

"Your mother's waiting for you," Sarge said.

"You know junk mail?" Trace said. "That's junk news."

While Chico was getting dressed and Sarge was watching television, Trace locked himself in his bathroom with his recorder and tapes. He hadn't recorded anything on the other side of the tape he had made while in bed with the countess, so he just stuck that tape inside his jacket pocket.

Chico was waiting for him when he came out.

"Did you erase everything you didn't want me to hear?" she asked.

"What do you mean?"

"I thought that was pretty straightforward, as questions go."

"I refuse to argue with you about it. Here. Take the tapes. You still have your own recorder?"

"Yes."

Sarge was watching a tennis match.

"I don't watch women's tennis anymore," Trace said.

"They're good," Sarge said.

"But it's always the Ovum twins."

"Who the hell are the Ovum twins?" Sarge asked.

"Whatever their names are. The Ovas. There's Martina Under-and-over and Hannah Hit-it-over. They're always playing, and who cares anymore? Where's Mother?"

"Waiting in the room."

"What was she doing?" Trace asked.

"When I left, she was looking at her watch every five seconds and getting ready to chew a drape."

24

"Hello, Mother."

"I suppose you ate breakfast," she said. They were standing in the lobby of the Araby Hotel and Casino.

"Actually, I don't eat breakfast much," Trace said.

"No wonder, probably, with no one to cook for you. You wouldn't want fish for breakfast. Or rice."

"You're right, Mother. People who eat fish for breakfast are uncivilized. Have you eaten? We could get bagels and lox."

"I got so tired of waiting that I had them send breakfast to my room. They charge terrible prices here. Just awful. I wouldn't splurge like that normally, but I thought if I went to the coffee shop, I wouldn't be in the room when you called and I might miss you."

"That would've been awful," Trace said solemnly. "Do I look any different?"

Suspiciously, she answered, "No, I don't think so. Maybe. Why?"

"I'm forty years old," Trace said.

"My uncle Phil died when he was forty," she said.

"Who could blame him?" Trace mumbled. He took his mother's arm and led her into the casino, where he saw an out-of-order sign on the second machine in the right-hand bank. He put his mother at a machine near it.

"Play here for a while, Mother. I want to do something."

"What?"

"You see, you have to pick these machines carefully. Some pay better than others. What you try to do is get a machine that's just been repaired and serviced."

"Why?"

"Because the wheels are still round and the electronic fabricator inside the devious speculum produces a much more honest count for the player."

"So you could win?" she said.

"Something like that. If you're lucky."

"I haven't been lucky yet. I keep losing ten dollarses. Even when I use the machines you tell me."

"Not today. Warm up. I'll be right back."

Trace left her playing, one grim nickel after another grim nickel, and talked to the pit boss, who called the slot-machine mechanic.

"Jerry told you that he rigged up Machine 186?" the pit boss asked, and the mechanic nodded.

"Okay. This is Trace. Go turn it on for him."

"All right," the mechanic said.

As they walked toward the machines, Trace slipped the mechanic twenty dollars.

"Mum's the word," he said. "She mustn't ever know."

"You won't hear it from me. What is it, a special occasion or something?"

"Yeah," Trace said. "It's my birthday and I'm investing in my own peace of mind."

The mechanic walked to Machine 186 and Trace whispered to his mother, "We're in luck. That machine over there has just been fixed. It's ready for plucking. Grab your nickels."

As soon as the mechanic had turned on the machine, Mrs. Tracy brushed by, shouldering him out of the way. The mechanic winked at Trace, who nodded back.

She won a dollar with her first nickel.

"Oh, yes," she said. "I can feel the difference already. The wheels feel round when they're turning. Why didn't you take me to this machine when I first got here?"

"Just waiting for the right moment, Mother."

He found her a chair to sit on and bought twenty dollars' worth of nickels at the change booth.

"Here. Stick these in your purse, in case you need reserves," he said. "Can I get you something?"

"They still have free stuff here, don't they?"

"Drinks and things. Coffee," he said.

"I'll wait for the waitress," she said.

"Okay, Mother. I've got to go to work. I'll see you later. Knock 'em dead."

"I'd be happy to get even after all the ten dollarses I lost," she said.

Trace kissed her on the cheek and walked away.

"Oh, Devlin."

"Yes, Mother."

"Happy birthday. And many more."

"Thank you, Mother."

Before he left the hotel, Trace was spotted by Bob Swenson, who was coming out of an elevator. "Trace. Hold up," he called.

"How are you doing? You look like hell," Trace said.

Swenson's face was drawn and his eyes seemed darker, deep set. "Not much sleep," he said.

"You going for breakfast?"

"No. A drink. Come on, have a drink with me."

"Maybe one," Trace said. "No, not in there. My mother's in there. The other lounge."

They ordered drinks at the bar and Swenson said, "I'm in love."

"Anybody I know?"

"Nash."

"I was going to ask you how your night went," Trace said.

"Well, I wasn't in love with her when we did it in the bed or even when we did it in the shower. I don't think I even loved her when we did it in the closet. But when we did it in the potted plant on the balcony, I think that's when I fell in love."

"Is she in love too?" Trace asked.

"She's sworn off donkeys," Swenson said solemnly. "I want to take her home with me."

"You mean home home?"

"No, I mean back to New York. I can set her up in an apartment somewhere. Shit, Trace, I'm rich. Shouldn't I be able to do that?"

"No," Trace said.

"What the hell kind of an answer is that? I bring you down here and make you buy me a drink and you give me a 'no'? I'm your employer. Don't be my friend. Be my employee. Say yes."

"No," Trace said.

"Have you forgotten that you still owe me three thousand dollars?" Swenson said.

"Stop worrying, you'll get your money. What

are friends for if not to say no? You think Groucho's going to tell you no?"

"He'd better not. Why did you tell me no? I think what I just had was a perfectly smashing idea."

"Never work," Trace said.

"Why not?"

"Only two things can happen, and both of them are bad. First, you set her up, and then, I know you, you start spending too much time with her. Or when you can't spend time with her, you start to wonder what she's doing. The next thing, I get called in to tail her and find out who she's seeing, what she's doing. She's going out and you're going nuts. You wind up doing something stupid and your wife finds out. You want your wife to find out?"

"That question's too dumb to deserve an answer, Trace."

"Okay. So maybe even your wife doesn't find out, but she's going to get on your back anyway because you're so nutty about climbing into the rack with National Anthem that you're trying to spend all your time there. And then it escalates."

"It sounded pretty bad already," Swenson said.

"It gets worse. You start doing dopey things just to hang on to her. You tell her that you'll back her next movie. The insurance-company board of directors hears that you want to back a film called *Sex Secrets of the Silent Stars* and they take a vote to throw you out. You're out on the street. Homeless. Only the suit on your back."

"I'll bring another suit. I've got a lot of suits," Swenson said.

"Your wife burned them all after you lost your job and became penniless. Anyway, that's the way one goes," Trace said.

"Is the other one as grim as this? I didn't like that one at all," Swenson said.

"The other one starts out better."

"Start it. I'll tell you when to stop."

"Okay. Nash falls in love with you. You're the older, sophisticated, skilled, and talented man she's always wanted. A man she can trust and look up to, someone who's not just trying to get into her pants."

"I still get into her pants in this story, don't I?" Swenson asked.

"Yes. Very frequently. More and more frequently, because she's crazy about you. She wants you all the time. She starts calling you at the office, making you come over for lunch. She comes to the office in the afternoons to see you. Soon, people start to talk. Who is this woman? Why is Bob losing weight and twitching a lot?"

"This is where it gets bad, right?"

"Sort of," Trace said.

"Go no farther."

"I've got to tell you how it ends," Trace said.

"Okay, make it quick, though. Bartender, another drink."

"Soon people are talking. Everybody's talking. Nash resents every minute you spend home with the family. One day, she can't take it anymore. She knows you're out and she goes to see your wife to tell her that you and she are deeply in love and your wife should just butt out. Your wife gets mad and sues you for divorce and gets everything and you wind up out on the street. This time, maybe if you're lucky, you get to keep two suits."

"I still have my job. My insurance company," Swenson said.

"No. Your wife gets the stock. The company

fires you because you've embarrassed them and they elect Walter Marks to be the next president. He fires me and the two of us are out in the street. And I'm bigger than you are and your suits don't fit me. We look like derelicts, the two of us, walking along the gutter, battling pigeons for peanuts."

"You're some way to start the day," Swenson said. "I thought I had everything worked out and you come and rain on my parade."

"That's not rain. Your parade is marching underwater," Trace said.

"I think I should tell you that I'm not at all happy with the way you've dealt with my life plan," Swenson said. "I'd say it was basically cavalier, this analysis."

"Nonsense," Trace said. "I've given this a great deal of thought. Ever since I saw you with her for the first time and noticed your tongue lashing the tops of your shoes."

"You think this is just sex, don't you?" Swenson asked.

"I wouldn't know what it is."

"Well, it isn't just sex. There's a lot more to it than that."

"You share a love of animals?" Trace asked.

"That's unkind. Really. So you've got all these terrible scenarios; give me a good one."

"There is no good one, but here's the best of a bad lot. You rent Nash an apartment here. Or in L.A. You make it a point to fly out to the coast a lot to do business. You don't really do business, though. That's just an excuse to get to see her. When you're with her, you screw your brains out. When you go home, you forget her till the next time."

"I've got to think about it," Swenson said.

"Give it a lot of thought," Trace said.

"You just missed your father and Chico," Dan Rosado said as Trace walked into the office.

"What'd they want?"

"They wanted to look at the pictures of Jarvis' body."

"Did you show them?" Trace asked.

"Why not? Everybody else in town has got a theory, why not them? Anyway, I wanted to see how Chico deals with blood."

"She's tough, isn't she?" Trace said.

"Not even a blink. I got out all the really disgusting close-up photos too. You'd think she was looking through a family album."

"They say what they were up to?" Trace asked.

"No. I figured you sent them on another mission, like the one yesterday. I told them, though, if they find any more bodies, they have to call me first. After that, they can call you. So what are you doing here?"

"I can't stop in to say hello to my old buddy?"

"That lie is received, noted, and filed. What do you want?"

"You still holding Hubbaker?" Trace asked.

"Let him go this morning. Somebody made his bail. The guy said he knew you," Rosado said.

"Walter Marks?"

"That sounds like it. Little guy?"

Trace nodded. "How much bail did he go for?"

"Twenty-five hundred," Rosado said.

"Good. I hope he eats it. Dan, I ask you a question, you don't ask me any questions?"

"I don't know. Try me," Rosado said.

"Did you find any money in Roberts' office? Money, casino chips, anything like that?"

"Why?"

"I don't know. I've got a hunch."

Rosado shrugged. "Just two hundred bucks or so in the back of one of the desk drawers. And that list, I guess it was his pimp list."

"That's all?"

"Yeah. What hunch?" Rosado said.

"What about Roberts?" Trace asked, ignoring the question. "You find out anything about him?"

"Yeah. You won't believe it."

"Listen, I've got a father who thinks he's Wyatt Earp. I work for a boss who's a sex maniac. I'll believe anything," Trace said.

"Roberts lived alone in a rooming house. He sent every penny he had back home to Pennsylvania to support his parents in a nursing home."

"That's rotten," Trace said. "It makes him harder to hate."

"That's the way life goes," Rosado said. "What hunch do you have?"

"Let me think it through first. Then I'll call you with it."

"You're not going to go out and get yourself shot or anything, are you? If you do, I won't know what your hunch was. Maybe the person in your hunch will do you in, too. What happens then?"

"With my last fleeting ounce of strength, I'll scribble the killer's name on a postcard and mail it to you. You can play a Caruso record over my grave."

"If I don't get the postcard, you get Mario Lanza. You know, I'll be glad when your father goes home and you go back to working out of town. No wonder cops in other towns hate you so."

"Gee, they never tell me that," Trace said.

The young woman was shapely and pretty, but it looked as if she had bought her clothes, by mistake, in the children's section of the department store. Her satin shorts were cut so high that the bottom of her buttocks peeked out. Her knit top was cut so low that almost all of her bosom was visible.

She slid into the diner booth across from him and said, "Hi, Trace. What brings you down here?"

"I need a favor, Margo."

"If I can," she said warily.

"Not good enough. You can and you owe me," Trace said.

"Okay. What is it?"

"I'm looking for a big blond hooker named Lip Service. Where do I find her?"

"Clara?"

"Is that her name? Roberts used to run her before he got it?"

The corners of Margo's mouth turned down in disgust. "Sleazebag. Him and that p.i. license."

"What did he do to you?" Trace asked.

"I've got my own old man. But he'd come in here all the time, always trying to round up girls, not caring whether you've got a man or not. He was always causing trouble. Who did him in?"

"Some jewel thief," Trace said.

"Why do you need Clara?"

"She was his top woman, I'm told," Trace said. "I think she might be able to give me a lead on the jewel thief."

"Maybe. I don't know. But she wasn't his top woman anymore. You know, she was the first woman who worked for him. She was with him all those years and he just slid her out to put in somebody else."

"Who?"

"Some cheap redhead who calls herself Blaze. A real bitch."

"So I need Clara," Trace prodded.

"I haven't seen her in a couple of days, Trace."

"Then I need her full name and her house. Where's she hang her hat?"

"When do you need it by?" Margo asked.

"Yesterday."

"It's not that easy sometimes," she said.

"A lot of things aren't easy. I did some things for you, too, that weren't easy," he said.

"All right. I'm not forgetting. I'm just saying—"

"You're just saying that you've got a lot of reasons why you can't do something, instead of doing it."

"All right, Trace."

"I need it right away," he said.

"I've got to get a telephone," Margo said.

"I'll wait here," he said.

It took her only five minutes. She slid back into the booth and slipped him a piece of paper.

"Her name's Clara Buxtable. She lives out in the Village section in those new houses. The address is on there. She's got a seven-year-old kid, a girl, but no old man."

"Thanks, Margo."

"You didn't get it here," she said.

"You don't have to tell me the rules," he said, standing up.

She touched his hand with hers. "Give me a call sometime, Trace. If your woman's out of town. I'm here most of the time. The taxi phone booth next door. They can always get me."

"I'll do that sometime," he said.

The thing that was going wrong with Las Vegas was houses like Clara Buxtable's, Trace thought as he parked in front of the neat little frame house on the neat little street with the neat little lawn in front.

When he had first moved to town, even though the late-August temperatures could top 110 degrees, it was still reasonably comfortable because there was hardly any humidity.

Then the city had a housing boom and every house had a lawn and every lawn had a sprinkler system, and all of a sudden there was all this sprinkle in the air, packing the city with moisture it didn't need, and 110 degrees wasn't bearable anymore. It was hot and sticky and he perspired. Why didn't people leave a desert alone? Why did everybody think that when he moved he had a right to bring his grass with him? If he wanted grass, let him move to Guatemala, not Las Vegas.

Nobody answered the door bell, so Trace walked to the house next door and summoned up a gray-haired man with a potbelly and thick eyeglasses.

"What do you want?"

In the background, Trace could hear a television roaring.

"I'm looking for Mrs. Buxtable," Trace said.

"What's that you say?"

Deaf, too, Trace thought. It was his luck. When he was driving and got lost, as he often did, the person he stopped to ask for directions would be the one person in five thousand square miles who didn't speak English. Now, he had to question a deaf man.

He shouted, "I'm looking for Mrs. Buxtable."

"She ain't home."

"I know that. Where is she?"

"What's that?"

"WHERE . . . IS . . . SHE?" Trace shouted again.

"Who wants to know?"

"I DO," Trace yelled.

"Oh," the man said, as if overwhelmed by the simple beauty of the answer. "She's gone back home."

The man glanced back inside as if a moment's letup in his vigilance and termites would come in and eat his furniture. The television set roared on.

"Where's home?" Trace asked.

"Listen, if you're going to talk all day, come in here. I want to watch the end of this show," the man said.

Trace went inside and sat on a flowered couch. The man sat down on a chair in front of the television and cheered on the contestants in a game show.

"Take the curtain. Take the curtain," he yelled.

The contestant, who was dressed to look like a sugar cube, took the first door and won an automobile.

"There was better behind the curtain," Trace's host shouted.

The master of ceremonies opened the curtain to display a camel, a particularly disreputable-looking beast.

"Camels are worth a lot," the man yelled. He turned to Trace and in an aside, as if he feared the contestants would overhear him, said, "You should always take the curtain. Curtain's always got the best behind it."

"I'd rather have a car than a camel," Trace said.

"You watch this show?"

"Never," Trace said.

"Take the curtain. What they do is they move things around when you pick, and if they want you to win, they put the good thing behind whatever you like. That's if they like you. If they don't like you, they give you a camel or something."

Great, Trace thought. He needed information and he had wound up with somebody with a conspiracy theory of game shows.

"All the games shows are like that," the man said. "They all cheat."

"I guessed that," Trace said blandly. "That's why I don't watch them."

When the show ended, the man leaned forward and turned off the roaring television set. "I don't like what's on next," he said. "They got all these celebrities, and they are the stupidest people you ever saw. I saw that Mister Spock once and he was so dumb he shoulda been arrested."

"I'm looking for Mrs. Buxtable," Trace said.

"Why are you yelling?"

"I thought you were deaf."

"I will be if you keep yelling," the man said.

"I'm sorry. I'll talk softly."

"Not too softly, sonny. I'm eighty years old. I hear good but not perfect."

"I'm looking for Mrs. Buxtable," Trace said again. "How's that?"

"Much better. She went home."

"I thought she lived next door."

"She does, but that ain't what I mean by home. Home is where you come from. Nobody comes from Las Vegas."

"Where's her home?"

"Minnesota. What do you want her for?"

"I talked to her last week about a job. I was thinking of hiring her."

"You a pimp? You don't look like no pimp," the man said.

"No, I'm not a pimp. Why should I be a pimp?"

"Because you want to hire a hooker."

"I thought she was a bookkeeper," Trace said.

"Maybe she told you that, but she's a hooker. Calls herself Lip Service. Ain't that a good one?"

"Sure is," Trace said. "Don't you mind living next door to a hooker?"

"Not if she's nice. Clara's nice. Even comes over here once in a while. Won't take no money neither."

"Why'd she go home?"

"She said she wanted to take a rest. I think somebody beat up on her, though. She had a black eye. I could see it under her sunglasses. Just left yesterday."

"When's she coming back?"

"She didn't say. Want a drink?"

"No, thanks," Trace said. "She own that house next door?"

"No. She just pays rent. I own it. I own six houses on this block."

"Suppose Clara doesn't come back?" Trace said.

The old man shrugged. "There's always hookers to rent to," he said.

25

His mother had her jacket off and, as if that weren't serious enough, her hat, too.

Trace stood across the casino entrance from the machine she was playing. A plastic tubful of nickels was next to her and there was a look of unalloyed joy on her face that he hadn't seen since the first summer she had sent him to camp. He left the day after public school closed and came back the day before it opened. Summer camp to his mother meant summer camp, not for one week or two but for the whole summer.

When eleven-year-old Devlin had gotten home, his father had asked, "How'd you like Camp Chicken Soup, son?"

"I hated it. All fat kids in green sneakers."

"Good. You're not going anymore."

"Good."

"Without you around, I didn't have anybody to talk to," his father had said.

"Did Mother go away too?"

"No. That's why I didn't have anybody to talk to."

The red light atop the slot machine began to flash, a bell rang, and a small avalanche of nickels began clattering into the coin tray in the front of the machine. His mother whooped and started scooping the money into the bucket.

Trace walked away into the casino. As he passed the blackjack pit, the day boss called him over. "Your mother's having a great time over there," he said. "I've been keeping an eye on her."

"Thanks. Is she doing any damage to my bankroll?"

"Not a chance. She won't bet more than a nickel. She's got a progressive machine, and if she'd punch up her bets, she'd be winning six, ten times as much. But she can't get herself to pop for more than one coin."

"Good. I just want her to be successful. I'm not paying for a windfall."

"You'll get out of it for a hundred dollars if she keeps going that way."

"It'll be worth it."

At the casino cage, Trace asked to speak to the head cashier. She was a tiny little woman with gray hair, iron-rimmed glasses, a pencil behind her ear, and a no-nonsense attitude that discouraged small talk.

"What can I do for you, Trace?" she asked.

"Sometime yesterday before noon, did any of your people cash in a woman with three thousand dollars in chips? Hundreds?"

"What kind of a woman?"

"A big blonde. She's on the hook, but she might have been dressed mousey. I'm not sure."

"Wait a minute." The woman began to talk to her cashiers. One at a time, Trace saw each of them shake his head. Finally, one woman nodded and the head cashier called Trace down to the window.

"Martha here had a woman yesterday."

"What'd she look like?" Trace asked.

"She was wearing some kind of leopard-skin suit or something."

Trace nodded.

"But it wasn't three thousand," the teller said. "It was nine thousand."

Trace grimaced. It was supposed to be only three thousand dollars.

"She caught a hot hand," the young woman said. "It was quiet here and I saw her walk in. You don't miss anybody who looks like that. She went over to the craps table, and a couple of minutes later there was a crowd gathered around and everybody's shouting and screaming. It didn't take ten minutes, she came over and dumped her purse on the counter. I checked her out at ninety-one hundred."

"Okay, Martha. Thanks a lot." Trace looked past her to the head cashier. "Did I ever tell you I love you?"

"All the time, but I'm saving myself for when I get married."

"You wouldn't want me. I snore and eat English muffins in bed."

"And you've got Chico too," the woman said.

"Don't remind me."

"The best thing that ever happened to you," the woman said.

"Did you two hire the same scriptwriter?" he asked.

Trace took a peek into the banquet room, where the insurance conventioneers had just finished lunch. Swenson and Marks were seated together at a table in the rear of the slowly emptying room.

"Hello, Groucho. Bob."

"Sit down, Trace. We were just talking about you."

"I knew that. I could tell by the scowl on Groucho's face."

"You really haven't done much on this Jarvis case," Marks said, "and the convention ends tomorrow."

"He'll still be dead by then," Trace said. "No need to hurry."

"I'm suggesting to Mr. Swenson that we call in somebody else who can get to the bottom of this," Marks said.

"The bottom of what?" Trace asked.

"This whole matter. The killing of Jarvis. The jewelry theft."

"Horseshit," Trace snapped. "In the first place, the Jarvis case is simple. If the countess killed him, she doesn't get any money from us. If she didn't, pay her up. She was in Europe when he got killed."

"She might have paid to have him killed," Marks said.

"She might have," Trace said agreeably. "And if she did, I'll find it out. I don't need any help. And if I don't do it today, I'll do it tomorrow or I'll do it when it's doable, but it'll get done. As far as the jewels go, that has nothing to do with us. It's not Gone Fishing's policy, we didn't have the jewels insured and I don't know what you're getting all twisted for."

"Because the two things are tied up together. That's obvious. And now Roberts getting killed."

"We don't know what's tied up with what," Trace said. "You're jumping to conclusions, and that's dangerous, particularly when the conclusions are,

243

like yours, so unfailingly stupid. And as for calling somebody else in, what happened to your big fancy insurance detective? I thought the baron was going to set the world straight."

Marks was silent and Trace said, "I'll tell you what happened. Hubbaker got his ass thrown in the slammer and you went bail for him. So we've got one detective who gets killed and the baron gets arrested. What are you going to ask me to have in next? Somebody with bubonic plague? Stay off my case, Groucho."

"We can't let this drag on forever," Marks said.

"No, we can't, because I'm planning to go to Paris for my new fall wardrobe, and if I wait too long, all the pedal pushers will be gone."

"I think Mr. Swenson and I would like a report of your progress," Marks said as he got up from the table.

"Will triplicate be all right?" Trace asked.

"That'll be fine." Marks slowly walked away and Swenson asked, "Why does he hate you so?"

"Because I don't need this job and I don't need him and he can't bully me because he doesn't own me. He'd like you to let him dump me."

"He said he's given you enough rope to hang yourself. Aaah, screw insurance. Let's talk about women. Where's Chico?"

"She's out working on the Jarvis thing. I needed her to do some legwork, so she got Flamma to fill in for her."

"I know it," Swenson said. "She came running up to me at this morning's session, threw her arms around me, and tongued me in front of four hundred people."

"She's just basically warm," Trace said. "It comes from dancing with Sterno in your navel. Have

244

you thought about what I said? About National Anthem?"

"Yeah," Swenson said. "I may get an apartment here in the company's name and put her in it. Maybe I'll talk to her about it tonight. Felicia invited us all to her place for dinner."

"I think you're on the right track now," Trace said.

"How does that story end?" Swenson asked.

"With you getting tired of her and letting the lease expire."

"No lawsuits? No public humiliation for me?" Swenson asked.

"Nope. None of that."

"Good," Swenson said. "I'll talk to you about working out the details."

Trace went home. There were no messages on his answering machine and he wondered where Chico and Sarge were. If either of them had any sense, they'd be eloping, on their way across the Mexican border, never to return.

He made a sandwich. As he was pouring catsup on his roast beef, he looked at the bottle and saw the black crud that formed around the mouth of the catsup bottle and it made him think of Walter Marks. What was there in catsup anyway that turned black? Did it turn black inside your stomach too?

And what was there about Groucho that always made it black midnight in Devlin Tracy's soul?

He ate his sandwich, drank a glass of milk, and put a tape of Joan Sutherland arias on the stereo and fell asleep listening.

"Da-daaaa," Chico riffled and flourished as she came into the apartment with Sarge, waving a pile of papers over her head.

"Please, I'm depressed," Trace said, looking up from the sofa. "Da-daaa me no da-daaas."

"What are you depressed about, you poor thing? Look at him, Sarge. He's aged ten years in a single day. I bet he's getting shorter too. The Incredible Shrinking Man. In a week he'll be smaller than me. Two weeks and Walter Marks can laminate him and use him for a paperweight."

"He was always depressed. A neurotic kid," Sarge said. "I tried to save him. I even kept him away from shrinks. His mother wanted to send him. His shoes are dirty, he needs analysis. His marks are low, he needs analysis. His marks are too high, he'll be unhappy as an overachiever, get him analyzed. And now he pays me back with this."

"Sarge, I'm forty years old. I'm lying around my house here, all by myself, nobody cares. Swenson's in love with a woman who loves donkeys. He doesn't care. My mother's off raping a slot machine somewhere. She doesn't care. My roommate and my father are out gallivanting around the countryside and no one cares about me. I'm lying here in my misery. I've heard this record a thousand times."

"Better hide the razors in the bathroom," Chico told Sarge.

"And the sleeping pills," Sarge said.

"Save one. People my age often have trouble falling off at night," Trace said.

"You'll sleep like a baby when you hear this," Chico said.

"No, I won't. What?"

"We've got it all figured out. Jarvis, the jewelry, everything," she said.

"I don't believe it," Trace said.

"It was all in your tapes. You just missed it," Chico said.

"I didn't miss anything. Tell me one single thing I missed."

"You missed everything," she said. "Did you look at the car-rental agreement Sarge got for you for Jarvis' car? Did you?"

"I glanced at it."

"You were wondering why Jarvis called for Spiro and then rented a car, right?"

"I might have had a moment's question about that, yes," Trace said.

"The rental agreement is stamped with the time. You remember what time it was?"

"It was late," Trace said.

"It was 11:46, you Mickey Mouse," she said.

"So?"

"And what was Spiro doing when Jarvis called to say pick him up?"

Trace sat up on the couch. "He was watching television in the kitchen."

"Right. And you know what show, don't you?"

"The midnight movie," Trace said.

"Quick. For two dollars, *Tuesday Night at the Movies* is on what night?" Chico asked.

"Tuesday?" Trace said.

"Correct. And now for the grand prize, what time does the midnight movie come on?"

"Midnight?" he said.

"Correct again. Give that man five hundred dollars' worth of overpriced junk patio furniture."

"I get your drift," Trace said. "Jarvis rented the car before the phone call."

"Right," Chico said.

"Then why'd he call?" Trace asked.

Chico looked at Sarge. "You want to tell him or should I?"

"You do it. I want to concentrate on watching him suffer," Sarge said.

Chico stepped forward and kissed Trace on top of the head. She said, "Jarvis didn't call."

"I give up," Trace said. "Senility is at hand. I thought I heard you say that Jarvis didn't call."

"That's what I said. And if that's got you confused, look at this." She shuffled through the small pile of papers in her hand and pulled one out and handed it to him.

He glanced at it. It was a list of names.

"Line eighteen," Chico said.

Trace looked at it. "Oh my, oh my, oh my," he said.

"Happy birthday, sweetheart," Chico said.

26

The dinner party was under way when Trace, Chico, and Sarge arrived at Felicia Fallaci's desert home. A twelve-foot-long oak table had been erected on the stone walk alongside the front of the swimming pool. Six large candelabra blazed with flame, casting shadows from the dinner guests across the yard and pool and illuminating the eerie parrots, who sat in a nearby tree, their eyes electrically watching, waiting.

Felicia was seated at the head of the table when the three guests stepped onto the patio. Bob Swenson sat next to her with National Anthem alongside him. Walter Marks was on the other side of the porn star, looking very uncomfortable, as if he expected her to make some crazed incursion on his groin at any moment. On the other side of the table, their backs to Trace, sat the Neddlemans and Ferrara and Willie Parmenter.

Hubbaker was not there and the table was barely half-filled. Six more seats at the table were empty.

Felicia saw them and half-rose from her seat.

"Come on and join us, all of you. There's plenty of room. I'm glad you could make it. Everybody, you all know Trace and his father, and this is Chico. You all know everybody here."

Trace stepped over to the countess, kissed her cheek, then went with his father and Chico to the other end of the table. Silver covered trays shielded large mounds of food: potatoes, corn, chicken, ribs, small steaks, vegetables, and salads. Chico started filling a plate for herself.

"Not that you're not welcome, of course, but what brings you here?" Felicia asked.

"Of course," Ferrara mumbled sarcastically.

"Just sort of revisiting the scene of the crime," Trace said. "We invited another friend. He'll be along soon."

"Any friend of yours et cetera, et cetera," Felicia said.

"Where's the baron?" Trace asked.

"Haven't seen him all day," Felicia said. "Dig in. There's plenty of food and more in the kitchen. And if you don't like the wines, ask, we've got others."

Chico's plate was already piled three inches high with food, in a masterpiece of balancing to rival Carmen Miranda's hats. She took a bite of food, then leaned over to Trace. He nodded and she rose, excused herself, and walked toward the house.

"Little girl's room," Trace said. "Heh, heh."

"Little girl's room," Ferrara said mockingly. "Would you believe that?" He turned to Trace. "So tell us, Super Shamus, how goes the detecting business? Solve any crimes lately? Commit any?"

"Solved a couple," Trace said. He poured wine for himself and Sarge, and club soda for Chico.

"Oh. Anything we should know about?"

"A couple of killings and a jewel theft," Trace said.

The background buzz of conversation at the table stopped.

"What's that, Trace?" Felicia asked.

"I think we've finally got things figured out," he said.

"You mean . . . Jarvis . . . the jewels?" she said.

"Yeah."

"Well, talk, man. Explain. Get me my money."

"Let's finish eating first," Trace said. "It's a better story on a full stomach."

"You can't do that to us," Felicia protested.

"Watch me," Trace said.

"Come on, Tracy," Walter Marks said peevishly.

"Eat, Groucho. Eat your little heart out."

Spiro came hustling in out of the kitchen with more food, recharging cold gravy into warm. He saw Trace, passed his end of the table, and whispered into Trace's ear, "Everything all right?"

"All under control, Spiro," Trace said.

Chico came back, apologized for her departure, and sat down. She put her purse under the table, nodded to Trace, and started to attack her food.

A large silence hung over the table. Trace realized his announcement had put a damper on the conversation and no one spoke except National Anthem, who kept babbling about her impending film career, and Felicia's parrots, who suggested once in a while that they might like a hit.

Night had fully fallen and the guests were into their coffee, brandy, and small cakes when Dan Rosado arrived.

Trace stood up and said, "Everyone knows my friend Lieutenant Rosado. Sit down, Dan. You hungry?"

"No, I ate." He sat in the vacant chair next to Trace and said, "What's going on?"

"You told me not to do anything without you," Trace said softly.

"You can eat dinner without me. That wasn't included."

"We're not here for dinner," Trace said.

"Come on, Trace, we're waiting," Felicia's voice rang out.

"By all means," Ferrara said in a sarcastic tone. "Night has fallen. Far off, the owls are screeching. Close by, the parrots are crapping all over the yard. We've got all the makings of a Hitchcock thriller, so do, let's get on with it."

"I'd like to do a Hitchcock thriller," National Anthem said.

"You'd make a wonderful victim," said Ferrara.

"Eeeeyou," National agreed.

"I wish Hubbaker were here," Trace said.

"Where is he?" Rosado asked sharply.

"Nobody knows," Trace said. Rosado began to get up from his chair, but Trace put a hand on his arm. "Let it go for a while. It doesn't matter."

"So who killed Jarvis?" Walter Marks asked from the other end of the table.

"Come on, Walter. We can't just plunge into it that way. Where's your sense of the dramatic?" Trace asked.

Chico was still eating.

"You mind if I start without you?" Trace asked.

Chico kept looking down at her plate, but she waved one hand over her head for him to proceed.

"One of the questions I just kept chewing over was why Jarvis didn't have a passport on him," Trace said aloud to the entire table. "It didn't make any sense that a thief with a million in jewels is going to stop and steal a passport. Well, the thief didn't. The fact was that Jarvis was traveling under a fake passport. He didn't want any records to show he had come back to town."

A deep voice rumbled, "Why not?" and Trace had to look twice to convince himself that the voice had indeed come from the hitherto-silent Francis Neddleman. He spoke and his wife nodded and they both stared at Trace.

"He was coming back on a secret trip to steal the countess's jewels," Trace said.

"That's ridiculous," Felicia snapped.

Trace said blandly, "I don't know. I hear a lot of people get jewels by stealing them."

He looked around the table. The Neddlemans and Ferrara and Willie Parmenter were staring at him. National Anthem was gazing off over the roof of the house, looking as if she expected to see her name being written in the sky at any moment. Marks and Swenson were watching him too, Marks looking disgusted, Swenson smiling slightly and nodding encouragement.

"So Jarvis said he got sick soon after he arrived in London, Felicia. You remember what you told me?" Trace looked down the table at her, their eyes locking for a moment. "That you told him to take a couple of days off in the country? Isn't that right, folks? Isn't that what she told him?"

"Yes," said Ferrara, "but so what?"

"When did any of you find out that Jarvis wasn't out resting in the British countryside but had come back to the States instead?" Trace asked.

Ferrara was thinking. Parmenter was silent. Mrs. Neddleman said, in a small timid voice, "When we heard he got killed."

"Thank you. Exactly," Trace said. "Nobody knew he had gone back to Las Vegas, and Felicia told you about it only when he turned up dead and she had to tell you about it. If he had done what he wanted to do and gotten back to London, all of you would have just believed he was in the countryside resting his poor stomach."

The other eyes at the table turned toward Felicia, all but Chico's; she was busy eyeing some glazed sweet potatoes on another tray.

The countess, for once, seemed to have lost some of her poise. Her voice crackled a little as she said, "Are you saying he wasn't sick?"

Trace nodded. "Yes. And that you knew it."

"You're forgetting something. Willie got sick too. I told you, it was food poisoning."

Trace turned to Willie Parmenter. "How'd you treat it, Willie? Did you go out into the countryside, too, to rest your tum-tum?"

Willie shook his head. "I went to spend a couple of days with friends," he said. "In London."

"Swell," Trace said. "We'll get to that. Anyway, Jarvis flew back here."

"You still haven't told us one thing about his missing passport," Walter Marks said.

"Jarvis had two passports," Trace said. "One was under his name of Early Jarvis. He didn't want to use that one because he didn't want any record of his coming back into the country. Remember, he came here to steal jewels and his alibi was being overseas. And he had a second passport, in the name of Edward Stark. That's the name he grew up with. It's the name he had on a police record in New York before he started working for you, Felicia."

"Jarvis? I never knew that," she said.

"Somehow I suspect that you did," Trace said.

Neddleman's deep voice rumbled again. "Are you saying Felicia had something to do with Jarvis' death?"

"No, I'm not saying that yet," Trace said. "But she knew what he was up to. He was going to fly back here as Edward Stark, steal the jewels, fly back out as Edward Stark, and let all the heat fall on poor Spiro. Why else would he have hired somebody with a police record for theft to work out here? It was all being set up," Trace said.

"The passport. The passport," Ferrara said. "So far, a lot of conjecture, but no passport."

"Remember he had two," Trace said. "Chico."

She quickly finished chewing and swallowing a large lump of chicken and potatoes and reached into her purse and handed him a passport.

"Here's the passport in the name of Early Jarvis," Trace said. "It shows his trip to London. It doesn't show any return to this country." He handed it to Rosado.

"Exhibit A?" Rosado said.

Trace nodded, and Felicia's face, even under the warming effect of candlelight, seemed to lose some of its color.

"Where did you get that?" she asked.

"You know. In your suitcase upstairs. Chico found it when I said she was going to the little girl's room, heh, heh. The other night you told me you hadn't unpacked your bags from London yet and I thought you might still have Jarvis' passport. Because, of course, he gave it to you when he was leaving England. He was using the other passport in the name of Edward Stark. We know that, for sure, by the way. Sarge found the flight manifest from New York to Vegas with Stark's name on it. Those flight manifests can be dangerous evidence, can't they, Mr. Ferrara?"

"I'm sure I don't know what you mean," Ferrara said.

"So the other passport, Trace? What about that?" Swenson said.

National Anthem seemed surprised at hearing a voice sound so close to her ear, and she looked around with what seemed to be interest, then concentrated on watching Trace.

"I'll get to that soon," he said. "I know it's puzzling. Isn't it, Mr. Neddleman?"

His voice boomed back. "It sure as hell is, but I like what you're doing so far."

"Now we had a problem," Trace said. "If Jarvis was sneaking back here—"

Neddleman interrupted him. "Why did he call Spiro from the airport, right? If his trip was supposed to be secret, that would reveal his presence here, wouldn't it?"

"Yes, it would, dear," his wife said. "It certainly would."

"At first," Trace said, "I figured he called Spiro and then rented a car so he could get here while Spiro was out. But that wasn't so. A minor thing, but for one thing, he rented the car first, *before* Spiro was called. And for another, he had the keys to this place. He could just have come out here and waited for Spiro to go to sleep and then sneak into the house, loot the safe, and beat it. No one would ever know. That's why he parked his car back up on the road—so that Spiro wouldn't hear it come up the drive or wouldn't see it and notice the license plate."

Trace noticed Spiro watching him from the kitchen door.

"Come on out, Spiro," he called. "You might as well have a front-row seat."

Spiro stepped forward, cautiously, and sat on a stone wall planter, back away from the mass of the crowd.

"So why did Jarvis call Spiro?" Felicia asked.

"He didn't."

"I swear he did," Spiro said, jumping to his feet. "I swear."

"Don't panic, Spiro," Trace said. "You didn't do anything wrong. Somebody called, but it wasn't Jarvis."

"But—"

"Remember you told me that he didn't really talk like himself on the phone. He was too polite? That's because it wasn't really Jarvis."

"Then who was it?" Rosado snapped. His patience had obviously been frayed to breaking.

"Coming to it," Trace said. "Another reason why the call couldn't be Jarvis. If he called, Spiro here would tell the police and so much for the secret trip to rob the jewels and make believe he was in England. That would have been stupid and Jarvis wasn't stupid."

He looked around the table. "Now everyone pay attention because this is where it gets tricky," he said. "Spiro goes to get Jarvis. Now the person who actually made the call is waiting, and when Spiro zips out through the electronic gate, he's waiting outside and he slips in before the gate closes behind Spiro. He's got a drill and he figures he'll be safe for a long time because he told Spiro to wait at the airport for Jarvis. He never counted on Jarvis coming back because he thought Jarvis was out throwing up all over the British country-side."

Trace poured himself more wine. "Anybody else?" he asked, but got no takers.

"So the thief gets into the house and he's trying to drill open the safe and Jarvis comes back. He parks out on the road and walks up the drive to the house. He lets himself in. He's very quiet because he thinks Spiro is home. Maybe asleep, maybe not. But when he gets inside, he hears the sound of the drill. He drops his bag, goes into the living room, and faces off with the thief. The two men scuffle and the thief slugs him, probably with his drill. Then the thief runs. He doesn't know if Jarvis is dead or alive or whatever, but he's no killer at heart, he just wants to get the hell out of here. So he leaves without ever getting into the safe."

"Then what happened to my jewels?" Felicia asked.

"Yes. Where are the jewels?" Ferrara echoed. "Do you actually know?"

"Maybe," Trace said. "I want everybody to come with me for a moment." He got up and walked toward the gate in the fence behind the swimming pool. The entire table followed him with the exception of Chico, who was still eating, and Sarge, who was taking off his jacket and rolling up his shirt sleeves over his massive arms.

At the fence, Trace said, "When the thief fled, he may have gone out through here. Or he may have just gone out the front door. I'm not sure."

"What the hell does that mean?" Rosado asked.

Trace looked past him back toward the dinner table, where Sarge was sitting back down. Chico nodded to Trace and he said to Rosado, "Never mind. It's not really important."

"This is ridiculous," Ferrara said.

"Come on. Go back and sit down," Trace said. "Almost done now."

When they were back in their seats, Trace said, "Remember, Felicia, Jarvis came to steal the jewels. As you well know. So now he's been knocked out, maybe badly hurt. He comes to. He's groggy maybe. The place is a mess. But he's thinking of only one thing: protecting you. He puts his gloves on. The gloves he carried to Las Vegas in July all the way from London when he didn't pack anything else. Or maybe he was wearing them all the time. He opens the safe."

"What would stealing my jewels have to do with protecting me?" Felicia asked.

"Remember. As far as Jarvis knew, Spiro was still in the house, maybe sleeping. Jarvis was in no condition to clean things up, and when Spiro came in and saw the mess, he was going to call the cops. Jarvis didn't want them ever to find out what was in that safe. Here's one everybody missed. The tree inside. The one that was knocked over in the fight? If you go look at the two trees, the one that was knocked over doesn't have the burlap wrapping around its roots anymore, like the other one does. Jarvis took the burlap and used it to wrap up what was in the safe. He threw his phony passport in there too, because he knew that might just cause trouble. Then he stashed them away."

"Where? How? His body was found over there?" Neddleman said. He was pointing to the fish pond.

"I thought it was strange," Trace said, "that Jarvis crawled out here. Why didn't he crawl to a phone to call for help? Maybe he would have, but he had to get rid of the stuff first. *That's* why he came out here. It was just his bad luck that he, well, maybe got dizzy and fell and bopped his head, and then he lay there and bled to death. While Spiro was waiting for him at the airport. Sarge, you want to do it?"

"Sure," his father said. The burly gray-haired man stood up and walked to the goldfish pool. He sprawled himself out on the stone deck and plunged his arm deep into the water. A moment later, he brought out a burlap package, dripping water.

"Christ, this smells," Sarge said. "Clean that pool, Countess."

He brought it back to the table and plopped it down on the clean dinner plate in front of Rosado. The policeman used a steak knife to cut away at the rough package and Felicia came down from the head of the table to watch. She was followed by the Neddlemans. It was the first time, Trace realized, that he had ever seen them move.

"I'd like to do Cleopatterer," National Anthem said, but no one was listening.

Rosado pulled out a blue-covered passport booklet.

"That should be the fake passport in the name of Edward Stark," Trace said.

Rosado cut some more fabric and then peeled back the burlap. There was a tiara and two elaborate diamond necklaces. And the white marble ashtray.

"My jewels," the countess said. "My jewels." She reached over and lifted the tiara over her head. "Your father's right. That water smells. But they're my jewels."

"Not exactly," Trace said. He took the tiara back from the countess and returned it to Rosado.

"What do you mean, not exactly?"

"They're yours, all right, but they're not jewels. They're just cheap paste, glass imitations of your jewels. You know this, Felicia, but nobody else does, so I hope you don't mind my explaining it. That's why Jarvis went to New York three weeks in a row before your trip to Europe. He was selling off the jewels in your pieces and getting them replaced with paste imitations."

"That's absurd," she said. "Really, Trace—"

"Is it? It's a great way to beat the insurance company. Sell the real jewels and steal the imitations yourself."

"Ridiculous," she snapped.

"We'll know when we have these looked at," Rosado said.

"Remember, Countess, you told me that you never do charitable work or served on boards or anything like that. But you went out of your way to be photographed wearing all this junk just before you went to Europe. That was part of it. Making sure that a lot of people saw you in the jewels. Then, when they were stolen while you were away, well, you had hundreds of witnesses that they really existed. Anyway, I don't think there'll be much trouble finding the jeweler in New York who replaced these real stones with glass. It's pretty specialized work."

"I resent this," Felicia said. "This whole idea of my stealing my own jewels—"

"Remember, Countess, how you got them," Trace said.

"They were gifts," she said.

"They were stolen," Trace said. Rosado looked at him sharply and Trace shrugged. "That's what Interpol thinks, anyway. They have the countess and Jarvis listed among their top suspected jewel thieves."

"Why steal the ashtray?" Ferrara asked sharply.

"It wasn't stolen," Trace said. "Jarvis used it as a weight to make sure the package would sink to the bottom of the pool."

Ferrara waved his arms over his head in disgust. "This is all moronic," he snapped. "Felicia a thief? You're an imbecile, Tracy. I've never liked you, but now I think you ought to be committed."

"Quiet, morgue-breath," Trace said. "To steal jewels, you have to be where jewels are. What better way than to be a beautiful woman? Especially one with a phoney title? The only better way might be to be a drug-dealer." He stared at Ferrara, who glared back.

"Anyway, Felicia and Jarvis aren't the only jewel thieves in the world," Trace said.

Mrs. Neddleman said softly, "I still don't understand who killed Jarvis."

"The insurance-company detective knows," Trace said.

"He's not here," Marks said. "The baron's not here."

"Sorry, Groucho, he's not your detective. In fact, Interpol says he's a jewel thief too."

"What?" Walter Marks said. He rose up out of his seat.

"He's got a record," Trace said.

"I put up twenty-five hundred dollars in bail money," Marks moaned.

"Not my problem," Trace said.

Neddleman was growling again. "You say the detective knows. Who's going to tell us?"

"The insurance detective will. Won't you, Willie?"

Ferrara's head snapped around toward his valet as if on a spring. "Willie? Him?" He pointed at Parmenter and laughed.

Parmenter ignored him. "Congratulations, Mr. Tracy. Very ingenious."

"I had help," Trace said. "You want to tell us anything or should I go on?"

"You go on, by all means," Parmenter said.

"How'm I doing so far?"

"I'd give you about a seven."

"That's not too bad," Trace said.

Walter Marks was pointing at Parmenter. "Him?" he said, and looked to Trace.

National Anthem said, "I think he's nice. Sort of. For a man."

Trace told Marks, "Yeah, he's your secret agent, Groucho. You want him to go now and fetch you a drink? Not too sweet."

"I don't believe it," Marks said.

Trace imitated his whine. "I don't believe it," he said. "Sorry for that. I'm not a very good mimic. You want to do your impression of Walter?" he added, looking at Willie.

The small man smiled.

"Remember," Trace said, "I told you all before it wasn't Jarvis who called Spiro? It was somebody imitating his voice. It was Willie here."

Parmenter was still standing at his place at the table.

"You made a mistake when you showed off the other night for Chico, imitating Groucho," Trace said. "She remembered. She remembers everything."

"Showing off always gets you into trouble," Parmenter said.

"I still don't believe it," Marks said.

"Believe it, Walter," Swenson said.

"Eeeeyou. This is getting exciting. I think," said National Anthem.

There was silence for a moment and one of the parrots squawked, "Polly want a hit."

Felicia was still standing near Trace, staring at Parmenter, and Trace looked up at her.

"You see, Felicia," Trace said, "Willie's been working for insurance companies for a few years working on big jewel robberies. You and Jarvis were two that kept getting away. So when you went to London, he was there. He thought this was the perfect chance to find out what you two had hidden back here. So he got make-believe sick and went away for a couple of days, supposedly to visit relatives. What he did was hop the first plane to the States and then to Las Vegas. He never expected that, just by coincidence, Jarvis would do the same thing."

Felicia sat down heavily in the chair next to Chico. She stared dully at the candelabra in front of her as she spoke. "It wasn't a coincidence. When Willie got sick, it gave us the idea. It could look like food poisoning and it was a great excuse for Jarvis to get sick too and get back here. We never knew who Willie was."

"Nobody did. Not even Ferrara, and Willie worked for him."

"He was convenient," Willie said. "He was entrée, you might say."

"So here you are," Trace said. "You're on your way to Las Vegas, and you never suspect it but so is Jarvis. You both have the same idea. *You* want to check Felicia's jewelry, and if it's stolen, steal it back. Jarvis, on the other hand, has already sold off the real stuff, exchanged it for paste, and he wants to steal the paste now to beat the insurance company. You get here before he does and you sit in your car near the gas station down the road and finally you call Spiro and send him off to the airport on a wild-goose chase. When he leaves, you slip in and go to work. Jarvis arrives, finds you, and then it's what I told you. Struggle, Jarvis drops, Willie runs, Jarvis dumps the jewels so that the fact they are fakes won't hurt Felicia, and he has the bad luck to hit his head and bleed to death."

"Can you prove any of these accusations?" Parmenter said.

"We've got the airline manifests of you flying into Las Vegas on the same day Jarvis got killed. You're on Line eighteen, William Parmenter. I'm sure your passport will show it too, or airline tickets or whatever. It won't be hard to nail down."

Parmenter, who had been the lone person standing at the table, sat back down. "It was an accident, you know," Willie said. "I didn't try to hurt him. I just wanted to get away without him recognizing me." His face seemed to brighten. "He bled to death after hitting his head. That doesn't have anything to do with me."

Ferrara looked over at him. "I think you've got one hell of a nerve. You're supposed to be working for me and you're off doing—"

"Oh, shut up," Willie Parmenter said. He picked up a bucket of melted ice and poured the water over Ferrara's head.

The curly-haired Italian shrieked, and National Anthem, said, "I love mystery movies. Don't you, Bobby, sweetheart?"

"Sure, sure," Swenson said.

Ferrara was drying his hair with a large cloth napkin. For a moment he looked as if he'd throw a punch at Willie, but his eyes met Sarge's for a moment and Trace's father gave him a look that meant that throwing a punch would only be the start of something big, and the Italian slumped back in his chair.

"The other night," Trace told Rosado, "Felicia told me that she was surprised that the thief hadn't contacted her. That didn't make any sense to me. But it does when you realize that the jewels are fake, and once the thief found it out, he had a good blackmail move against her. That's why she was surprised she hadn't heard anything. Isn't that so, Countess?"

She was still staring at the candelabra. "Yes," she said softly.

"And, Willie, you had a problem too," Trace said. "Felicia's jewels were gone, but you didn't get them. Who did? Where were they? You knew there was something going on, so you got the insurance company to send you in here. Probably you figured you'd be able to pick up an easy fee, because you had the one piece of information that the cops didn't have: that the thief never got the jewels. That's why you were always lurking around, listening in, trying to find out something. The obvious choice in your head was Spiro, and that's why you broke into his apartment to see if he had the jewels. But he didn't, of course. They were here all the time."

Trace poured more wine into his glass and turned to Rosado. "Good luck, Dan. Now it's all yours to sort out. I don't know who gets charged with what and I don't care. And, Walter—"

Marks looked up.

"I think you probably owe Felicia the insurance money on Jarvis' death," Trace said. "Unless your legal beagles figure out some way she shouldn't get it." He leaned over to Felicia and said, "I told you I'd try to get it for you."

Rosado stood up and said, "I'm calling for some help here. Don't anyone try to leave."

"They won't," Sarge said.

A few minutes later Rosado returned. The guests were still sitting around silently, as if the main course had just been served and when they lifted the top of the serving tray, they had found a corpse.

Trace noticed Rosado beckoning to him and walked over to him.

"One thing everybody forgot," Rosado said softly.

"What?"

"R. J. Roberts. Who killed him?"

"It had nothing to do with this," Trace said. "It was most likely a hooker named Lip Service. They had a fight. I think he slugged her and she cut him. She's skipped town to go back to Minnesota."

"Oh. And what about Hubbaker and Roberts?"

"This is only a guess. I think Roberts found out that Hubbaker had a record. That's what that note in his files meant. Maybe he was going to blackmail the baron, or maybe he thought Hubbaker could help him find out about Felicia's robbery. I don't know."

"I don't know either, and I can't find out because Hubbaker's gone," Rosado said.

"He's probably skipped," Trace said. He talked very softly. "You could do me a favor if you wait before putting out a want on him," Trace said.

"Why's that?"

"First of all, he didn't have anything to do with anything. Second of all, I wouldn't mind if his bail was forfeited."

Rosado looked past Trace toward Walter Marks, sitting at the dinner table, looking disgusted.

"I understand," Rosado said. "I will pursue the baron with all due slowness."

"Polly want a hit," one of the parrots squawked.

It's probably skipped," Trace said. He talked ... ... You could draw a favor. If they had before putting out a warrant on ... Trace ...

... but he didn't make anything to ... police, anything ... ... wa ...

... ed past ... utter tax ... "Rosa ... ... the slo ...

27

The annual convention of the Garrison Fidelity Insurance Company was over. It had ended with a gala banquet at which Bob Swenson, company president, had praised the dedication and zeal and intelligence of the men who had made the company what it was, among them none other than Walter Marks, "our brilliant vice-president for claims."

After the dinner, Marks pleaded an early plane and passed up the opportunity to come to Trace's apartment for an after-dinner party to celebrate the convention and also Trace's birthday, now one day past.

Swenson came. Alone.

"Where's National Anthem?" Trace asked.

"It's all over," Swenson said.

"What happened?"

"She's leaving the country."

"Why?" Trace asked.

"Why? Because she got a goddamn offer to star in some Zulu epic or something. *The Queen of the Apes*. I guess she never balled a gorilla before. Anyway, she left, and I don't want to talk about it. Where's your phone?"

"Use that one," Trace said.

Swenson dialed long distance. As he was dialing, he said to Trace, "You hear what I said about that dingaling, Marks?"

"Every word. I nearly threw up," Trace said.

"You've got to praise the little people," Swenson said. "It keeps them in line. You know, he told me he was going to give you enough rope to hang yourself. Poor bastard, he gave you forty-seven miles of rope and you wrapped it around his neck."

Trace said, "I had a lot of help."

"I'll give him rope," Swenson said. "Hello, Deirdre, this is Mr. Swenson. . . . Yes. Everything's fine here; we finished everything up tonight. Monday morning, first thing, I want you to send one of the office boys to a hardware store. . . . Listen and I'll tell you. I want one mile of rope. . . . That's right. Rope. Clothesline. Deliver it to Walter Marks' office. . . . That's right. And put a note on it. 'Better luck next time.' . . . No, no. Don't sign it and *don't* let him know it came from me. . . . Yeah. I'll be back Sunday. . . . Okay. Good-bye."

He hung up and took the drink Chico offered him.

"Ain't revenge grand?" Swenson said.

"Sure is," Trace said. "Listen, there'll be a lot of expenses on this one, Bob. No matter how it goes. Pop and Chico and me."

"Whatever it takes. Just remember you owe me three thousand dollars."

"I've got it. The check just cleared."

Later they were joined by Dan Rosado and his wife, and last of all by Sarge and Mrs. Tracy. Trace thought she had a look on her face that would make a basset hound look absolutely jovial by comparison.

"What's the matter, Mother?"

"It's all your fault."

"What is?"

"Last night, after I won all that money, I went to bed and I was thinking, If I bet more, I'll win more. So today I went back to that machine and tried again."

"How'd you do?"

"I gave everything back that I won yesterday. And I lost ten dollars besides. I'll be glad to get home."

"I'll hate to see you go," Trace said.

Later, Chico poured each of them a glass of champagne. Mrs. Tracy examined her glass carefully for dirt spots.

Chico led the toast. "To the man I sometimes love," she said, raising her glass, which held barely a teaspoon of wine.

"To my friend," said Bob Swenson, raising his glass.

"And mine," Rosado said, lifting his glass, but not drinking.

They all looked at Mrs. Tracy, but she was still busy examining the glass. Sarge lifted his glass and said, "To my son."

After they drank, Chico started singing "Happy Birthday." Everyone joined in except Trace's mother.

Chico clicked her glass against Trace's. "All's well that ends well, partner," she said.

"All's well that ends," he said. He leaned forward and whispered in her ear. "I love you."

"That makes us even," Chico said.

JOIN THE TRACE READERS' PANEL

Help us bring you more of the books you like by filling out this survey and mailing it in today.

1. Book title:_____

   Book #:_____

2. Using the scale below how would you rate this book on the following features.

Poor		Not so Good			O.K.			Good		Excel-lent
0	1	2	3	4	5	6	7	8	9	10

Rating

Overall opinion of book . . . . _____
Plot/Story . . . . _____
Setting/Location . . . . _____
Writing Style . . . . _____
Character Development . . . . _____
Conclusion/Ending . . . . _____
Scene on Front Cover . . . . _____

3. On average about how many adventure books do you buy for

   yourself each month?_____

4. How would you classify yourself as a reader of adventures?
   I am a ( ) light ( ) medium ( ) heavy reader.

5. What is your education?
   ( ) High School (or less)   ( ) 4 yrs. college
   ( ) 2 yrs. college   ( ) Post Graduate

6. Age_____   7. Sex: ( ) Male ( ) Female

Please Print Name_____

Address_____

City_____State_____Zip_____

Phone # (   )_____

Thank you. Please send to New American Library, Research Dept, 1633 Broadway, New York, NY 10019.